BEFORE IT'S
TOO LATE

Also by Sara Driscoll

Lone Wolf

BEFORE IT'S TOO LATE

SARA DRISCOLL

KENSINGTON BOOKS
www.kensingtonbooks.com

KENSINGTON BOOKS are published by

Kensington Publishing Corp.
119 West 40th Street
New York, NY 10018

All Kensington titles, imprints and distributed lines are available at special quantity discounts for bulk purchases for sales promotion, premiums, fundraising, educational or institutional use.

Special book excerpts or customized printings can also be created to fit specific needs. For details, write or phone the office of the Kensington Special Sales Manager: Kensington Publishing Corp., 119 West 40th Street, New York, NY, 10018. Attn. Special Sales Department. Phone: 1-800-221-2647.

Library of Congress Card Catalogue Number: 2017944852

Kensington and the K logo Reg. U.S. Pat. & TM Off.

ISBN-13: 978-1-4967-0443-6
ISBN-10: 1-4967-0443-6
First Kensington Hardcover Edition: October 2017

eISBN-13: 978-1-4967-0444-3
eISBN-10: 1-4967-0444-4
Kensington Electronic Edition: October 2017

10 9 8 7 6 5 4 3 2 1

Printed in the United States of America

To my mother, Edith Danna, who opened up the magic of the creative arts for all her children by showing us the joy of books and music from our very first days. Our successes are only possible because of the gifts you gave us.

Prologue

Monday, May 22, 7:47 PM
Glencarlyn Park
Arlington, Virginia

Sandy Holmes took a deep breath of spring air as the sun sank low over the rise of the hill overhead. Glancing over her shoulder, she gauged the distance back to her car in the lot at the far end of the park. *Time to head back before we lose the light.* But she paused, giving herself a moment to enjoy the tranquility of the small, forested valley, an oasis in the middle of bustling urban life. It was a cool evening, the breeze carrying a dampness that hinted at rain, and Lubber Run Trail, a narrow paved path that hugged the curves of the meandering creek, was quiet. Deserted, actually. Now that she noticed it, all the other hikers must have already headed in for the night.

Pressure against her knee had her glancing down and smiling. Ruby, her Heinz 57 service dog—heavy on the hound—gazed up at her, her dark eyes full of love and concern. Sandy reached down and ran a hand over the dog's head, her fingertips dropping away just where caramel-colored fur met the camo-patterned service dog vest. "It's okay, I'm good." Trained as a PTSD service dog, Ruby was always alert and ready to either protect or soothe, depending on the situation, but Sandy had been feeling pretty steady over the last few weeks. Maybe it was the coming of spring, but her post-traumatic stress—a souvenir from serving with the marines in the Iraq War— seemed better lately. This past winter had come with some rough patches, but hope apparently dawned with warmer weather and longer days. It had been weeks since her last severe panic attack and, for the first time in years, Sandy felt like she was coming out of a fog and stepping into brilliant sunlight.

"Come on, girl. Time to head for home." She started to tighten the lead, but Ruby was already circling around behind her, her body stiff, her nose pointed forward as if at a target, and her eyes locked on the path behind them.

"Excuse me?"

Sandy jerked around at the sound of the man's voice, stepping back a pace as gut-wrenching fear spiked her heart rate. She looked up to see a man about fifteen feet up the hill to her left, backlit by the setting sun. He stood on the short access path that ran up to the corner where North Columbus Street met 3rd Street North. Behind him, a large white van was parked with the back doors thrown open.

Ruby gave a low growl, her head dropping lower between her shoulders, and her weight shifting to her haunches as if preparing to spring.

"Animal Control," the man said calmly, his eyes locked on the dog instead of the woman. He pointed to the insignia on his baseball cap. "We got a call about a rabid raccoon in one of the backyards up on North Columbus, but it got out before I could get here. It's in pretty bad shape and we're afraid it's very infectious. Have you seen any raccoons down here?"

Sandy surreptitiously blew out a breath heavy with relief and gave herself a mental kick for overreacting. *Just because a strange man startles you doesn't mean you're under attack. He's just doing his job.* She laid a hand on Ruby's back. "Ruby, it's okay, girl." The tense muscles under her fingers relaxed in response to the soothing tone. Sandy looked back up at the Animal Control officer, his face shaded even further in the dim light by the brim of his cap. "I'm sorry, no." Sandy cast her eyes around for any sign of the animal, pulling Ruby a little closer as if to protect her with her own body.

"I'm pretty sure it came down here. If I could suggest, maybe skip the creek-side path and head up to North Columbus Street if that's the direction you're going. Not so much cover up there and you'll see him if he takes a run at you. Your dog is up to date on his vaccines?"

"She is, yes. Thank you for your concern. Come on, Ruby. We'll cut across North Columbus and dip back down into the park on the other side of Arlington Boulevard."

"Thank you, ma'am. Wouldn't want either of you getting bitten." He stood aside on the access path as if to allow them to pass. "I'm going to search down here some more. I'd prefer to put the poor creature out of its misery, rather than leave it to suffer."

Sandy gave the leash a gentle pull and Ruby reluctantly trotted along at her side, her eyes staying locked on the stranger. They passed the man—now she could see he was in full uniform—whose face was turned away as he scanned the bushes, and they pushed up the short hill.

The street above was just coming into view when a vicious hold suddenly wrapped around her. She struggled against the vise, but a hand slapped over her nose and mouth, smothering her with something cold and wet. The deep breath she was drawing to scream pulled in a suffocating cloud of chemical fumes instead of fresh air.

Ruby barked furiously, but the man landed a brutal kick to the side of her head. With a broken whimper, the dog staggered backward.

Panic, that terrifyingly familiar friend, rose and clawed at Sandy's throat as her vision started to blacken. She reached for her injured dog, but even as her fingers stretched out, darkness closed over her.

CHAPTER 1

Opening Volley: The first shots fired in a war.

The hound dog mix was found wandering alone on N Wakefield Street. Sporting a service dog vest, she dragged her leash behind her as she staggered down the sidewalk, her head sweeping from side to side as if searching for her owner. One of the neighbors, a dog owner herself, spotted the dog and lured her closer with a treat before catching her leash. It was only by chance that she noticed the note peeking out from the small plastic bone containing waste bags:

> *To: Meg Jennings, Forensic Canine Unit, FBI:*
> *IMHFL HVVGJ RVYUL HHCGW FSGGX*
> *RAUUL LRAVS QWBQY VICPE OIRCR*
> *GVCCX KIWNS FOCUX LGEKR JSHJI UPCHI*

The FBI's Cryptanalysis and Racketeering Records Unit wasted no time running the code through their big computers while special agents discovered the identity of the missing woman: Ms. Sandy Holmes, a veteran of the Second Iraq War who suffered from occasionally debilitating bouts of PTSD, and never went anywhere without her dog. To find the dog alone was a significant concern.

An hour later, the cryptanalysts confirmed her disappearance as they revealed the real message behind the string of eighty capital letters addressed to the FBI search-dog handler: "Find her before she dies. Come to Washington's House in Alexandria. The clock is ticking on her life."

Monday, May 22, 9:44 PM
Forensic Canine Unit, J. Edgar Hoover Building
Washington, DC

"Washington's House? Do they mean Mount Vernon?" Brian Foster asked.

Craig Beaumont nodded. The supervisory special-agent-in-charge of the Human Scent Evidence Team, part of the Forensic Canine Unit, cast his gaze around his team of handlers and dogs gathered in the bullpen. "That's what the CRRU cryptanalysts are saying. Mount Vernon is near the city of Alexandria, and they think Ms. Holmes is being held on the property. I don't know what we're looking at, so I want you all to go. Scott, we've got the dog's leash, so you'll be able to use that for tracking."

Scott Park laid a hand on the head of Theo, his lanky, droopy-eyed bloodhound. "Nothing he loves more than a good hunt." To punctuate Scott's words, Theo gave a huge ear-slapping head shake, his jowls flapping in concert.

Meg Jennings stared down at the driver's license photo of the missing woman, which she gripped in one white-knuckled hand. "Craig, is there anything that indicates why he sent the message to me? I don't even know this woman."

"Nothing so far, and I really don't like the fact that one of my team has been specifically named in this. Stay in pairs for now. I don't want anyone on their own until we know what's going on. The last thing I need is my people brought out to a site, only to be picked off."

The teams doubled up—Brian and his German shepherd, Lacey, with Meg and her black Labrador, Hawk; Scott and Theo partnered with Lauren Wycliffe and her border collie, Rocco—and set out. The drive was just a half hour down the George Washington Parkway, but they'd only been on the road for ten minutes when Meg's phone rang through her SUV's audio system.

"Jennings."

"Meg, we've got a problem." Craig's voice boomed through the speakers.

Meg and Brian exchanged a sideways glance. "More than our missing victim?"

"We might be sending you to the wrong place."

Meg checked her mirrors and then smoothly pulled into the right-hand lane. "The Beltway is coming up. Do I need to redirect?"

Craig paused as if weighing his decision. "Get off, go west, and then circle back north on I-395."

"Where are we going?" Brian asked.

"Arlington."

"The county or the cemetery?" Meg shot them down the exit ramp and then merged into Beltway traffic. "What happened to George Washington's house?"

"The coded message never said, 'George,' just 'Washington.' One of the cryptanalysts wanted to make sure we weren't missing anything obvious, so he ran the message by a buddy of his, a history professor at Georgetown University, without telling him why the information was important."

"Unless the buddy is an idiot, he's going to question his FBI friend asking such a left-field question," Brian muttered under his breath.

"What?" Craig's echoing voice filled the passenger compartment.

"Nothing," Meg said, shooting Brian a look that clearly said, *Behave*. "What did the professor say?"

"He said Washington could also be George Washington Parke Custis, Martha Washington's grandson and the father-in-law of Robert E. Lee."

"Lee's mansion on the grounds of Arlington Cemetery. You think that's the clue?"

"This guy does. He says Arlington County used to be called Alexandria County, but the name was changed in 1920 because it was too confusing also having a city in Virginia named Alexandria. He said Custis's mansion went to his daughter and therefore, upon Custis's death, to Lee. Mount Vernon never occurred to this guy."

"But it could still be right," Brian reasoned.

"It could, which is why Lauren and Scott are still headed there. Scott's got the leash, which means you won't have anything on hand to provide scent, so I know this makes it a bigger challenge for you—air-scenting and tracking an unknown target. Get to Arlington. Emergency Services is waiting to let you in. Move fast. As the note says, 'the clock is ticking,' and we just lost time." The line went dead.

Meg flicked a glance at Brian, seeing the unease she felt reflected in his eyes, and pressed down harder on the accelerator.

Monday, May 22, 10:23 PM
Arlington National Cemetery
Arlington, Virginia

They arrived at Arlington National Cemetery hours after it had officially closed. The grounds of the cemetery were dark, lit only by the light of a full moon; however, the main entrance was ablaze with lights. Several Arlington Emergency Services vehicles lined the main driveway. They ushered Meg's SUV through the main gates and then jogged over to meet the K-9 handlers as they let their dogs out of the SUV's special compartment and shouldered their search-and-rescue packs.

"Jennings and Foster?"

"That's us." Brian snapped Lacey's lead onto her FBI vest. "What are we looking at here? Are we expecting any one inside the grounds?"

"We've cleared the cemetery of all emergency personnel. Professional military mourners who attended today's burials, as well as grounds and admin personnel who were in during regular hours, went home hours ago. The only person who should be on the premises is the officer on duty at the Tomb of the Unknown Soldier. Please try not to disturb him, unless absolutely necessary."

"We'll let the dogs lead us," Meg said. "But if they don't go in that direction, we won't interfere." She turned to Brian. "You and Lacey go north, and then circle around to the west and then south. I'll go south first and then circle around from there."

The handlers were of equal rank, but because of Meg's past experience as an officer with the Richmond PD, she naturally took the lead, which suited Brian just fine. "Check. Lacey, come." Brian jogged off, disappearing into the gloom outside the circle of lights surrounding them. Meg saw him pause inside the far gate by the gold shield of the US Marine Corps as he unclipped Lacey's leash. He flipped on his small, powerful flashlight; then he bent down to her, giving her the command to search, and she was off, Brian following at a light jog.

"Is there anything we can do?" the officer asked as Meg turned back to Hawk.

"Just stay out of the grounds for now. We need to find

the only other person inside, except for the officer at the Tomb. We'll let you know if we need assistance. Hawk, come."

They walked away from the lights and officers and into the darkness. As Brian had done, she paused by the massive wrought-iron gates and removed Hawk's lead. She ran a hand down his back and met his gaze. "Find her, Hawk. Find Sandy." Hawk tipped his nose into the cool evening breeze momentarily, and then trotted down the road, into the darkness. She turned on her flashlight and followed.

Meg followed Hawk, pacing herself, knowing this could be a long search, if they were even in the right place. The cemetery was over six hundred acres—just less than one square mile—but packed with over four hundred thousand graves, monuments, outbuildings, an amphitheater, and a mansion. They might have to cover all that ground two or three times over in pursuit of an elusive wisp of scent, just to start the search proper.

Meg found herself studying Hawk's gait, looking for any impairment. He'd only been back on the job a few weeks, after being shot during their last case. It was only a flesh wound, but the hairless white scar arrowing over his hindquarter was a constant reminder of how close she'd come to losing him. She'd already lost one K-9 partner in her career; she was not about to lose another. But Hawk was strong and healed quickly, showing no sign of weakness as he loped along.

Hawk suddenly cut to the right, off the pavement of Roosevelt Drive and onto grass. As he arrowed between the pale, ghostly rows of headstones, Meg's eyes were drawn to the distant lights parting the darkness. Ahead, John F. Kennedy's eternal flame danced on its stone base in ever-shifting tones of red and orange. Above it, high on the hill keeping watch over the dead below, General Robert E.

Lee's majestic columned mansion shone, lit by both spotlights and moonlight.

Come to Washington's House in Alexandria.

She turned back to her dog and the task at hand. "Find
her, Hawk," Meg encouraged. She was very conscious of the
fact she had to let Hawk lead, but the house was right there.
She could help keep his spirits up and spur him on to—

He suddenly cut left, crossing back over Roosevelt Drive
and then onto grass again. Meg cast one last look at the
Greek Revival mansion and then turned her eyes back to
her dog. *Trust him. He knows what to do.*

They ran through the moon-tipped granite headstones,
and under the spreading boughs of trees, some hundreds
of years old. Hawk's breath was coming louder now, but
his gait was steady, only occasionally slowing to scent the air,
then speeding back up again as if he understood the press of
time.

To the west, the Memorial Amphitheater glowed at the
top of stark white steps. Meg couldn't see the Tomb of the
Unknown Soldier, but she'd been there in person enough
times to picture the solitary soldier on his march, his rifle
on his shoulder, his steps sure. Honoring the dead and
their memory every hour of every day.

Ahead, Hawk started to zigzag between the rows of
stones, and Meg focused sharply on his body language. Up
to now, he'd been running in a fairly straight line in search
of scent. But now as his pattern changed and he wove back
and forth, Meg knew he'd found part of a scent cone and
was trying to distinguish the outer limits of the cone and
the strengthening concentration as they closed in on the
source. She praised him quietly, but hung back to let him
work without distraction. Time was dripping away and
every second could mean the difference between life and
death.

As Hawk crossed Eisenhower Drive, his search became

more focused, his body tense, his movements more sure and directed. In the peripheral light of her flashlight, Meg noticed the sharpness of the engraving in the headstones and, slowing down, shone the light on several nearby stones, noting the recent death dates. Meg pulled the radio off her belt. "Brian?"

A moment's pause, then, "I'm here. Found something?"

"I think so. Hawk's caught a scent. Where are you?"

"Lacey circled us behind Arlington House, but there's nothing here. Maybe this isn't the Washington House the guy meant. Where are you?"

"Heading into section sixty, due east of the Memorial Amphitheater. From the look of things here, this is where the recent burials are. I've seen several from this year and last. Just wanted to give you a heads-up. I may need you."

"I'll be there. We'll stay on this until you say otherwise. I know where you are and can be there within a few minutes."

"Thanks. Over and out."

Hawk ran faster now, his nose skimming the ground, and Meg had to scramble a bit to catch up. Then, all of a sudden, he angled to the right, straight toward a fresh grave. Clearly, it was from a funeral earlier that day; even in the diffuse light of the flashlight beam, the grass was pressed down on both sides of the grave as if trampled by many feet. While dirt filled the grave to the grass line, it had yet to be turfed over. Out of respect, Meg started to circle around the grave, not wishing to disturb whoever had been freshly laid to rest. But she jerked to a halt when Hawk gave a single sharp bark and launched himself directly at the grave, landing at one end, his front paws already furiously digging.

She's in the grave? Buried alive?

Meg frantically scanned the area, her gaze coming to rest on a landscaping truck, twenty feet away, parked at the side of the road. The groundskeeping team had likely run out of time to close the grave completely before dark and had left everything in place to finish up tomorrow. She sprinted across the grass, darting between headstones, her gaze locked on the shovels standing upright in the truck bed. Snatching a shovel, she raced back to the grave, pulling her radio free.

"Brian, come in." She didn't even give him a full second before she barked his name again. "Brian!"

"I'm here. What's going on?" he gasped with a panting breath. "Lacey, hold."

"Get down here. I think Hawk's found her. He zeroed in on a fresh grave here in section sixty. He's digging, trying to get her out."

"She's *in* the grave? Holy sh—" He cut off his own profanity and she could hear the sound of his footfalls speeding up. "Lacey, come! I'll be there as soon as I can. Keep your flashlight on hand to guide me in."

"Will do." Meg cut the transmission, dropping her radio and flashlight onto the damp grass and dug in with her shovel as fast as she could, tossing spadefuls of earth out on the grass. Beside her, Hawk kept his head down, digging faster, a cloud of dirt flying out from between his back legs. Every once in a while, he'd tip his nose down as if to reconfirm the scent and then would be back at it, if possible with even greater urgency.

Meg's head shot up when she heard Brian's call and turned to see light bobbling about fifty feet away. She picked up her flashlight and waved it at him. "Over here." Brian jogged closer and she jabbed an index finger in the direction of the truck. "Grab a shovel."

Brian tore off toward the pickup as Lacey jumped in to join Hawk, immediately starting to dig. Returning, Brian dropped his flashlight on the grass, light spilling into the slowly deepening hole. For a full five minutes, there were no words, just the scrabble of paws and the repetitive stab of shovels.

Thump.

Meg and Brian froze as his shovel made contact with something solid with a hollow echo.

"Finally," he muttered. "Lacey, time to get out, girl."

"Hawk, out." Meg motioned for him to jump out. "You're awesome, but this job is for us." She patted a grimy hand on the grass at the edge of the four-foot hole. "Good boy," she praised as he leapt out, Lacey on his heels. She met Brian's eyes. "Let's finish this."

The relatively unpacked dirt allowed them to work quickly, revealing the top of the dark wood coffin. Brian cleared the hinges on one side, while Meg worked on the other, digging back far enough for them to perch on a narrow band of dirt to open the box.

They tossed their shovels on the grass, crowding together at the side of the coffin.

The silence around them and at their feet made Meg's stomach clench nervously.

Together they bent down, curling fingers under the rim of the coffin lid to heft the heavy lid upward. Hinges protested slightly, the dirt-caked hardware jamming briefly, but then they yielded and the lid lifted smoothly.

The wash of illumination from the flashlights at the edge of the grass fell over the inside of the coffin where a woman lay limp. Meg dropped to her knees into the dirt, pushing aside clothing and torn strips of a satiny material, searching frantically for a pulse. Her shaking fingers slid across flesh that was still warm, smearing splotches of blood as she pushed in further.

Nothing.

"Let me try." Brian shouldered in beside her, his hands sliding in under hers.

Meg pulled back, horrified, taking in the contents of the coffin, as Brian desperately looked for signs of life.

There were two bodies in the coffin. A soldier buried in full dress blues, complete with shiny brass buttons and devices, light blue cord, and a starched white shirt. Above the shirt was nearly translucent skin on one side of the face and catastrophic burns on the other. Here was a man, clearly lost in the fury of battle, meant to finally rest in peace in his solitary grave, surrounded by countless row upon row of his fellow soldiers.

Solitary no more.

The woman from the picture Craig had showed them lay on top of him, jammed into the small space below the lid. She wore black yoga pants, sneakers, and a hooded sweatshirt—exactly what you might wear on a cool spring evening while walking your dog. Exactly how Meg herself dressed to walk Hawk more times than she could count.

"Goddamn it." Brian sat back on his haunches beside Meg, his shoulders drooping, his head bent. "She's gone."

"She's still warm." Meg's words were hoarse, forced through a throat thick with emotion.

"Not fully. I'm no expert, but we didn't just miss her. We were close, but not that close. Maybe a half hour ago. Possibly less."

Meg shifted back to sit on the edge of the grass. "He buried her alive. She was a pawn in his game. A disposable pawn."

Brian pushed to his feet, stepping clear of the grave. "I'm going to call Craig. And the Evidence Response Team."

"We need to bring Lauren and Scott back in."

Brian's hand dropped to land briefly on Meg's shoulder. "Craig will know what to do. Climb out of there. Nothing more we can do for her now, and the crime scene team will already be put out that we disturbed the scene as much as we did."

Meg clambered to her feet to stand beside the grave as Brian moved away, but she couldn't take her eyes off the woman. The black-and-white driver's license photo had given her some idea, but now the shock hit her full force: pale skin; dull, staring blue eyes; long, straight black hair. Black Irish, just like Meg and her sister, Cara.

It was like looking down at her own corpse.

The combined light of their flashlights told a tale of terror in horrifying detail: from the woman's fingertips, nails cruelly ripped off, the ends of her fingers worn to stumps and studded with splinters of wood, bloodied flesh torn away to reveal the ghostly glint of bone; to the crimson droplets splattered over face and clothes; to the ragged gouges in the lining of the coffin, right through to the wooden lid.

They'd come too late. She'd died while they wasted precious time.

A soft whine drew her gaze down to the black Labrador at her side, restlessly shifting his weight. Hawk, still in his dirt-caked navy-and-yellow FBI vest, looked up at her with sad eyes. He'd come to find life, but all they'd found was death. For a search-and-rescue dog, nothing was more devastating.

She crouched down beside him, slinging an arm around him to tip her head against his. "I know, bud, I know. You tried so hard and did everything right. We let you down too. I'm sorry." Her gaze slid across the open slice of earth to fall over tumbled black hair and deathly-white skin. "I'm sorry," she whispered.

Footsteps sounded behind her. "Craig's bringing Lauren and Scott back in. And agents and Evidence Response are on their way."

She turned to find Brian standing behind her. Even in the dim light, his green eyes seemed even more luminous than usual, highlighted by the paleness of his skin beneath his untidy dark hair. He held out his hand, as filthy as hers, and met her eyes. They'd worked, side by side, as part of the FBI's Human Scent Evidence Team for so long, tracking suspects and rescuing the lost, that words weren't needed. They could read each other like open books, and Meg knew instinctively Brian was suffering as much as she.

She slid her hand into his, fingers clamping tight, and let him pull her to her feet. But once upright, he didn't release her hand. Shoulder to shoulder, they stood with their dogs, trying vainly to fathom the unfathomable.

Meg finally broke the silence with the question that had haunted her for hours, but now only grew more complex and horrifying. "Why me?"

"I don't know." Brian rubbed his free hand over his forehead, unmindful of the dark smudge his fingers left behind.

"I don't just mean the coded message. *Look* at her."

His gaze flicked sideways at her, then down into the grave, but he remained silent.

"Am I crazy? Am I the only one seeing it?" she pushed.

Suddenly he turned on her, the anger from a night gone badly wrong glinting in his eyes and in the punch of his words. "You need me to say it? That he not only sent you a message to find her, but she looks like you as well? That he sent you in search of your own death?"

Meg expected his words to compound the darkness crowding her, but instead, to her surprise, the gloom lightened fractionally. *I'm not crazy.* She gripped his hand tighter. "I knew you'd be with me on this."

Solidarity met her grip, strength for strength. "Always." Anger washed away under the weight of the same guilt and exhaustion she felt, and his voice was calmer now. "This scares me. Assuming it's a guy, what the hell is he trying to prove?"

"I don't know. But we have to find out before he takes someone else."

"You think he intends to take more?"

"I can't say for sure, but I have a bad feeling. He goes to all this trouble, leads us on this kind of wild-goose chase, and plans on only killing once? No. He'll strike again, and intuition tells me he won't wait long."

Thirty minutes later, Meg and Brian stood under the spreading boughs of a nearby massive white oak in the diffuse wash of spotlights when they heard a familiar voice call out to them. They turned to find Lauren, blond and statuesque, striding toward them; Rocco was trotting at her side. Not far behind slouched the tall, lanky form of Scott, with Theo heeling beside him.

"Craig filled us in, but neither of us could just go home. We needed to come, to see the end of this."

Meg's gaze traveled across the thirty feet separating them from the grave, now surrounded by Evidence Response Team members in white Kevlar suits, brilliantly lit by a half-dozen portable spotlights. "We're staying out of their way while they're collecting evidence and the body."

"Craig told us some of it. She was buried in a soldier's grave?"

"Arlington's executive director came in when he heard what was happening and he stopped by and shared some information with us. The US Army officer in the grave, Lieutenant Henry Ranger, was buried this afternoon in a ceremony with full honors. He was one of twenty-three burials today and the groundskeeping team filled the grave, but it got dark before they could seal the grave with turf. They left the truck to come back first thing tomorrow morning to finish up."

"And in the meantime, someone got into the cemetery with the victim. How? The gates would have been locked."

"They were. But the cemetery is bounded by a three-foot fieldstone wall. The front sections of the cemetery have four feet of wrought-iron spikes for additional security, but the back sections of the cemetery are just the original wall. You can't drive in, but you can get close, park off the street, and hop right over the wall. Our perp would have done it with the victim tossed over his shoulder or in some sort of bag to disguise her. If she was unconscious and still, no one might have thought twice about it. And assuming he went in after sundown, no one would have seen him."

"The cemetery is closed at dusk," Brian added, "but they know sometimes people are in there when it's closed. They rarely have any problems because of it, and if Emergency Services finds them and asks them to leave, they usually do without any fuss. But this time, nobody saw anything."

"So he came in with the victim," Scott said, "found an open grave by chance, dug it up, put her in, and closed it again?"

"If he scouted out the area at all, then he would get a feel for how funerals work here." Meg looked out into the darkness away from the blinding spotlights. "He'd know where the majority of recent burials are, and he'd know this section is where most of the War on Terror burials are located. He'd know how they handle closing the graves and how often graves are unfinished at the end of the day. He could just look like a mourner coming later in the day and leaving just at closing time, but he'd be scoping out his surroundings and making plans. If he took her from somewhere nearby, he could have confirmed the open grave before the cemetery closed tonight, and then doubled back later with the victim."

"Convenient of the grounds staff to leave that truck right there overnight." Lauren studied the truck and the landscaping equipment protruding from the back. "Although you have to think, he must have had a backup plan."

"Any folding shovel would have done the job, but why use something like that when you have professional landscaping tools right there? It wouldn't have taken him that long if he worked fast. And I suspect we're looking at someone with a certain amount of strength to be able to kidnap victims and carry them around like this."

"It took you and me, what . . . around seven or eight minutes in total?" When Meg nodded, Brian continued. "One guy, relatively strong, maybe fifteen minutes max to dig it out and less to put it back. I never noticed traces of dirt on the grass around the grave, but you were already into digging when I got there, and no one cared where the dirt went except out. Did you notice?"

"No. Hawk and I were so focused on digging, we didn't have time to take in our surroundings in detail." She sighed, discouragement riding heavily on the mournful sound. "Maybe we'd have more information if we had." She sagged back against the tree trunk. "I just can't help but feel we could have done better. But how? If we'd found the dog earlier? Solved the riddle faster? Figured out its meaning right from the start? How could we have stopped this?"

"We couldn't." Meg looked up sharply, but Lauren kept her voice level and calm. Lauren was always the least emotional of the group, but Meg could sense she was shaken nonetheless. "We worked as fast as we could with limited information. And when that information was inconclusive, we split up to better our chances."

"If we'd gone for Arlington right off the bat, we might have gotten here in time."

"You can second-guess yourself through every step we took tonight, but that's not going to bring her back."

"Lauren's right," Scott agreed. "Everyone did the best they could. The only thing we can do now is figure out how to do better the next time."

"Because there will be a next time." Brian's tone was grim as his eyes traveled back toward the grave where death, old and new, lay. "Whoever he is, he's not even close to being done."

CHAPTER 2

Regroup: The reassembly of an army into organized units after an attack or battlefield retreat.

Monday, May 22, 11:56 PM
Jennings residence
Arlington, Virginia

Meg pulled her SUV into the double driveway, but then sat blinking in confusion at the unfamiliar pickup truck parked in her spot. Glancing at the house, she found it fully lit, instead of dark as expected. It wasn't that late; maybe her sister had a visitor. If so, she'd politely say hello and then disappear.

She was not in the mood for company.

She was also exhausted, discouraged, and filthy. And before she could take care of herself, she needed to deal with her equally filthy dog, who needed a bath and an extra meal, in that order. Grabbing her SAR bag, Meg slid out of the driver's seat, stumbling slightly as she reached for the back door. She pulled it open to find Hawk already on his feet and ready to jump down.

"You've had enough of tonight too, haven't you?" Meg patted her thigh. "Come."

Hawk leapt from the compartment to land at her feet,

tipping his head up to her for praise and an affectionate scratch.

"Come on, let's clean up and go to bed."

They headed for the side door with dragging steps. Meg fumbled her keys, nearly dropping them, but caught them just before they tumbled from her fingers. Muttering under her breath, she jammed the key in the lock and opened the door. Hawk preceded her into the dim mudroom, illuminated only by light filtering in from the living room. She closed the door behind them and locked it. Then she tipped her head against the door and simply breathed in the comfort of home.

"Meg?" Cara's voice behind her had her turning to find her sister standing silhouetted in the open doorway.

"Hey."

"Bad one?"

Meg couldn't help the bitter laugh from escaping. "Yeah."

"Worse than the Whitten Building?"

"Not in terms of sheer numbers, but definitely in terms of horrific ways to d—" She cut off as a second backlit form filled the doorway. It was undoubtedly a man, inches taller than her sister's nearly six-foot frame and easily twice as broad. "Sorry, I didn't know you had company. I'll get out of your way."

"I'm not her company. I'm yours."

As she heard the man's voice, comprehension dawned. Todd Webb, the firefighter she met on her last case. They had plans to go to a movie together on their mutual night off. She'd totally forgotten.

This was just not her night.

"I'm sorry. I got called out on this case and—"

Webb stepped forward, holding up a hand. "You never need to explain emergencies to a first responder. Cara told me you got an unexpected case. She didn't know when you'd be back, so I volunteered to wait. We got to talking, and before we knew it, a few hours had passed. And here you are."

"I'm sorry you waited all this time. It hasn't been a good night and I'm not feeling very social."

Cara reached over and flipped up the light switch on the wall. Bright light flooded the small room, revealing rows of natural wood shelves, stacked cabinets, and hooks bearing everything from rain gear to dog leashes. Her gaze ran first over Meg, from head to toe, and then Hawk, taking in both dirt-caked clothes and fur. "What on earth were you into tonight?" She started toward Meg.

"A soldier's grave at Arlington."

Cara froze partway across the room, caught by not only the words, but also by Meg's flat tone of voice. "You said it was a 'horrific way' to die. But the occupant of a grave is usually already deceased. Someone else died?"

Can't talk about it. Don't want to talk about it. "I can't tell you any more than will be in the papers tomorrow after the media liaison releases the basics. Someone was buried alive. We didn't find her in time." Her hands curled into fists. "But we were close enough that she was still warm."

"You did your best." Webb's words drew her gaze. He still hung back in the doorway as if unwilling to intrude, but couldn't resist trying to help, even from a distance.

"Sometimes your best doesn't get the job done," Meg answered.

"You can't beat yourself up about that." When her jaw tightened and her eyes dropped from his, Webb stepped forward. "If I let every smoke inhalation or fire death get to me, I wouldn't be able to get the job done. Same thing with medical calls. You give your all with the situation and tools you've been given. And then you have to let it go and set your sights on saving the next person who needs you or you'll go crazy. And they'll suffer the consequences."

I don't think I'm going to be allowed to let this one go.

As if hearing her thoughts, her cell phone rang. She closed her eyes for a second, trying to center herself. Unless there was a life-or-death emergency with her parents, there was only one group of people who would be calling at this time of night. She pulled out her phone—"Craig Beaumont" was displayed on-screen.

"Jennings."

"Are you home yet?"

"Just walked in the door. What's happened?"

"We've got another one. It's addressed to you again."

"Already? We just barely finished the last one." She could hear the mounting fury in her own voice. From the quizzical looks she was getting from Cara and Webb, they could hear it too. She turned her back in some semblance of privacy and steadied her tone. "Same type of message as last time?"

"Yes. The CRRU boys are on their way back to Quantico to crack it for us. But there's a problem."

"This whole thing is a problem."

"I couldn't agree more. But this vic was taken two days ago."

"*What?*"

"I know. A woman disappeared two days ago, and her dog was found outside alone. No one found the note, so no one knew to connect us to the case or where to look for her. One of the special agents working tonight's case was smart enough to put two and two together and followed up with the local PD, which sent someone out to take a better look at the dog's leash. That's when they found the note. It was tucked away so well, no one spotted it."

"The chances of her still being alive . . ."

"Near zero, I know. But 'near zero' means there's still a chance. Get back here. Hopefully, by the time everyone is back in the office, Quantico will know where to send you."

Meg glanced at her watch. "I need to take the time to feed Hawk or he won't make it through another search. I'll be there in forty-five minutes. If you get new intel, we can redirect en route." She ended the call and turned around to find Cara and Webb staring at her. She gave them a crooked smile. "No rest for the wicked. No time to clean up either, apparently. I have to go."

"I'll feed Hawk," Cara said. "You just worry about you. Hawk, come." She left the mudroom, Hawk trotting at her heels.

Webb stepped closer and tipped Meg's head up with an index finger so he could see her eyes. From his expression, he didn't like what he saw there. "You okay?"

"Have to be."

"It doesn't sound like you're walking into a very hopeful situation."

"I think this will be a recovery, not a rescue."

"So do your best. It's all anyone can ask. And if you want to talk it out later, you know I'm here." When she started to protest, he cut her off. "Even if you can't discuss the case, there are still things you can talk about. I've been there, done that, so I'll get it. No pressure, but the offer stands anytime you need it."

Meg forced herself to stop for a moment before responding. He was trying to share his own struggles and experiences to help lighten her burden. Refusing out of hand was not only stupid, but it was hurtful. She reached up on tiptoe and pressed a brief kiss to his jaw. "Thank you. I don't know what I'm walking into, but I appreciate the offer and I'll seriously take you up on it if I can." She stepped back and straightened her shoulders. "Now Hawk and I need to get to work."

CHAPTER 3

Horology: In current usage, the art and science of making precision mechanical timepieces. In the decade prior to the start of the U.S. Civil War, American watch manufacturing was transformed based upon the "armory practices" of the United States Armory emphasizing machine-based mass production of identical, interchangeable parts to allow rapid assembly and repair. The American Watch Company, which had manufactured and sold only twenty thousand watches before the start of the war, sold an additional 160,000 pocket watches by 1865. The "Model 1859"—sold as the "Wm. Ellery grade"—was worn by President Lincoln and marketed to Union forces. The company emerged from the war as the main supplier of precision railroad chronometers in the United States and over fifty other countries.

Tuesday, May 23, 12:48 AM
Forensic Canine Unit, J. Edgar Hoover Building
Washington, DC

Lauren, Rocco, Brian, and Lacey were already at their desks in the bull pen when Meg arrived, Hawk trotting at her heels. After a quick meal at home and a power nap in the SUV, Hawk looked much perkier than Meg was feeling.

Meg collapsed into her desk chair and gave Hawk the hand signal to lie down. He flopped at her feet and put his head down on his crossed paws with a sigh.

"Scott called to say he's on his way," Brian said. "Should be here any minute."

Meg swiped a hand over gritty eyes and swiveled her chair to face Craig's closed office door. "He's in there?"

"He got impatient waiting for Quantico to call, so he thought harassing them would speed them up." Lauren's voice was flat with exhaustion.

"He wants us out there ASAP. The longer this takes, the less chance we have of saving her," Brian said. "Do we even know who 'she' is?"

"I'm sure that's one of the details he's getting," Meg said. "Though, really, I'm not sure that really matters right now. All that counts is saving her. We can figure out the rest later when we have the luxury of time."

"Agreed." Lauren leaned back in her chair and closed her eyes. "This has the possibility of being a *really* long night, so I'm just going to rest for a few minutes. Wake me up when—" Her eyes flew open as Craig's door crashed against the wall. "Scratch that." She sat up, blinking rapidly as if to clear blurry vision. "We've got something?" she called to Craig.

"We do." Craig strode out of his office just as Scott and Theo came through the door. "Good, everyone's here. Thanks for extending an already-long day." His gaze slid across the group of exhausted handlers and the snoozing dogs at their feet. "I know you're tired."

"We are, but that won't stop us." Scott pulled up a chair.

"Don't sit down. I want you all out the door in ninety seconds." As Scott shoved the chair back toward his desk, Craig glanced quickly at the scribbled notes in his hand.

"The victim's name is Michelle Wilson. We found this picture of her online." He pulled out a sheet from behind his notes and flipped it so the group could see it.

Meg's stomach clenched and she glanced at Brian to find him already staring at her. *Black hair, pale skin and light eyes. Black Irish.*

But Craig continued on, as if he hadn't seen the silent exchange. "She was taken Saturday night, sometime after ten PM, while walking her dog on the beach in Cape Charles, on Virginia's Eastern Shore. Someone heard the dog barking outside Ms. Wilson's house around midnight and went to investigate. They found the beachside house locked up, and the dog outside, his leash still attached to his collar. They called the cops who entered her residence, but there was no trace of her. Her car was in the garage, and nothing was out of place. It appears she took the dog out for a walk and simply vanished."

"Just like Sandy Holmes," Scott said.

"The Cape Charles PD opened a missing person report right away, instead of waiting the usual twenty-four hours, because of the circumstances. They didn't believe that she was simply off somewhere on her own. But their investigation led to nothing notable, and they had no evidence of foul play."

"Until the note was found," Meg said.

"And that was missed during the initial investigation. It was found in the same location—a small container attached to the leash for waste bags—but pushed so far in, no one saw it. The note is in the same code as the one used for the first victim."

"Except she wasn't the first," Brian interjected. "She was actually number two. The note was addressed to Meg again?"

"Identical addressing to Meg here at the FBI. CRRU reports this as the decoded message, 'She is on John Smith's Island in a place known to her family. Will she die there too? Not if you hurry.' "

Brian leaned forward on a groan, his elbows braced on his knees as he grabbed twin handfuls of hair and pulled in frustration. "And what does *that* mean? Could it be more vague?"

"It means who she is does matter," Lauren said. "The clue is clearly directly related to her. But how are we going to narrow that down? I'm a long way from high-school history class, but didn't Smith discover a lot of islands as one of America's early coastal explorers?"

"He did, and that's causing some trouble. Apparently, he discovered a number of islands from the Chesapeake Bay area, right up the eastern seaboard to New Hampshire."

"We don't have time to search every key location he found," Meg protested. "Are the CRRU boys confident in the search location?"

"There's maybe more guessing than I'd like, because we're short of time, but they have a theory. It's the best we've got, so we're running with it. It's the middle of the night and we don't have time to interview her friends and family, so they pulled this information off her personal Facebook page. Ms. Wilson is the senior vice president of the Daughters of Union Veterans of the Civil War. She's related to a Corporal George Wilson, of Company L of the First Maryland Cavalry, who died at the Confederate prison camp on Belle Isle, Virginia."

Meg sat up straighter, suddenly awake as hope and a feeling of some semblance of control filled her. "I know Belle Isle. I've been there many times. It's right across the river from Richmond. It was one of John Smith's discoveries?"

"Yes."

Lauren pushed to her feet. "And it matches the clue. Her family knows of it, and one of them died there."

"There are probably other possibilities we don't have time to explore yet, but we're going to go with this one and hope we'll be lucky. It's relatively close and it makes sense. I told them I needed something to start you on, but they're still going to keep looking for any other possibilities. If anything else seems more likely, I'll let you know on the way. It's going to take you over an hour to get there, as it is."

By this point, all the handlers were on their feet, their dogs awake and alert, feeling the building tension in the room.

"Any idea as to where she might be on the island?" Scott asked. "The clue doesn't really help there."

"No." Craig met Meg's eyes. "You know this island. Suggestions?"

"A few." Meg picked up her SAR pack and pulled it on. "It's now a city park, but there are still some ruins on the island. There were ironworks and a power company in the nineteenth and twentieth centuries. And there is still some Civil War era brickwork left. The abandoned power plant would be the best place to hide someone for several days, as it's the only intact building on the island and it's been locked up for the past few years to keep urban explorers out." She glanced down at Hawk. "But we'll let the dogs lead us. They didn't fail us at Arlington, and they won't fail us now." She looked back up at the team. "We've still got a chance at this. Let's roll."

CHAPTER 4

Tailrace: The downstream side where water exits below a turbine or hydroelectric dam. In 2012, the National Park Service's Archeology Program explored and documented the mostly intact tailrace of the second National Armory commissioned by the government in 1798. The surviving ruins are located in the Lower Armory Grounds at Harpers Ferry National Historical Park.

Tuesday, May 23, 2:16 AM
Belle Isle
Richmond, Virginia

Moonlight guided the teams as they jogged across the footbridge crossing the tributary of the James River, the sturdy wooden planks vibrating under the thump of boot and paw as tumbling streams of water washed underneath the steel trusses.

"There!" Meg threw the word over her shoulder as she pointed at the pale three-story building on the far side of the bank, set deep into the encroaching forest. "That's the old power plant."

"Looks like a good choice!" Brian called back. "Now let's see if the dogs agree with us."

Even with lights and sirens going, and minimal late-night traffic, it had taken the team over an hour and a quarter to reach their destination. They parked in the lot just south of the James River, crossed the short bridge over the train tracks, and followed the riverside path until they reached the footbridge. The night was quiet and dark, with only the moon and their flashlights for light, but the dogs' steps were sure and they loped along easily beside their handlers.

Meg pulled up as they came to the end of the footbridge, waiting until everyone was grouped around her. "Quick overview to orient yourself in the dark." She pointed to the northeast. "That was where the Confederate prison camp was. There's not much left of it now, as there were no buildings for the prisoners, only a bunch of tents that were insufficient for the thousands held here. A huge number of men died and were buried on the island. Those graves have now been moved, but their location is marked. The ironworks was also over on the east end of the island and there are several metal structures left from it, including the ruins of both the old oil house and the rolling and milling facility. But that would be a harder place to hide anyone, as neither building is complete or has a roof. The old power plant is the only intact building because it's the newest and was used until the 1960s. There are also the remains of several quarries on the island, the biggest of which is on the western tip of the island and has been flooded to become a deep man-made pond, so be careful in the dark. Let's split up so we can cover ground more quickly, but keep your radios on. Call out if you run into trouble or if you find her."

One at a time, each handler unleashed his dog and gave the animal the command to search. One at a time, they headed off into the darkness, following their dog's lead. Lauren and Scott headed out first, both of their dogs choosing the main path that led northeast to run under the

Robert E. Lee Bridge. Lacey chose due north, heading straight into the brush, much to Brian's discontented muttering about always taking the hard way.

Then Meg and Hawk were alone. In the distance, over the north fork of the James River, the lights of Richmond glowed, even at this time of night. Her old stomping grounds. She rarely came back after Deuce's death, finding it still too painful. But somehow, standing here with Deuce's legacy at her side, it was the love that remained, rather than the pain.

Meg unleashed Hawk and bent down to meet his eyes. "This is going to be hard, buddy. No fresh trail to follow, and if she's trapped inside, probably no decent scent cone until we're practically on top of her." She stood, gazing down the path that ran southwest to the power plant. *Hell with it.* Normally, she let Hawk lead, but time was desperately short, so she was going to point him in the direction her gut told her was not only the right way to go, but was the only section of the island not already covered by a K-9 team. "Hawk, come." She led him along the main hiking loop toward the western end of the island before giving him the command. "Find her, Hawk. Find Michelle."

He lifted his nose, sampling the air, and then trotted down the path in the direction of the power plant. She could tell he didn't have a scent at this point, but, as far as she was concerned, she was stacking the deck in Michelle's favor, especially since the teams were well distributed over the length and breadth of the island. *If time hasn't already run out.* She pushed that thought away. After one unsuccessful search tonight, she really hoped that she wouldn't have to comfort her dog a second time.

Another woman who looked like her might die tonight. Might already be dead. And the thought that the death might be in her stead was too horrifying to contemplate.

Focus.

"Find her, Hawk."

The dog's ears pricked, indicating he heard the command, but his stride didn't waver. They jogged down the hard-packed dirt path lined by thick forest, the leafy canopy blocking out nearly all the moonlight. The beam of Meg's flashlight lit a ghostly circle on the ground in front of them, dissipating into blackness into the trees.

The first indication that Hawk had something came with the waving flag of his tail, paired with the slowing of his steps.

"Got something, buddy? Good boy!" Meg hung back, not wanting to disturb any air currents, waiting with bated breath to see which direction he'd go. She gave a small fist pump of triumph as Hawk cut left, right into the foliage, his head low now, his steps hampered by bushes and jutting tree roots. But he was unmistakably headed toward the abandoned power plant.

She knew within minutes that he'd lost the scent, but she wasn't concerned. This was part of his process, especially in a search where she suspected the victim was inside a structure. She quietly encouraged him, doing her best to light his way as he pushed through the forest before them. Suddenly he broke out onto a narrow dirt path, hardly wide enough for either of them single file, but he immediately turned toward the looming bulk of concrete rising above the trees. He had the scent again.

Meg pulled her radio off her belt. "Meg here. I think we have something. Anyone else?"

"We're at the quarry, and nothing so far." Brian's voice seemed overloud in the still night air.

"We're under the bridge, almost all the way to the edge of the island. Rocco doesn't have anything," Lauren reported.

"Theo neither. We're just past the oil house. Where are you?" Scott asked.

Meg ducked and pushed under a low branch. "Coming

up on what looks like a fieldstone wall. But beyond it is the power plant."

"You called it," Lauren said. "Want us to come in?"

"Not until I've got better evidence that he's really onto something. One of the reasons they locked up the power plant was because people used to sit in there and smoke weed at all hours of the night. Let me make sure it's not a bunch of stoners."

"We'll keep looking then. Lauren out."

Scott and Brian signed off and then it was just handler and dog again. Ahead of them, the thick fieldstone wall loomed out of the darkness, the path passing through a low, semicircular opening lined with corrugated metal. Hawk shot right through, but Meg had to bend over double to clear the low ceiling. She scurried through the four-foot channel and then took a moment to take in the moonlit buildings that filled the clearing.

The larger building to her right was constructed of concrete and rusting steel, the outside walls covered with multicolored graffiti. She remembered coming here years ago with a mechanical-minded friend who explained all about hydroelectric-power generation, and those odd details helped fill in strategic gaps as to possible victim location. The concrete-lined "millrace" carried water from the James River through the plant, where it turned the huge turbine blades, before falling out the front of the plant and back into the James. The turbines were connected to massive generators inside the building that produced electricity. That power was carried through the smaller transformer building beside it and then off to Richmond to power the early twentieth-century streetcar system.

She closed her eyes, listening for any sound that could indicate a human presence, but there was nothing. Opening her eyes, she spotted Hawk, fifteen feet ahead and moving faster and faster as he arrowed straight for the gated entrance. She sprinted to catch up to him. Years ago, when she'd last been inside this building, this had been an open doorway, but metal bars now covered all the windows and formed the metal gate. A thick, dull silver chain was wrapped between the gate and the grating, which made up a section of the wall. With a gasp, Meg realized the ends dangled free and the padlock, which normally locked the entrance, lay on the ground below, the heavy U-shaped shackle cut in half.

He knew to come with bolt cutters. This is it.

Hawk stood at her knee and whined as she pulled off the chain and draped it over the iron bars, in case there was any evidence to be recovered. She yanked open the metal gate, with an ear-piercing squeal, and Hawk was through the moment the gap was wide enough. Meg stepped into the huge, cavernous space—three stories overhead and lit by moonlight flowing through the barred windows to fall on the floor at her feet. Using her flashlight, she made quick work of her initial search, her light bouncing off colorful graffiti, iron barred windows, and three massive concrete pads that once supported the generators. Opposite the footings, three heavily riveted concave steel semicircles, each easily eight feet across, protruded into the space beyond. Hawk made a beeline for the nearest steel circle, and as Meg trained her light on him, she saw that where the other two massive steel circles were sealed, this one was missing the middle steel plate that should have enclosed the center two feet of the dome. Hawk went right to it, jumping up onto the built-in platform, which was part of the structure, and stuck his head into the void beyond. Pulling back, he gave two piercing barks, the sound echoing off the bare walls and high ceiling of the generation room.

"Good boy. Out of the way a second." Meg gave Hawk a gentle push to the side of the platform and knelt on it herself. She leaned her upper body through the gap, leading with her flashlight. The room on the other side was only a third of the width of the building, but it had the same empty height above. Meg trained her light on the floor below. And that's when she saw her.

The woman was a little older than Meg, and carried a few more pounds, but her long, straight black hair was pulled back into a braid to reveal the gag that sunk between her lips. She sat on the edge of the steel-lined concrete pad that had once housed the turbine, her legs dangling down into the void below, where the turbine blades would have spun in the water passing through. Her hands were tied behind her back and then strapped to a metal pole behind her, high enough to force her shoulders nearly down to her knees.

She wasn't moving.

"Ma'am! Ma'am, can you hear me? I'm with the FBI."

Nothing.

Meg couldn't tell if she was unconscious or dead. She pulled back through the hole and ripped her radio off her belt. "It's Meg. I'm in the power plant and I've got her. I need more hands and I need 911. I can't get to her yet, so I don't know her status, but get a medical team here now in case she's still with us."

"I'll call for help." Lauren's voice was crisp and calm.

Both Brian and Scott reported they'd be there right away and Meg signed off. She wriggled out of her SAR pack, knowing she'd have trouble getting through the gap with it on. She pushed it through the hole and lowered it down onto the concrete platform below; then she turned to her dog. "Hawk, stay. I'll be right back." Gripping the narrow metal sill around the opening, she swung both legs in and wriggled through and down to concrete.

The turbine pad was in the middle of the room, but was surrounded by dark, murky water. Meg couldn't tell how deep it was, as her flashlight only bounced off the surface.

She eyed the four-foot gap between the narrow pad and the platform on which she stood.

She'd have to jump it. And she'd have to stick the landing or she'd end up in the turbine shaft, and who knew how deep that was?

She put her pack back on, backed as close to the wall as she could, pushed off in a single step, and leapt across the flooded space. She only had about eighteen inches to land on, but managed to not only land, but also to catch her balance and keep herself from tumbling forward. Already sliding out of her pack and ripping it open in the search for her spring-loaded military knife, Meg rushed to the woman. Even as she pushed the button for the blade to pop free, she was laying a hand on the woman's cheek.

Chilly, but that could be from exposure rather than from death. Maybe they weren't too late after all.

Meg put down her flashlight and sawed at the cords binding her hands. Once released, they fell limply to her sides and the victim slumped sideways. But Meg was ready for her and smoothly rolled her onto her back, pulling her legs out of the shaft to lay out prone.

Bending over, she yanked down the gag and pressed an ear to the woman's mouth. *No breath sounds.* But two fingers pressed to the pulse at her throat rewarded Meg with what she hoped wasn't an imagined weak pulse. Quickly lacing her fingers together, she planted them over the woman's sternum and started CPR.

She heard her name being bellowed through the hole into the adjoining room. Brian was here.

"In here! Look through the hole into the next room." She looked over when a beam of light struck her, blinking until he lowered the light a bit with the command to Lacey to stay. He clambered through the hole and made the jump over to her, hurrying around the far side of the gaping hole to kneel at her side.

"She's alive?"

"Faint pulse. She's been here for days and is dehydrated at the very least. And we don't know what else he might have done to her. Ambulance coming?"

"Yes."

They both looked up to find Lauren leaning in through the hole in the wall.

"We need to keep her going until they get here. We're not in the easiest place to reach."

"We will." Brian nudged Meg over a bit. "Let me take over. We're going to be at this for a while, I suspect, so we'll do best spelling each other off."

They made the switch without missing a beat, and Meg sat back, letting her hands fall into her lap, saving strength for when Brian needed a break.

"You okay?"

Meg looked up to Brian's serious gaze as he bobbed up and down with the compressions. "It's better than it could have been. Honestly, the chances of finding her alive were small. If she'd been buried alive like Sandy Holmes . . ."

"She would have been long dead. I hear you. But he just had her tied up here? I don't get it. If we'd found the note right away, what would be the big deal?"

"I'm not sure, but maybe it's too early to see the pattern yet." She glanced back to where Lauren still watched them, Hawk's head pushed under her arm to keep his eye on her as well. She turned back to Brian. "I'll tell you what I don't like—that this was guesswork. What if the CRRU was wrong? They're lucky they hit on Michelle's background so quickly, but this was never a sure thing. We need better intel if we're going to keep doing this."

"But how? You know they're doing their best."

"I know. But I'm afraid next time, the best simply isn't going to cut it."

CHAPTER 5

Strategic Planning: The process of defining a strategy and allocating personnel and resources to achieve specific goals.

Tuesday, May 23, 3:52 PM
Forensic Canine Unit, J. Edgar Hoover Building
Washington, DC

"Didn't Craig say three-thirty?" Brian tapped his cell phone, the time prominently displayed in stark white numerals on a black background. "You think he forgot?"

Lauren looked up from where she sat at her desk, Rocco tucked into the space around her feet. "Not a chance in hell."

"He's probably in a meeting himself," Scott said. "Maybe Peters needed to see him about last night." Executive Assistant Director Adam Peters was the head of the Criminal, Cyber, Response, and Services Branch, which oversaw the Criminal Investigative, Cyber, and International Operations Divisions, as well as the Critical Incident Response Group, which included the Forensic Canine Unit.

"He could be talking to the hospital to get an update on Michelle," Lauren said. "A coma . . . What happened there that we don't know about? I know she wasn't breathing when you got there, but she didn't seem outwardly injured."

"We don't know how long she wasn't breathing. And we don't know if he drugged her or hurt her in ways we couldn't easily see." Meg leaned back in her chair, feeling like she'd been hit by a Mack truck. The scant few hours of sleep she managed left her feeling exhausted, and the news first thing that morning that Michelle had never regained consciousness at the hospital had been an unexpected further blow. Defeat snatched from the jaws of victory. One dead victim, and one close to death who might not pull through. Discouragement rode her like a physical weight. *Perp, 2. FBI, 0.* She gave herself a mental head shake and pulled herself back into the conversation. "Craig may be down with the investigative boys to pump them for answers so we know what we're looking at."

"That's exactly where I was."

All four handlers swung toward the bull pen door, where Craig stood in his usual uniform of a suit and tie. Not an actual handler himself, Craig always dressed to the nines.

"You were down in CID?" Meg asked.

"I've been everywhere today. I've talked to the cryptanalysts in the CRRU about the code, been down to Evidence Response to find out where we are with scene processing, and I've even had a quick word with SSA Rutherford from the BAU."

Eyebrows rose at the mention of the Behavioral Analysis Unit—the FBI's criminal profilers—but the team waited for Craig to elaborate.

Craig came into the room, shrugging out of his suit jacket and laying it neatly across an unused desk, before he grabbed a spare chair and rolled it up to the group. Hawk raised his head, tilting his nose up to Craig in greeting. "Hey, buddy, good job last night." He ran one large hand down Hawk's back.

"Every time I think Hawk can't surprise me anymore, he does something like find a victim four feet underground in a box." Meg smiled down at her dog, the only thing that lightened her soul in the midst of this case. "Or inside a room with minimal air flow."

"He has a damned fine nose." Craig sat back in the chair. "Now, before we start, because I know it will be your first concern, let me tell you that I just talked to the charge nurse for Michelle Wilson and there's no change in her condition. I have more information on what happened to her, but let's do this stepwise and break down what happened yesterday, starting with victim selection in the order they came to us. First was Sandy Holmes. Ms. Holmes was ex-military. She served with the marines in Iraq in 2012."

"They let women do that back then?" Scott asked. "I thought women in service weren't allowed in Iraq at that time."

"Not on the front lines. But they needed service women working the checkpoints. They'd do body searches of any women and girls going through, looking for explosives, since anyone could be a suicide bomber by that time."

"Dangerous job," Lauren commented.

"That wasn't the hard part of their day, from what I understand. The men working the checkpoint could hunker down and sleep there overnight, but the women had to be ferried back and forth daily between the checkpoint and their bunker. That made them a predictable target. One morning, on the way in, their convoy was hit by a suicide bomber. He rammed his explosives-packed car into the first armored vehicle in the convoy. Everyone in that vehicle died in the explosion. Ms. Holmes was in the second vehicle and sustained some pretty significant injuries. Got an honorable medical discharge and came home to recuperate. She healed physically, but suffered from severe episodes of post-traumatic stress disorder. So she got herself a PTSD service dog named Ruby. From what agents learned, Ruby could stave off a panic attack simply by her presence. When things started getting bumpy, Ruby would be right there and would calm Ms. Holmes down. She never went anywhere without her dog."

"So Ruby being found on her own yesterday really was a red flag." Meg reached for the coffee mug on her desk. "Do we have any idea how the perp separated Ms. Holmes from her dog? It doesn't sound like something she would have done willingly."

"We don't have anything there yet," Craig replied. "Ms. Holmes and Ruby were walking in Glencarlyn Park near their home. They were seen there often, and we've got witnesses corroborating their presence there last night, around seven-thirty."

"Just as dusk was falling," Lauren said. "And I know that park. Off-leash spaces for dogs, but also lots of forest area and a creek. Multiple access points to a road or vehicle. And it connects to Lubber Run, to the north, so she could have been picked up there as well. Who knows how far Ruby ran on her own before she was found?"

"Exactly. Agents will be out there again tonight, canvassing to try to catch a few more who might have been there last night at the same time, so that's still evolving. Related and also ongoing is the autopsy. I've got some very preliminary results. The victim died from oxygen deprivation in a small space, but there were signs of trauma while still alive. The problem is, it's difficult to tell what was a result of her struggle to free herself and what happened during her capture. What was undoubtedly from her capture is the small needle mark inside her left elbow."

"The ME is thinking she was injected with something?

Maybe an anesthetic while the suspect moved her, or a hallucinogen to terrorize her inside the coffin?" Lauren frowned. "Not that something like that would be necessary. It was a self-fulfilling prophesy."

Craig nodded his agreement. "He's a careful man, our ME, and samples have been sent for tox screening. Fibers and swabs have been collected and are being analyzed. But we all know how long that can take."

Meg's mug thumped down with more force than required on the desktop. "What if we tell them we're looking at a repeat offender? Would that light a fire under them?"

Craig sent her a flat look that clearly said, *Settle down.* "This isn't their first rodeo, Jennings. They know what they're doing, and they're doing it as fast as they can." When she opened her mouth to speak again, he raised a hand to stop her. "Moving on to Michelle Wilson. Mrs. Wilson is a widow, living on her own, with only her dog, in Cape Charles. She works in real estate and is well known in town as being a walker. She and that dog go all over town, but their habit during better weather is to walk at night on the beach."

"So she's predictable," Brian said. "If anyone wanted to go after her specifically, there'd be a pattern."

"Yes. She was seen by neighbors as she was heading out toward the beach. Investigators canvassed the area, but no one else saw her. There were multiple access points for both foot and vehicle traffic that crossed or came very close to the beach, so we're not sure where she was taken from."

"We've got two different abductions in two separate locations," Meg reasoned. "There must be a vehicle involved."

"I agree," Craig said. "So we're acquiring any security

footage of the areas available. As far as Mrs. Wilson's physical condition goes, she also had a needle mark inside her elbow. Blood was drawn and tox screens are in process."

"Why is she in a coma?" Meg could hear the words were too harsh, too forceful, but couldn't seem to hold herself back. Women who looked like her were dying and they were losing the game. "What did he do to her?"

"Not much, but it was damned effective. It was all in her positioning when he restrained her. The doctor said it was something called 'positional asphyxiation.' Based on how she was restrained, her ability to breathe was inhibited over a prolonged period of time. Essentially, she suffocated in a room full of air because she couldn't draw enough air into her lungs. Then she went into cardiac arrest." He turned to Meg. "You arrived shortly after and saved her life by unfolding her and starting CPR. But the doctors say it's too early to really understand the amount of damage done. She's not brain dead, but she's in a very deep coma. Only time will tell there."

"So that's two for two, then," Brian said.

" 'Two for two' what?"

"Asphyxiation deaths. Different method, but the same result. This is his goal?"

"That's what Rutherford at the BAU thinks."

"He's taking this case?"

"Normally, they profile after three victims, but this is happening so fast, the pattern is coming together quickly. He's asked us to send him everything we have so he can look at it in much more detail. In his opinion—and it's worth something because he's seen a lot of this kind of thing—with two victims coming this close on top of each other, we should expect the next one soon."

Meg closed her eyes, unable to speak. Soon another woman who looked like her would be in danger. How could she possibly stop it?

Craig either didn't notice her distress, or chose to push onward, since dealing with the case was their only method of offense. "Now let's look at how organized this perp is. The CRRU boys say the code in both notes is a Vigenère cipher, which is a form of polyalphabetic substitution—code substitution using multiple alphabets. This is a really simple form of polyalphabetic substitution, developed in the sixteenth century, but you may be more familiar with a much more complex version of the same type of substitution—the Enigma machine."

"If this is so simple, how come it took them nearly an hour to crack the first code?" Lauren asked. "And not that much less for the second."

"Well, the first time they had to figure out what kind of code it was. From then on, for both messages, they didn't have the keyword for it, so they had to figure it out backward. They ran through the process with me, but I admit I stopped listening about two minutes in. That's their department, and as long as they get the job done, I'm happy to leave it to them."

"Have you got a copy of the messages?" Meg asked.

"Yes."

"Can you get me a copy? My name is on them, so I'd like to know what I was supposed to see. Actually, it might be best if you sent it to all of us. We want everyone on the same page."

"Agreed." Craig pulled out his cell phone, and bent over it for a moment. "There you go. The original and deciphered text and an image of each note."

During the pause while Craig was looking for the report, Meg noticed Brian staring at her. When he didn't take his eyes off her, she finally turned to him. "What?"

"You're not going to bring it up, are you?"

Meg knew exactly what he was talking about; after all, she'd shared it with him. But that was meant to be between them, not for the whole team. She hoped he wouldn't push it, so she played it light. "I think we're covering everything."

"Uh-huh." Brian swung around to face Craig. "No one in this room has said the words out loud, so I'm going to. We all know the notes are addressed to Meg, but the victims also look like her. For Sandy, maybe not so much in the driver's license picture you showed us, but in real life, she looked startlingly like Meg. And Michelle . . ." He turned to meet Meg's narrowed eyes. "Maybe you thought I didn't notice last night, but I did. By that point, I was looking for it. She's a slightly older version of you, but still striking in resemblance. It needs to be said. I'm not suggesting you shouldn't be on this case. It's just another angle we need to keep in mind, and we all need to be aware of, because whoever partners with you needs to keep their eyes open for anything odd."

Lauren sat up and leaned forward. "You think Meg is a target."

"I don't know for sure, but this guy seems to have his sights set on her for some reason."

Meg threw up her hands in frustration. "Why? Honestly, I'm not that special."

Brian gave her a familiar *Don't you dare go dissing yourself* look. "Some of us think you are. And maybe this guy does too. The question is *why*? I mean, it could be a coincidence a single vic looks so strikingly like you, but two? No way. So why is he singling you out?"

"Could be the notoriety from the Mannew case," Craig hypothesized. "Her picture was in the *Washington Post* the morning after the first bombing. Then after she actually caught Mannew, Peters dragged her up in front of the media for that press conference. Her face was in every newspaper and on every news network for a few days."

Meg groaned and sat back in her chair, tipping her head back to stare at the ceiling. "Ugh. Don't remind me."

"Peters loved it," Craig continued. "And so did Director Clarkson. Great publicity for the Bureau. So the question becomes—with you so far out in the public eye, could you have caught someone's attention? We can't discount it. Have you received any threats, of any kind?"

"Of course not. I'd let you know if I had."

"Then I think it's time to start thinking about anyone who might hold some sort of grudge against you. Especially since no one thinks this is the end for this guy. The only question now is *who* and *when*?"

CHAPTER 6

Cipher Disk: The Confederate cipher disk was a mechanical-wheel cipher machine consisting of two concentric brass disks, each with the twenty-six letters of the Latin alphabet, which was used to encrypt messages. Created by Francis LaBarre and based on the Vigenère cipher, only five disks are known to exist today.

Tuesday, May 23, 5:32 PM
I-395 South
Washington, DC

Meg's cell phone rang just as she was merging onto I-395 South, heading for the Rochambeau Bridge over the Potomac and toward home in Arlington. She glanced at the name displayed on the small screen on her dash—C. McCord.

Part of her wanted very much not to answer, but, truthfully, she'd expected his call before now. "I guess it was only a matter of time, right, Hawk?" She answered the call. "Jennings."

"It's McCord."

"What can I do for the *Washington Post*'s finest?"

McCord, already a well-known investigative war correspondent for the *Post,* shot to renewed prominence during Meg's last case when the bomber threatening the eastern seaboard used McCord as his personal communication channel. "I'm being stymied by the FBI's media liaison, so I thought I'd come to the source."

"You do realize that's her job, right? To keep the media hounds at bay?"

" 'Media hound'? You wound me, madam."

His over-the-top dramatics drew a much-needed smile from her. "Not a chance in hell. So you're looking for information?"

His voice grew suddenly serious. "Partly. I also wanted to make sure you're okay. All the liaison would say is that the coded notes from yesterday were addressed to a member of the FBI. But that made me curious so I pulled in a favor. She said a 'member of the FBI,' not an agent. And lo and behold, it turns out to be one of the Forensic Canine Unit handlers. It turns out to be *you*."

"They were trying to keep that information under wraps."

"And it will stay that way, at least by me. Can you tell me about what's going on?"

Meg paused, torn. Part of her wanted to do a cop's knee-jerk reaction to any reporter and to tell him to back off. But part of her recognized the man who'd helped so much in the last case and had been utterly trustworthy.

We need better intel if we're going to keep doing this.

Her own words to Brian as they knelt over Michelle Wilson rang in her head. Two victims; both times they were too late, one fatally. The code was taking too long to crack, the messages too long to solve, and women— women who looked frighteningly like her—were dying in her place. She knew what her answer should be: As a member of the FBI, she knew all case details were confidential. Bringing anyone else into the case was a breach of protocol and could cost her job. But it was a battle between her heart and her brain. She knew the rules, but at what point did the end justify the means? How many women saved would justify crossing the line? Two? Four?

One.

"Meg? You still there?"

Meg glanced at the clock on her dash, and cemented her decision.

"McCord, it's been a long day after an even longer day yesterday." When he started to speak, she cut him off. "So give me some time to go home, eat dinner, and recharge, then I'll tell you what I can, but you'll have to keep it under wraps for now. You kept details of the Mannew case quiet until I could give you the green light to release them. Can I get your promise to do that again?"

"Scout's honor. And maybe I can help you. You know us news guys . . . we've got contacts in all sorts of places."

"That's what I'm hoping for. Write this down." She rattled off her home address. "Give me two hours and then come on over. And bring Cody. I haven't seen him in a few weeks and Cara tells me he's coming along really well," she said, referring to McCord's enrollment in one of Cara's puppy obedience classes.

"Your sister is a miracle. He hasn't eaten one of my shoes in over a week now."

"Congratulations. I'll see you at seven-thirty." She ended the call and glanced back at Hawk. "Hope you're up to enthusiastic company tonight, Hawk. Nothing like a puppy to liven things up."

After the past twenty-four hours, a little puppy chaos might be just what the doctor ordered to keep the conversation they were about to have from going over to the dark side.

Tuesday, May 23, 7:28 PM
Jennings residence
Arlington, Virginia

Meg answered the knock on the door, opening it to reveal tall, blond Clay McCord and his eleven-month-old golden retriever, Cody, who immediately jumped up, bracing his front paws on Meg's thighs. Before she could even open her mouth, Cara's voice sounded behind her. "Remember, Clay, consistency. Whether he's testing his limits or is just excited, you're still in charge."

"Cody, down," McCord ordered, and the dog dropped to all fours. McCord stared at Cara in wonder. "It always amazes me when he actually listens."

"He's a smart boy. He just needs to know you're the alpha dog." Cara stooped to give Cody a rub. "How's my growing boy? I swear you're an inch taller than last week."

"It seems like it. He's certainly eating me out of house and home."

"Until you get him neutered, no harm in feeding him what he wants. He's burning everything off."

"Subtle push there. Don't think I didn't catch it." Despite his words, McCord grinned. "So, before you ask me again, his surgery is booked for week after next. I wanted to wait until we finished your first intensive class before we interrupted his training."

"Great idea," Meg said. "I hear he's coming along nicely, so you don't want to sabotage that. Do we want to send them all out to run around and tire him out?"

"Yeah, let's give them some time out back. Come on through." Cara led the way through the mudroom and into the living room, where Hawk, Saki—Cara's therapy dog—and Blink, a retired racing greyhound, all flopped on the couch together. She clapped her hands to get their attention. "Playtime."

At the word "play," Blink's rangy brindle body was off the couch and running for the back door. "You can take the dog out of the racetrack . . ." Cara muttered. "Saki, Hawk, playtime."

Saki, a dusky gray stubby American bully with startling blue eyes and a cleft palate and lip that exposed her teeth, raised her head and gazed steadily at Cara. Cara gave her rump a playful nudge. "Yes, I know you just came in and were already settling down. But now we've got a baby on our hands and he needs to play. Come on." Saki jumped down and ambled after Blink toward the back door.

Meg simply gave Hawk a silent hand signal—*off you go*—and he, too, followed. Cara opened the door and all four dogs shot into the backyard. Cody tore in the direction of a piece of rope and Blink went after him and then proceeded to spend the next minute in a happy game of tug-of-war. The three humans crossed the back deck to lean against the railing and watch the organized chaos down below in the large fenced space.

"Nice yard you've got here. I'd kill for a place I could let Cody out that didn't involve three flights of stairs."

"That's what you get for having a dog in a three-story walk-up." Cara was unsympathetic. "On the other hand, it's great exercise for both of you."

"There is that." McCord leaned an elbow on the railing, resettled his wire-rimmed glasses on the bridge of his nose, and fixed a level gaze on Meg. "So? What happened yesterday? The real story and not the sanitized version fed to us by the media liaison."

"Nothing in print until I say so."

"Didn't I already say that?" Irritation sparked at the edge of his words.

"You did, but I just need to be sure. I'm about to cross a line that could get me into pretty big trouble."

" 'Trouble'?" Concern colored Cara's tone. "How?"

"I want to tell you about this case. About the *whole* case."

McCord's eyebrows arched, but he kept his mouth shut, clearly not wanting to look a gift horse in the mouth.

Cara, however, knew this wasn't standard procedure. " 'The whole case'? Craig gave you permission to discuss it?"

"No."

"But—"

"No 'but.' I have to do something. I won't be able to live with myself if we lose another one."

" 'Another one'?" Cara laid a hand on her arm. "Did the second victim from last night die?"

"No, but she's in a deep coma, which is almost as bad. They don't know if she's going to come out of it."

"That's not the story the media liaison told me. We were told she was stable."

"She's been stable in that coma since we found her."

"The media liaison said messages were coming into the FBI and the note was addressed to a member of the FBI, which we now know is you. Why?"

"Wait, what?" Cara whipped around to face her sister. "The victims you're going after, there are messages about them, and they're addressed to *you*?"

"Yes. I couldn't say anything about it before, shouldn't say anything about it now, but we're losing this game fast and McCord offered to help." She turned back to McCord. "We're not sure why they're addressed to me. It might be because I was highlighted in the *Post* during the Mannew case. Or it could be something I did in the Richmond PD years ago, who knows?"

"What was in the notes?" McCord asked. "We know they were encrypted, but that's all."

"The messages are in code?" Cara asked. "Can I see it?"

Meg glanced sideways at her sister, suddenly seeing a

new avenue opening she hadn't focused on before—her sister, the puzzle fiend. The one who could blow through a crossword or Sudoku in a fraction of the time regular people, like Meg, would manage it. The one who could see patterns where none apparently existed, until she proved they did.

She pulled out her cell phone and opened her mail, searching for Craig's e-mail. "Here it is. The messages come in as a string of capital letters in clusters of five with no punctuation."

"You wouldn't want to give away any clues as to the structure of the message by indicating beginning or ends of sentences." Cara held out her hand, a tacit request.

Meg passed over her phone and Cara angled it so both she and McCord could see it. "It's something called a Vigenère cipher."

"Polyalphabetic substitution," Cara said. "And half a millennium old. So, not incredibly complicated."

"If it was more complicated than this, we'd have never had a chance. For our first victim, we barely had a chance to begin with, and it was dependent on the riddle getting solved right away. We missed the boat there. For the second victim, it was pure luck and nothing to be proud of."

Cody had run up the stairs with a Frisbee in his teeth for McCord. After taking it, McCord paused, one arm partially wrapped around his middle in midthrow. "Wait, what riddle?" He launched the Frisbee and Cody tore after it as he turned back to Meg. "The liaison didn't say anything about a riddle. She just said each note contained the location of the victim."

"Not directly. The first deciphered note read, 'Find her before she dies. Come to Washington's House in Alexandria. The clock is ticking on her life.' "

McCord paused for no more than two seconds. "Arlington Cemetery is the logical answer to that. You could have been there in fifteen minutes. Did something go wrong?"

"The cryptanalysts thought it was Mount Vernon."

McCord shook his head. "Mount Vernon isn't *in* Alexandria. It's near it, but not in it. So the only Washington house *in* Alexandria is what is now Arlington House, overlooking Arlington Cemetery."

Meg simply stared at him. "How do you know that? We had to have a history prof from Georgetown tell us."

"I've always been a military history buff, especially Civil War history. My dad started me young and used to take me out on weekends to tour Civil War battlefields. Do you know the rock formation at Devil's Den in Gettysburg is virtually unchanged from 1863? Standing there is like being a part of history." He ground to a stop as both women stared at him with nearly identical expressions of bafflement. "Anyway, back to this clue, Arlington is the only thing that makes sense. Lee's mansion, passed down to him by Washington, his father-in-law, taken over by the Union, which then turned the grounds into a cemetery, guaranteeing Lee would never return to his own home after the war."

"I wish you'd been on hand yesterday. Sandy Holmes might still be alive."

"You only have to call. What about the second victim?"

"Her clue was 'She is on John Smith's Island in a place known to her family. Will she die there too? Not if you hurry.' "

"That one is a little harder," McCord said. "John Smith discovered a lot of geography in his day."

"The connection was apparently her position as a Daughter of Union Veterans of the Civil War. That cross-referenced to Belle Isle in Richmond, Virginia, because she had a great-great—et cetera, et cetera—grandfather who died there as a Union officer."

McCord whistled. "Belle Isle. That place was a hell-hole."

"In what way?" Cara asked.

"It was a Confederate prison in the Civil War. Way over-crowded, overrun with disease. In just two years, estimates of the number dead range anywhere from one thousand to fifteen thousand of the total thirty thousand prisoners housed there. The men rescued were barely more than skin and bones. Horrifying. It was right up there with Andersonville for barbaric practices."

"And now it's a city park," Meg said.

"Yeah, kind of blows your mind, doesn't it? But they moved all the Civil War dead to Richmond National Cemetery a long time ago, so there's no relic of that nasty time there now. And speaking of the Civil War, that Vigenère cipher is related."

"How? I was told it originated in the sixteenth century."

"It did. But the Confederate Army used it during the war for most of their coded communications. The Union tended to use route transpositions, but the rebels used Vigenère." He looked from one woman to the other. "Am I the only one seeing the Civil War connection? Arlington to Lee's mansion to the Belle Isle camp to the cipher?"

"You aren't now. Damn, we didn't pick up on that at all."

"You guys needed someone on hand with a real knowledge of history for this one."

Meg propped her elbows on the railing and looked out at the dogs frolicking in the grass in the cooling spring evening. She felt a little jealousy at their ability to just *be*. "I'm not sure that's exactly the right way to put it."

"You don't think that would have helped you?"

"Oh, it would have helped. I just don't think the need has passed. He's going to hit again, and when he does, we need to be ready. If he hints at another Civil War connection, we need to be able to make that leap quickly."

Cara stared down at the phone still cradled in her hand. "So you expect him to send another message."

"Yes. And so does my team."

"You'll use the victim connection then?"

"The victim connection?"

"I heard on the news that Sandy Holmes was a veteran?" At Meg's nod, Cara continued. "She was buried in Arlington in a soldier's grave. And, as a veteran, she could rightfully be returned there for her own burial. Arlington isn't just a connection to the Civil War. It's a connection to the victim herself. And Michelle Wilson's family is connected to Belle Isle through a relative who died there. Another Civil War connection and a victim connection."

McCord bent down as his dog bounded up the stairs, panting and bright-eyed, with a bright red rubber ball in his mouth. He dropped the slobbery sphere into McCord's hand and was racing down the steps, even before McCord had the ball in the air for him. He wiped saliva onto his pants as he turned back around. "If he's really going to do this again, that could help us."

" 'Help *us*'? Look, I'd love to use you as a consultant, but this has to be totally under the radar. The FBI can't know I have a reporter on this, or I won't have access to case details when we need them. And you can anonymous-source me as much as you like, once I give you the green light, but they can't know I'm feeding you information, because the case details are going to be crucial." Meg studied her sister, who was contemplating the phone screen with narrowed eyes. "I'll need those details to give to you, Cara."

Cara looked up. "The coded messages?"

"Yes. You think you can solve a Vigenère cipher?"

"I'd like to have a go at these ones, now that I can see the raw code. I know a little about these ciphers, and I know there are some tricks you can use to play around with the cipher when you don't have a keyword. Having the keyword is . . . well . . . key. If you have the keyword, you can decode the cipher quite easily. Without it, it's a lot harder, but not impossible. And I think that's the point."

"What do you mean?"

"Whoever your killer is, he doesn't want the code to be so difficult you have no chance of saving the victim. Where's the fun in that? If it takes days or weeks to solve it, your victim is already dead. There's no urgency. So make it something to slow you down, versus something to stop you in your tracks, and now you've got a game worth playing."

"That's what this whole thing is, isn't it," McCord said. "One big game to him? And a game is no fun if someone isn't playing with you."

"And he's really playing with you," Cara said. "Like a cat plays with a mouse. This isn't supposed to be fun for you. It's supposed to be hell."

"Well, bully for him. He succeeded."

"You failed this time, lost a couple of battles, but the war is still up for grabs," McCord pointed out. "Remember that. Set yourself up for success."

"Which is exactly why the three of us are having this conversation. Don't think I didn't second-guess this decision. It's risky, but we're struggling to get the job done in time by ourselves. Cara might be key to getting the code cracked. The cryptanalysts are good, but the more heads on this, the better. And, McCord, I was thinking I might need your contacts once we had the decoded message, but maybe what I need is you and your knowledge of history."

"When this happens again, don't just think about the message," McCord said. "As Cara pointed out, the victims are also linked to the burial site. We need to investigate both the message and the victim in parallel, because either could lead us to an answer."

"God, I hope so. You have no idea what it was like standing at the edge of that grave, looking down at the life you missed saving by such a narrow margin that the body was still warm."

"I can't imagine it. But I'll do my damnedest to make sure it doesn't happen again."

"We'll all do our damnedest," Cara agreed.

Little did they all know, in under twenty-four hours, another young woman would be taken and those efforts would be put to the test in the worst possible way.

CHAPTER 7

Tanning: Tanning is the process of turning animal hides and skins into leather. During the mid-nineteenth century, there were two primary methods of tanning: vegetable and chrome. Vegetable tanning takes several weeks or months to complete, and produces stiffer leather suitable for luggage, footwear, and belts. Chrome tanning uses acids and chromium sulphate to produce flexible, stretchable leather for a wide variety of uses, and takes just a few days to complete.

Wednesday, May 24, 10:56 AM
Forensic Canine Unit, J. Edgar Hoover Building
Washington, DC

"He's got another one."

Craig's raised voice and the sound of a handset being slammed down in its cradle attracted the attention of the handlers. As Craig turned to his computer, Meg, Brian, and Lauren ran into his office to crowd around him.

"When was she taken?" Lauren asked.

"Within the past half hour," Craig said. He refreshed his in-box, but the stream of messages was unchanged. "Come on, come on."

"What are you waiting for?" Brian asked.

"The field agent who took the call is snapping a picture of the coded message to send to me and the CRRU."

"What do we know so far?" Meg asked. "Is my name on it again?"

"Yes."

"I want a copy of it, Craig."

"We all want a copy of it." Brian perched one hip on the corner of Craig's desk. "Meg's name is on it; we're all involved."

"No disagreements from me." A small window flashed in the corner of his screen as a new e-mail arrived. "Finally." Craig opened the e-mail and then the attached image.

A long white paper strip was pictured. On it was typed: "To: Meg Jennings, Forensic Canine Unit, FBI," followed by a long string of capital letters in five-letter clusters similar to the first two messages.

Lauren leaned in to study the picture. "Can we assume the same code is being used?"

"We can't assume anything, but it's a place to start." Craig closed the image and then forwarded the e-mail to the whole team. "You guys need to be ready to leave at a moment's notice."

Meg stood up. "I'm going to run home and pick up some additional supplies. Keep me in the loop."

Brian was staring at her, eyes narrowed in suspicion. "You're sure that's a good idea? We should stay in pairs."

She met his gaze, trying to convey a silent message with her own. *Don't make a big deal about this. Trust me and go with it.* "More than likely, I'll be back before they send us out anywhere. You know how close I am. Depending on the location, I may end up being closer."

He seemed to get the message and gave her an imperceptible nod and a look that said, *Fill me in later.* "Sounds good."

"Hawk, come." She waited while he trotted after her. "Back soon."

Then they were out the door. She picked up her pace, jogging through the hallway, pulling out her phone and forwarding the message from Craig to both her sister and McCord. She followed it up with a text just to be sure: **Another one taken. Just sent the note via e-mail. Meet at home ASAP. Clock is started and we're already behind.**

Wednesday, May 24, 11:16 AM
Jennings residence
Arlington, Virginia

Meg slammed through the mudroom door. "Cara! How are you coming with the code?"

"I'm right here. No need to shout. Come in, but keep it down for another two minutes, I've just about got it."

Meg quietly closed the door behind Hawk. Entering the living room, she found her sister at her desk under the big picture window, which faced out into the backyard. Her laptop was open to the picture of the message and a pad of canary paper was in front of her, covered in scrawled letters. At her feet was a small mountain of crumpled balls of yellow, testament to her effort over the last twenty minutes.

A knock sounded at the back door and Meg went to open it. McCord stood on the doorstep, his laptop bag over his shoulder, concern creasing his forehead over his wire-framed glasses.

"Come on in," Meg said, sotto voce, as she held the door open for him as he crossed the threshold. "Cara says she's just about got it."

"That was fast."

"What can I say? She's good. She's in the living room." Meg led the way back.

Cara continued to ignore them, scribbling furiously, occasionally referring to a large block of letters laser-printed onto a single white sheet at her elbow. Meg pointed to the sofa and then to the coffee table, miming for McCord to open his laptop there.

He had just booted up when Cara slapped her pencil down on the table beside the pad of paper. "Got you, you bastard!" She pushed an errant strand of hair behind her ear from where it had escaped her ponytail holder. "I don't understand what it means, but I've got your message." She picked up the pad of paper and came to join them, stepping over Saki, where she sprawled on the floor in a sunbeam, to flop down onto the sofa. "There's something I need to tell you. Not now, there's no time. It's crucial to the case, but it won't make a difference to this particular victim, not anymore."

Meg pushed back the feeling of dread that rose based on nothing more than her sister's expression. Something was very wrong, but it was going to have to wait, at least for now. "I'll call you from the car. Okay, what's the message?"

Cara picked up the pad of paper. " 'Fruit of the earth used to kill the sons of the earth. She is like Calvert's sons, lost in the serpentine wilderness. Tick tock.' " She tossed the pad of paper onto the coffee table so McCord could read it for himself. "It doesn't mean anything to me."

McCord pulled out his cell phone and snapped a photo of the deciphered message. Then he sat back and stared at the pad of paper for long seconds.

"Well?" Meg pressed, her voice pitching higher than normal as the pressure intensified with each passing second.

"Give me a second. I'm trying to connect this to anything Civil War–related. Okay, first of all, Calvert."

"It sounds like a person. 'Calvert's sons.' "

"Bingo, it is a person. George Calvert, the first Lord Baltimore."

"The man who founded Maryland?" Meg asked. "*That* Lord Baltimore?"

"The very one. That's why you not only have Baltimore, but also the town of Calvert and Calvert's Cliffs, all in the state of Maryland."

"Good start." Cara leaned forward, her hands braced on her knees. "So it's relatively close geographically. Meg, when and where was the dog found?"

"Less than an hour ago, right here in DC." Meg shot upright as she grasped Cara's point. "Depending on how long she was taken before they found the dog, he may not be there yet. He hasn't had her long enough to get to most places in Maryland."

"Depending on where he's headed, no. And that buys us a little time. Clay, what else?"

McCord waved a hand carelessly, then bent over his keyboard. "There are a few clues in that message, so give me a minute. Talk between yourselves."

"What do we know about the victim?" Cara asked. "We need to look at that too."

Meg sat back against the couch cushions, feeling utterly drained. Hawk, who had been holding back as if sensing the pressure in the room, now came to nudge at her hand with his nose. He laid his head on her thigh and gazed up at her with liquid brown eyes filled with total trust. She ran her hand over his head and down his back, the repetitive motion calming. "Craig called me in the car. Her name is Catriona Baldwin, but most people know her as Cat. She's Wiccan and volunteers at an AIDS hospice with her dog, a Cavalier King Charles spaniel. They visit weekly."

McCord looked up from his searching. "Wiccan? As in Witch?"

"They consider themselves white witches. Anyway, they're

there every Tuesday morning, like clockwork, visiting patients after breakfast. They were in this morning as usual,
stayed for about two hours and left around ten-thirty. One
of the nurses noticed the dog running around the property
about ten minutes later and went out to see what was
going on. She was worried Cat was in an accident or was
hurt. But she couldn't find her. Then she found the note on
the dog's leash."

"Okay, so Wiccan. We know we're looking at Maryland,
so something like Salem, Massachusetts, isn't a reasonable
clue. What's local in this area specific to Wiccans?"

"What about the Firefly House?" McCord didn't take
his eyes off the screen as he clicked through Web pages.
"Aren't they some kind of community witchcraft organization?"

"I've never heard of them, but let's look it up. And there
must be other places. Don't Wiccans like to do some of
their ceremonies skyclad?"

" 'Skyclad'?"

"Naked—as in, *clad* in nothing but the *sky*—so out-
doors in what they consider to be spiritual places, private
places. A forest, a meadow."

"So, outside a city—"

"I've got 'outside a city' for you," McCord interrupted.

"You've got it?" Meg jerked upright so quickly Hawk
looked up at her in confusion.

"I think so. Once we knew it was Maryland, the next
clue was 'serpentine wilderness.' "

"As in related to a serpent?" Cara asked.

"No, in this case, 'serpentine' refers to the type of soil."
He was reading and paraphrasing from his laptop. "It's
soil that came from serpentinite rock and has a very high
concentration of nickel and chromium and very low nutri-
ent concentrations. So only the hardiest plants live there.
This isn't land where you grow wheat or corn."

"And this serpentine wilderness exists in Maryland?" Meg settled back on the couch.

"In the serpentine barrens at Soldiers Delight Natural Environment Area."

"Named because of its involvement in the Civil War?" Cara asked.

"Actually, no. It was named that in the late sixteen hundreds by King George's men. No Civil War action took place there."

Disappointment flooded Meg. "Then how could it be involved if the Civil War is the key?"

"Because there's a mine there called the Choate Mine. Remember I said the soil was rich in chromium? The Choate Mine was a chromium mine, and chromium was crucial during the Civil War for tanning leather for all those saddles, boots, belts, and ammunition cases." He looked up. "I could research more, but I think this is our best shot. Clock's ticking."

"It is. Okay, Hawk and I are heading out there now. And . . . what are you doing?"

McCord was packing his laptop back into his bag. "I'm coming with you."

"You are not."

"I am. I can either drive with you or follow you, but you're being targeted here and you currently have no backup. Two sets of eyes looking for a crackpot are better than one." When Meg opened her mouth to speak, he just kept right on talking. "Now we can waste precious seconds arguing, or we can move now. Either way, I'm going with you. It's a public space—you can't stop me from picking today to visit. Cara?"

"Works for me," Cara agreed without missing a step. "You need someone at your back. Right now, you don't have one of the other team members, so Clay will do in a pinch."

McCord sent her a squinted look. "Thanks . . . I think."

"Hey, I'm on your side. Now stop arguing and go." She met her sister's eyes. "Get out of the city, then call me from the car."

"You can be sure of it." Meg grabbed her SAR go bag and called her dog. She went out the door with both Hawk and McCord on her heels.

Wednesday, May 24, 11:52 AM
I-95 North
West Laurel, Maryland

Using the Bluetooth voice recognition system in her SUV, Meg called her sister as soon as they'd cleared the worst of the capital traffic.

"Okay, spill," Meg said, the moment her sister picked up. "What couldn't you tell me before?"

"It's about the cipher itself and how I solved it," Cara said.

"That's why it didn't matter anymore for this victim. You'd already solved it."

"Right."

"So what's the issue?"

"You're sure you're okay to do this while driving?"

"Cara . . ." It came out more growl than spoken word.

"Okay, okay. In a nutshell, the Vigenère cipher substitutes letters in the original message for other letters based on a key, which is a series of numbers of indeterminate length, of which each is a number from one to twenty-five. That key tells you how far from the actual number you have to count back to decipher the code. For example, if the first letter you have is *D*, and if the first number in the key is three, then you count backward three letters to get *A*. Make sense?"

"So far," McCord answered for both of them from the passenger seat.

"Counting forward is how you build the code into ciphertext, counting backward is how you decode the ciphertext into plaintext. Last night, I went through both the encoded and the decoded messages. I worked out backward that the key for the first message was four, five, twenty-one, three, five. The key was applied to each letter of the message in order. Of course, with only five numbers in the key, when you got to the sixth number, you circled back to the first number in the sequence and kept going until you finished decoding the entire message. If you are not given the key to decipher the code, then you have to figure it out. I won't get into that process in detail, but there are longhand ways and ways for a computer to brute force it, based on coincidence occurrences in the ciphertext and the frequency of certain letters in the English language. The computer will always be faster because the human brain can process at only a fraction of the speed."

"Which is how the cryptanalysts are doing it, but there's been no call yet. So how did you figure it out before them?"

"That's what I wanted to tell you. Because I know something they don't. Sure, they're faster than me at the computer work, but I have you and our family history."

Meg's mouth went as dry as the Sahara. "Why do you need that?"

"Because while the cryptanalysts are going on their merry way, simply dealing with algorithms and numbers, I noticed something special about the first key, the one for Sandy Holmes. The numbers are, in order, four, five, twenty-one, three, and five."

"So you said before."

"Meg, when you translate those numbers back into letters, the key spells 'Deuce.'"

Silence reigned for several seconds. McCord, taking in Meg's wide, shocked eyes, must have sensed he'd missed something crucial. "What? What does that mean?"

"Deuce was my K-9 partner when I was with the Richmond PD. He died in the line of duty." Meg's face was as colorless as her voice. "He used 'Deuce' as the key?"

"Yes. So I worked the second code, the one that was actually intended to be the first, for Michelle Wilson, to determine the keyword. This one had a four-digit pattern." She paused, as if unwilling to speak before pressing on. "The keyword spelled out 'Hawk.'"

McCord swore quietly. "I didn't think 'Deuce' was a coincidence, but now it's absolutely clear it's not."

"I agree. So for this newest code, where you would normally then go through the alphabet frequency to figure this out, I skipped that step. I ran the eighty-four-letter message through a Vigenère cracker online. Once I knew it was another five-number key, I didn't try to figure out the random numbers. I tried to figure out a five-letter word that applied to you personally and then translated that backward into numbers and tested each word out separately. I hit pay dirt with 'Haven.'"

Meg clutched the steering wheel until her knuckles shone white and struggled to speak through the panic clawing at her throat. "Mom and Dad—"

"Already done." Cara's voice was calm and pitched loud enough to cut through some of Meg's panic. "I talked to Dad, told him I couldn't be specific, but there might be a threat to them or the animals because of your work. A *serious* threat. He will take all precautions needed and will make sure the volunteers do too. They won't let it stop their work, but no one will get the jump on them. They did, however, ask for a better explanation when you could manage it."

"I have to go see them, as soon as I can swing it."

"It's all taken care of. You know Dad—he's as steady as a rock, and as pragmatic as they come. And he's got guns on hand. The guns are loaded, he and Mom know how to use them, and they won't hesitate to shoot if they need to. We'll go together to see them as soon as we can and we'll lay it all out for them then—"

"I'm lost again," McCord interrupted. "What is 'haven,' and how does it apply?"

"It refers to the animal rescue our parents run outside of Charlottesville, Virginia," Meg answered. "The full name is Cold Spring Haven. He's not only addressing the messages to me, but he's basing the keyword on my personal information. This isn't just someone who's read a newspaper article or two—this is someone who has a personal connection to me."

"Or thinks he has one," McCord clarified. "The name of your current and late dogs. The name of your parents' rescue. All of that is public information in one way or another. When he comes out with the name of your preteen crush that only your sister and your diary knew about, then you really worry it's someone you know. Cara, anything else?"

"No, that's it. I just needed you to know. You're trying to get inside this guy's head, but it appears he's already in yours."

"He can get the hell out." Meg's tone was rock hard. "Thanks, Cara. We'll let you know as soon as we've got something." She disconnected the call.

McCord glanced at her as the silence in the vehicle became stifling. "You okay?"

"I will be, once we find Cat. I just wish we had the rest of the team. Only one pair searching lowers our chances."

"If you call them, they'll know you have an inside track."

"I know. That's why I can't. They're right behind us, so

we'll get started. It's still getting the job done faster than if I'd never brought you in."

"What about the information about the keywords? Do you need to pass that on to the CRRU analysts?"

Meg took one hand off the wheel to rub her pounding temple. "Should I? Yes. But if I do, the cat is out of the bag and I'll lose all access to the case. Which means none of us will be able to help any future victims. Does it slow the teams down, putting the victim in greater danger? Honestly, it might. But if it comes down to the life of the victim versus my keeping quiet on the keywords, I'll speak up. Because the life of the victim is the only thing that matters."

Keeping her gazed fixed unblinkingly on the road, Meg wound up the combination of fury and fear churning inside and focused it into a deadly calm determination. She was not going to let this bastard get to her.

She would not let him win.

CHAPTER 8

Tunnel Warfare: The use of mining and tunnels as a battle-field tactic dates back to at least the Romans. During the Siege of Vicksburg, Union troops dug a tunnel beneath Confederate lines and packed it with gunpowder. The resulting explosion killed about three hundred Confederate soldiers, but the tactic was ultimately unsuccessful because Union soldiers rushed into the resulting crater, were unable to climb the steep sides, and were killed by gunfire from above.

Wednesday, May 24, 12:41 PM
Soldiers Delight Natural Environment Area
Owings Mills, Maryland

"Wait! That was it. Pull in there." McCord pointed out through the windshield to a shallow parking lot on the far side of the road overlooking a scenic vista. Then he clutched at the door handle as Meg hit the brakes and swung across the deserted road to pull in next to the only other car in the small gravel lot. Opposite them, a valley tumbled between rising green hills, a narrow path meandering from the parking lot down into gently waving grasses. A sign beside it proclaimed: THE SERPENTINE TRAIL.

Meg rolled down her window and craned her head

through the gap, squinting back across the road and at a similar sign with blocky white letters emblazoned on the brown placard. "I can't see what it says."

"According to this map, that's the Choate Mine Trail. Let's go."

As McCord climbed out, Meg followed suit and pulled open the back door to let Hawk out of the SUV. She shouldered her pack, grabbed her hard hat, and attached his leash to his vest. She glanced down the road, but there was no sign of any other vehicle. The CRRU team had come to the same conclusion as Cara and McCord, and Brian and Lauren were on the way to Soldiers Delight as well, but she wasn't sure how far out they were. "We can't afford to wait for Brian and Lauren and the dogs. They'll find us, or if we find her before they get here, we'll let them know. Let's move."

They jogged across the road, down a short service access, and around the yellow gate barring the way to vehicular traffic. As she ran past, Meg glanced at the sign emblazoned with the symbol of the Maryland Park Service and the designation CHOATE MINE TRAIL.

Bingo.

"Are you going to let him off the leash?" McCord puffed a bit as they jogged.

Meg checked Hawk as he ran easily beside her, the leash swinging loose as he stayed at heel. "Once we get to the mine, but here there could be too many conflicting scents with various hikers and park rangers about, and nothing to give him anything specific to look for. It will be a test of your theory, once we get there. How much farther is it?"

"Not far according to the map." He waggled his cell phone at her, showing a picture of a stark white map with black lines highlighted by different colored trails.

The dirt path led them beneath overhanging trees, shading them from the midday sun. Meg scanned each clearing they passed, searching for the mine. She'd seen pictures, and knew it wasn't a big, imposing structure, but rather a rocky tear in the earth. She wasn't sure how it was marked and didn't want to miss it. The dirt path they traveled was cleared and smooth, but around them was thick underbrush, fallen trees, lichen-covered boulders pushing free of the earth, and even a small pond from which dead trees sprang from the center of the stagnant water, mirrored eerily on the surface.

"There, that cleared section." McCord pointed ahead and to the right, picking up his pace. "I think that's it."

The forest opened up onto a grassy meadow with sparse trees. Bare, craggy rock was exposed between uneven patches of grasses and small, scrubby bushes fought for ground with short, scraggly pines. A wood and mesh fence enclosed what appeared to be an open grassy space, in front of which was a sign placed by the Baltimore Historical Society, signifying this as the site of the Choate Mine.

It was only once they got closer that Meg recognized the mouth of the mine as she'd seen it in pictures—a narrow slit set low into the rocky earth, disappearing into darkness.

Could he have gotten her in there?

Only one way to find out.

Meg eyed the wood fence. It was locked, but that wasn't going to stop them. With a good run, Hawk could likely leap over it, and she and McCord could climb over, but—

The sound of wood splintering had her spinning toward one side of the fenced area. A short gate, previously in line with the fence, now stood open, its latch and lock dangling drunkenly.

"Clock is ticking," McCord stated. "Kicking it in seemed like the fastest option."

"Sure does. We'll deal with the park rangers later."

They crossed into the enclosed area. Untrimmed grasses grew tall here, springing up around metal tracks that ran from the mine entrance, no doubt for ore carts. The long-disused path ran down into the slanted shaft of the abandoned chromite mine. Small rocks poked from the earth's surface like half-buried bones, and small bits of rotted timber from the old mine railroad bed lay scattered among the rocks.

As they made their way down the path, the ragged rock walls rose above them and they went from sunlight into shade at the gaping dark mouth of the mine. Half-height timber posts supported the roof, but only feet into the mine, the supports disappeared into an engulfing darkness.

They each pulled flashlights from their pockets and Meg bent to remove Hawk's leash before putting on her hard hat. She ran a hand down his exercise-warmed fur. "Hawk, find Catriona." Hawk put his nose into the air, sniffed the new smells, and stepped into the gloom. Meg and McCord switched on their flashlights and ducked to clear the low ceiling. The air suddenly stilled and the temperature dropped, causing a chill to skitter up Meg's spine. The beam from her flashlight bounced over rocky walls and ancient tree trunks placed every six feet or so to shore up the ceiling. Farther into the gloom, a single carved rocky pillar, shaped like an hourglass and banded in the middle with a dark layer of minerals, added to the roof support.

"I don't know about this."

Meg turned to find McCord staring suspiciously at the ceiling only inches over his hunched form.

"You'll go to Iraq, get shot at and nearly bombed, but a mine scares you?"

"I'm feeling less safe in here than I did over there sometimes." He shone his flashlight farther into the dim recesses, but the light was swallowed by the darkness less than fifteen feet out. "But that's beside the point. We're doing it anyway."

"Yes, we are. Just keep your head down. I don't have a spare hard hat in my gear for you." Meg stepped over debris and rubble littering the floor of the mine, her eyes and flashlight locked on her dog. The main shaft immediately tipped downward at a significant angle. "Slowly, Hawk. We have to stay with you, and you're as black as this mine, so don't lose us."

Hawk picked his way carefully over the uneven rocky floor, but his direction clearly had purpose.

"Has he got something already?" McCord asked.

"I think so. Keep in mind, the scent is trapped down here, so it's not diffusing far. On the other hand, it might be wafting down corridors that will lead us nowhere. Whatever happens, don't lose your sense of direction."

Hawk followed the downward shaft toward a cloying organic odor that even the humans could detect. Up ahead, the shaft forked, going north and south. The southerly fork angled steeply downward, disappearing into murky flooded depths.

"Flooded out." Keeping his head out of the range of jutting rocks from the ceiling, McCord moved to the edge of the water, shining his light down into it, but the light simply bounced off the surface, revealing nothing. "Spring rains maybe. Any chance she's under there?"

Meg watched Hawk who barely glanced at the water, but instead took the north shaft. "Hawk doesn't think so. And he's in charge."

They made their way around crumbling rock and rotting timbers, between rough walls still bearing the marks of the chisels and pickaxes that created their shape centuries earlier. A loose rock shifted under Meg's foot and she went down on one knee, strangling the cry rising to

her lips, which would be explosive in such a small, reso-
nant space. She pushed back to her feet, one hand over her
head to avoid banging her hard hat on the low ceiling.

Hawk's whine pulled her attention sharply from her
own struggles and she focused the beam of her flashlight
on his hindquarters, easily fifteen feet ahead. But instead of
just her dog, the beam of light fell across the pale flesh of a
limp hand, the fingers dragging in the loose stones of the
mine floor.

"McCord—"

"I see her. Sweet Christ, quickly."

They leapt forward over rubble and broken timbers
until they reached a cavern with a slightly higher ceiling.
In his rush to move forward, McCord carelessly rammed
his head against a rocky outcrop overhead. Grinding out a
curse, he moved toward the woman who lay underneath a
crushing load—a stack of heavy rocks was carefully balanced on the piece of wood positioned over her chest.

Even from the door of the mine shaft, Meg recognized
what she was looking at: a Wiccan victim, slowly suffocated by "pressing"—the addition of more and more
weight onto a body until the lungs couldn't draw air any
longer and the victim died. Just like Giles Corey, one of the
last of the Salem victims of 1692, killed for the crime of
witchcraft. A family trip to the Salem Witch Museum
when Meg was thirteen had taught her everything she
needed to know about 1692. The panoramic reenactments
were still vivid in her mind, all these years later.

She circled the woman to help from the far side, even as
McCord was reaching for the first boulder, pulling it off,
and tossing it carelessly aside. He held his narrow flashlight clamped between his teeth, freeing his hands for the
heavy lifting, his breath coming hard around the metal
cylinder lighting their work. Meg set her flashlight down
nearby and reached for a rock. Hawk gave another whine

and snuffled around the woman's face, pushing under her long, dark hair to her face, as if searching for life the only way he knew how.

"Cat? We found you. We're here to help." *Keep talking to her. If she's still alive, she needs to know she's not alone.* Meg hoisted another rock, which had to be at least twenty pounds—*how much weight could a body take before compression asphyxiation stilled her last breath and stole her life?*—and dropped it on the ground. "Cat, we have your dog. He's waiting for you. Stay with us. Don't leave him."

McCord yanked the flashlight from his teeth. "I've got this. Check her." He went back to clearing rocks.

Meg dropped to her knees beside the woman's shoulders. She had a brief flash of cooling flesh and an absent pulse from two nights ago, but she swallowed the fear rising with the image. Her fingertips found the spot in the hollow of Cat's throat and pressed.

And felt life flutter under her fingertips.

"She's still alive. Hurry."

McCord simply grunted and continued hefting rocks, and then he dragged the board off the woman's limp form to reveal a slight figure, dressed in dark-wash jeans and a pretty floral blouse, with a mystic crystal on a chain at her throat. With strength fueled by fury, he tossed the sheet of wood yards down the shaft, where it landed with a clatter. He crouched opposite Meg and reached out to touch the woman, but he froze with his hand an inch away from her shoulder. "How badly is she hurt?"

"Can't tell, but it could be bad. Don't move her. We've got to get an ambulance team in here." She looked to Hawk, who stood still at Cat's head, his nose down by her cheek as if trying to give comfort without touching her. "Hawk, lead me out of here. Outside, Hawk, outside." She glanced back at McCord. "I need to go out to get a signal. Stay with her?"

"Of course. Go."

Meg followed Hawk back through the same mine shaft, moving from utter darkness to gloom, to dim light, and then into the weak sunlight falling through the mouth of the mine. She rushed up the incline, back into sunlight that made her squint after the darkness below, and punched in the numbers for 911, giving not only her FBI designation, but their location and the status of the victim. Then she made a quick call to Craig to update him, and asked him to pass the message on to Brian and Lauren.

She climbed back down to McCord, who sat beside Catriona, talking quietly to her.

"Is she awake?"

"Barely. I don't know if she's been drugged or is hurt, but she's very confused. I've been talking to her to keep her calm."

Meg knelt down beside the woman and shone her flashlight toward her own face so she could be seen. "Cat, I'm Meg Jennings from the FBI. We've got you, and he won't hurt you again."

"Lachlan . . ." Her voice was a hoarse whisper that broke on the single word.

"Is that your dog?" The tiniest of nods was her response. "We've got Lachlan. He's safe and we'll get him to you as soon as we can. For now, just rest." Meg looked up at McCord. "I need to get back out there to meet the paramedics. Nine-one-one estimated they'd be about fifteen minutes out, max."

"We're fine here."

"Brian and Lauren should be almost here too."

"We can have a party."

The laugh that bubbled was buoyed on relief. "Leave the balloons and the seven-layer dip to me." She dropped a hand onto his shoulder. "Seriously, McCord, thanks for coming. I was wrong to try to get in your way. You've been a big help."

McCord nodded at Hawk, who stood still while Cat reached out to touch his fur. "Nah, he was the big help. I just came to be the muscle."

"Whatever, I'll take it. But don't tell Brian and Lauren about your part in figuring this out. They don't know you're involved. Hawk, stay with Cat. Stay. I'll be back."

When she stepped back into sunlight, she heard her name being called. "Over here!"

Brian, Lauren, and the dogs came into view as she climbed the hill out of the mine shaft. "Craig said you found her!" Brian called. "She's okay?"

"She's hurt, but she's alive, and paramedics are on the way. I think she's going to make it."

"Oh, thank God," Lauren said. "What was it this time?" Her gaze shifted over Meg's shoulder to the mouth of the mine. "A mine cave-in?"

"He's consistent on asphyxiation as his way to kill. Keep in mind she's Wiccan, and practices the art of witch-craft."

"Surely, you don't believe that stuff." Lauren's tone was rich with cynicism.

"I don't have to. It only matters that she does. He tried to kill her like one of the last of the Salem witches."

"He hanged her?"

"No, but that might be another method to watch for. One of the people accused of witchcraft, an old man in his eighties, was killed by pressing. They covered his chest with a board and then piled on rocks on top and kept adding more and more weight until his lungs couldn't expand and he asphyxiated."

Brian grimaced. "That's awful. And slow. *Really* slow."

"Depending on how fast you add the weight, like *days* kind of slow."

"And that's what he did to her in there?"

"Yes. Whether he meant to leave her alive, or whether we arrived too soon, we'll never know, but he picked a method of death to match the victim."

"He's clearly put some serious time and thought into his research ahead of time. It must have been hard work getting her out from under all that weight."

Here we go. Make it good. "Actually, I wanted to mention something to you guys. Hawk and I didn't come on our own."

"What do you mean, you *didn't* come on your own?" Lauren asked, her gaze narrowing. "Who's with you?"

"Clay McCord."

"*The reporter?* Are you out of your mind?"

Meg held up both hands in a placating gesture. "He was at my place when I got there, doing a lesson with my sister and his puppy, Cody. They were there when the call came through. He'd been at the media briefing earlier, so he knew something important was going down. I couldn't get him to stay behind." *Partly true. We'll just ignore that he was in the SUV with me when Craig called to give me the search location.* "He said he was either coming with me or he'd simply follow me here. So I swore him to secrecy. You remember how he helped with the Mannew case. He'll keep these details on the down low, or he'll never get a scrap of information from us again. He knows which side his bread is buttered on." She looked from Brian's questioning expression to Lauren's suspicious stare. "Look, in the end it was a good thing. He helped save her life. I needed the extra set of strong hands. And he's in there with her now, keeping her calm and from being terrified."

"Or trying to scoop a story," Lauren muttered.

The rising wail of a siren sounded in the distance, and both Lacey and Rocco pricked their ears toward the sound.

"Here they come," Meg said. "Brian, can you go flag them down and bring them over to speed things up?"

"Will do. Lacey, stay." Tossing his SAR pack beside the fence, Brian jogged toward the path and then disappeared into the trees.

"I'm just going to go check on Cat," Meg said, turning away from Lauren. "I'll be back to take them in."

She felt Lauren's pointed gaze on her back with every step toward the mine.

Wednesday, May 24, 1:27 PM
Soldiers Delight Natural Environment Area
Owings Mills, Maryland

"Easy. Watch your head. That's it. Slowly now, slowly."

Brian, Meg, and Lauren stood at the edge of the fence, their dogs sitting at their feet and staying out of the way, watching as two paramedics, with McCord supplying an extra set of hands, eased the backboard through the narrow mouth of the mine and out into sunlight. They trudged up the hill with their precious burden and settled her carefully on the stretcher.

The three FBI handlers approached, being careful to stay within the victim's field of vision; she'd had enough surprises for one day. Meg took her hand and leaned in a little closer. "Cat, you're in safe hands now. The paramedics are going to take you to the hospital in Randallstown." The woman nodded. "Is it okay if Hawk and I stop by to check in with you later?" Another nod. Meg gave her hand a squeeze, then laid it carefully along her side on the gurney. "We'll see you later."

Thank you. No sound came out, but the woman's lips moved in an unmistakable message of gratitude.

Meg simply smiled and stepped back as the paramedics

speed-walked the gurney back along the path to the waiting ambulance.

Brian held out his hand to McCord. "Brian Foster. Meg's told us a little about you and how you helped in the Mannew case."

McCord first shook hands with Brian, and then Lauren, who did not match Brian's easy smile, but instead fixed him with a flat stare. "I'm happy I was able to lend a hand today." He glanced over at Meg with a sheepish grin. "I admit I didn't give Meg any choice when I insisted I come, but I swore to her I won't report on any of this until she clears it." He shrugged. "It works for me."

"You're in it for the story, then?" Lauren said pointedly.

"I'm a reporter, the story is always the endgame. But sometimes it can't be the priority. Helping Meg save a life was the priority. I know you're law enforcement, and you guys consider reporters to be the enemy. But sometimes our motives aren't as nefarious as you assume them to be." He seemed satisfied with the slight softening of Lauren's expression because he turned back to the victim's ordeal. "It's amazing she survived. How did that not kill her?"

"It would have," Meg said. "Compression asphyxiation works by mechanically limiting the air and the oxygen you can inhale. As the weight stresses the rib cage, ribs break, compressing the lungs yet even more. Oxygen deprivation sets in. When it gets high enough, the victim passes out."

"She was unconscious when we got here."

"Exactly."

"With enough deprivation, the brain dies. We got the weight off her in time. Once her lungs had room to expand, even if she has broken ribs, her oxygen levels came back up and she regained consciousness."

"She's going to be okay." Brian's words were hopeful, but the expression on his face considerably darker. "I assume her appearance wasn't lost on you."

Meg had seen it in the flashlight's beam, but she had pushed it away. Leave it to Brian to insist on bringing it back into the light. She loved him and knew it was his love for her that kept him nipping at her heels like a persistent puppy, but part of her wished he'd just let it go. Of course the Brian she knew would never let it go. "She looked like me. Again."

"Wait." McCord grabbed her arm. "What do you mean 'again'? This has happened before?"

Brian answered McCord's question before Meg could force herself to do so. "The first victim looked like Meg. Scarily similar, in fact. The second wasn't quite as close a match, but it was there."

"I noticed Cat's coloring, but I didn't connect it." McCord pinned her with a narrowed gaze. "You mean he's killing you, over and over?"

"That's my theory," Brian said. When Meg turned on him with a cold stare, he simply shrugged. "I'm not letting it go. Get used to it. If you're not going to take it seriously, I will."

"I *am* taking it seriously," Meg shot back. "But all that's for the BAU to work out. It doesn't get in the way of what we do. It *can't* get in the way, or we risk losing a victim."

McCord held up a placating hand. "Okay, I get that part of it. But you have to keep everyone in the loop, so we can help you."

"That's what I keep saying," Brian said in a singsong under his breath, earning another acidic glare from Meg.

"You need to tell your sister," McCord added. "You can't just keep something like this away from your family."

"I didn't tell you guys earlier because I was disturbed by it and what it might mean. We've hardly had time to get our feet under us with this case and that was layered on top of it all. Also, time was of the essence and it wasn't worth getting into a big, emotional discussion about it.

Cat was already missing, so what she looked like wasn't relevant."

"It is now," Lauren said. "He didn't win this time, we did. And I don't know if that will piss him off or excite him, because now he knows we're up to the challenge, which will make the game more fun. Either way, someone else will be in his sights. Including you."

Meg understood Lauren was opting to be proactive, not reactive. But the frustration and fury building in her was reaching a fever pitch and she was honestly waiting for steam to start shooting out of her ears like a cartoon Wile E. Coyote. She paced two steps away and gave herself five seconds to look past the mine to the hills and forests beyond. The beauty beyond the horror. Feeling marginally steadier, she turned back. "It's too soon."

"What?"

"It's too soon. He's taken three victims over only a handful of days. I may be his last target, but he's not going to come for me just yet. Where's the fun in that? Why make a move like that now, when he can torture me more? No, I'm not his target—at least not yet."

"But someone else is," Brian said. "I think we need to talk to Craig about getting out a bulletin so people know what's going on. Women who fit the description need to be careful."

"There's something else to consider," McCord said. "Something started this maniac down this path, so let's say it was the Mannew case from last month. You had enough media attention at the time to focus on you, for whatever reason. So he's had a month to get this organized. There's a specific victimology being followed. It's not just a crime of opportunity. This required advanced planning. He's picking them off in short order, and the only way to do that is to have them already selected, to know their schedules and where to find them. On top of that, he's had to choose death sites for them that are not only related to them, but which also have a Civil War connection."

"A Civil War connection?" Brian asked. "That's a thing in this case?"

"It's beginning to appear so," Meg said.

"My point is"—McCord continued—"I think he's already chosen his victims, researched them, and planned where they'll die. This shows a scary amount of organization. That has to say something to your FBI profilers."

"I'm sure it does. We've got one watching the case, and I'm sure Craig is already making contact with him. Speaking of which, we'd better check in with Craig again."

"Agreed. Rocco, come." Lauren shortened her leash and headed for the gate and away from the mine, Brian and Lacey behind her.

McCord fell into step with Meg as they followed. "I know you don't like the issue of the victims, but you need to tell Cara," he said gently. "You don't want to scare her, but she needs to know."

"I know."

"No, I don't think you're seeing the whole picture. You're missing a crucial point."

"How so?"

"She looks like you. Besides some mysterious doppelganger out there, no one looks more like you than Cara."

Meg stopped dead, Hawk automatically following her lead, but McCord took another few steps before he realized he'd lost his companion.

"I've been so fixated on the puzzle, the game, that I didn't see what was right in front of me." Meg's hand rose to the necklace she wore around her throat, her fist closing over the pendant, a glass sculpture of electric blue and dusky black, intertwined with the soft powdery gray of all she had left of Deuce—a memory pendant made from his ashes. "What if—"

"Don't." McCord strode back to her, grasping her forearm and giving her a little shake, forcing her to release the pendant. "Cara's smart and she's brave. And with an alarm already raised about your parents, she has to be already on her guard. Tell her about her specific risk and she'll be ready for it."

"Okay."

They hurried after Brian and Lauren, Meg's hand already in her pocket, curling around her cell phone. She'd call from the car, just to hear Cara's voice. Surely, the maniac wouldn't act again this soon, because he wouldn't yet know he'd lost this round. But once he did know, how much time did they have?

CHAPTER 9

Field Dressing Station: Dr. Jonathan Letterman, appointed medical director of the Union Army in 1862, created a staged, three-tier treatment plan for wounded soldiers evacuated from the battlefield by the newly formed Ambulance Corps. Stage one, the mobile field dressing station, was located close to the battlefield and manned by medical personnel capable of applying tourniquets and rudimentary field dressings.

Wednesday, May 24, 3:34 PM
Northwest Hospital
Randallstown, Maryland

"Thanks again for this," McCord said with a sideways glance.

McCord and Meg moved through the hospital corridor, Hawk heeling on Meg's left. They stepped to the side to give an orderly with a gurney more room; then they continued toward their destination—room 327.

"This time, we've got a story you can run with in real time. Craig is absolutely on board—so much so, he gave the green light even before talking to Peters. We need to warn any woman who might be vulnerable, and the best chance is to get the story out there in as big a way as possible."

"The *Post* will be perfect for that. Here we are—room 327."

The door leading into the private room was open, but Meg knocked on the door before leaning into the room. "Cat? It's Meg Jennings from the FBI. May I come in?"

"Yes."

Meg and McCord entered the room to find Cat, cleaner and with considerably more color in her face, lying in the bed. The monitors around her were all dark, but a hanging IV bag dripped fluid steadily at the head of the bed.

Meg motioned to McCord, who hung back a bit. "I'm here with Clay McCord. Do you remember him from the mine?"

The smile Cat gave McCord was full of gratitude. "Of course I do. You were there when I woke up. You kept me company in the dark."

"That was me." McCord moved forward, holding out his hand. They shook, but even Meg could see her grip was weak. "I feel like I should introduce myself properly. Clay McCord, from the *Washington Post*."

The hand in McCord's grasp went completely limp. "You're a reporter?"

"Yes. And I want to make that clear, because I'd like to do a story on you." When Cat drew back, McCord threw a *Help me* look at Meg.

Meg circled the bed with Hawk to come up on Cat's other side. "I hope it's okay we brought Hawk. He does hospital visits all the time. He's very well behaved."

"I love dogs. I miss my own. We're rarely apart." Cat held out her hand, being careful not to tug on the IV, and Hawk slid his head under her palm, allowing her to stroke him. "The FBI agents here earlier said he found me."

"Mr. McCord figured out where you were. Hawk tracked you down, once we got there. Teamwork."

Cat looked back up at McCord, most of the suspicion gone now. "You found me?"

"I worked out where you might be from the clues." He shrugged. "No special skills. Just a well-read history buff, with a pretty good memory for mostly useless facts."

"Don't sell yourself short," Meg said. "Cat, the agents here earlier, did they tell you about the case we're working and the first two victims?"

Cat nodded.

"And they told you the person who took you has a specific victim type he's choosing?"

"Yes." Cat's gaze narrowed on her face for several seconds. "They said the victims looked like one of the FBI handlers. They meant you, didn't they? Fair skin, light eyes, and long, dark hair."

"Black Irish, through and through. Yes, that's the current theory."

"Why is he doing this?"

"We don't know yet. But we're working on it."

"That's part of why we want to get the word out there," McCord cut in smoothly. "We don't think he's finished. We think other women might be at risk. So we want to warn them. And I can use my position at the *Post* to do that. I can leave your name out of it, but, honestly, it's going to be out there already."

Cat blew out a long breath and stared up at the ceiling for a moment. " 'Mother, Maiden, and Crone, grant me strength. As you will, so mote it be.' " She looked directly at McCord, her eyes sparking with anger. "Let's do it, all of it, name and everything."

McCord grinned and pulled up a chair. "You're amazing. And after all you've been through today!"

"No one else should go through this." Sadness replaced the anger. "I was luckier than the first woman he took. But there's no guarantee the next one will be."

"There isn't," Meg agreed. "So let's try to keep him from taking her in the first place." She pulled up another chair and sat down, Hawk settling on the ground at her feet with a gusty sigh of contentment.

Cat smiled down at the relaxed dog. "He's had a busy day."

"He has. But he's a ball of energy. Give him ten minutes of downtime and he'll be raring to go again. He's used to grabbing whatever rest he can, whenever he can."

"My dog is just like that." Concern filled her voice. "The agents said they have Lachlan and would arrange to have him dropped off at my parents' home. The doctors tell me I have two broken ribs and an incomplete fracture in a third, so they want to keep me overnight just for observation. We won't be separated for long, but I just want to make sure he gets there safely."

"Would you like me to follow up on that for you?" Meg leaned forward and laid a hand over hers. "Trust me, I get it. If I was separated from Hawk, I'd be going crazy until I knew he was okay."

Cat gave a rueful laugh. "Exactly. Do you mind?"

"Not at all. I'll find out before we leave today so you're not worrying about it." Meg saw McCord was ready and had not only a pad of paper open on his knee, but his phone out.

"Cat, do you mind if we record this? We don't have to, but it would help capture the whole conversation."

"I don't mind at all." She shifted slightly on the bed and a soft moan of pain escaped her. "Sorry, it's not that bad with the painkillers they've given me, but if I move, or, worse, cough, it's like someone stuck a sword right through me." Biting her lip against the pain, she shifted once more, and settled before turning to McCord. "Okay, I'm ready. What do you want to know?"

"Let's start from the beginning. You were at Joseph's House this morning with Lachlan."

"Yes. Lachlan is a certified therapy dog and we volunteer weekly." Cat looked back toward Meg. "I'm Wiccan, and we have very strong beliefs about community service. Everything we do will be returned threefold. And I happen to have a fantastic dog, so we trained and certified for therapy dog work. He's such a sweetie. The patients love him and look forward to his visits."

"So this is a regular thing. Same time, same day, every week?" McCord asked.

"Like clockwork. It's important to the patients that they have something to depend on, something to look forward t—" She stopped suddenly. "You think he knew my routine."

"We think he's selecting his targets ahead of time. Possibly has had them selected for a while. So now that it's time to act, he can set up the abductions quickly."

"He's been watching me?" Her tone rose in alarm.

"We can't be certain," Meg said, "but we think so. However, you're safe now. He's done with you."

"Thank the Goddess."

"So you went to Joseph's House for your regular visit."

"Yes. Eight-thirty to ten in the morning. Although this morning, I didn't leave until about ten-fifteen because one of the patients wasn't doing so well. He's in palliative care at this point, and the doctor was in with him. So we waited because I didn't want to disappoint him." Her eyes grew shiny and she blinked furiously. "I don't think he'll be there next week when we go."

"I'm sorry," McCord said quietly. Cat blew out a long breath and gave a small laugh at herself. "I'm ridiculous. It's just . . . some of these patients have been around for years, since we started. They're friends now, and it's hard to lose friends."

Meg handed her a tissue. "It is. Take your time."

Cat dabbed at her eyes, then blew her nose. "Sorry, I'm not usually this emotional. It's like I've had a difficult day or something." She gave a shaky laugh. "Keep going."

"So you left Joseph's House at ten-fifteen. Then what happened?"

"I always park around the corner on Ontario Road Northwest. So we were walking back to the car and were just passing a white panel van with the back doors open."

"Any markings on the van?"

"I don't remember any. No name or logo."

"Any preexisting markings might have been covered over. Do you remember what was inside the van?"

Cat's gaze narrowed on the far wall, her eyes going unfocused. "Wire cages. An installed shelving unit on one side, with drawers in it to keep stuff. Maybe a net?" Her eyes snapped back into focus as she looked at Meg. "I'm sorry, I didn't really take a good look at it."

"That's okay. For not taking a good look, that's a great rundown. What else do you remember?"

"I remember a man standing near the van, staring at his phone. Standing with his back to me."

McCord looked over at Meg. "Probably using the front-facing camera to track her progress down the street so he could keep his head down and his back to her."

Meg gave a short nod of agreement.

"Can you tell us anything specific about the man?" McCord asked. "Hair color, height, weight, build?"

"Honestly, I didn't really see him, if you know what I mean. I saw the persona he wanted me to see. He was wearing all navy blue—pants and a short-sleeved shirt. He had on one of those heavy utility belts, like police officers wear with all the attachments. But no gun, I don't think. There was a shoulder patch on his left shoulder that very clearly said, 'Animal Control.' It looked official, and had a city crest on it, but I didn't recognize the crest. He had a baseball cap on, with 'Animal Control' on it in big letters. When he turned around, the sun flashed off the badge he wore." Cat patted her chest just above her left breast. "It was the shape of a police badge, but I didn't see what it said. He turned in my direction and asked if I knew where 2650 Ontario Road was, and when I turned to look at the house number beside us, his arm came around my neck and he pressed something wet and cold over my mouth and nose. After that, it all went fuzzy."

"Inhaled anesthetic," Meg said. "Probably a soaked gauze pad. So you heard his voice."

"Yes."

"You're certain it was a man?"

"Yes."

"We've been hypothesizing the suspect is male, but we didn't have any actual proof. Did you get a look at him?"

"I didn't. He had his head down so the brim of his cap shaded his face. He had a map open on his phone and was moving it up and down the street, like he was trying to find the specific address. When he looked up to talk to me, he only barely tipped his face up. I saw his lips move and could see he had light skin, but that's about it. And then I turned to look at the addresses, and that was it."

"Enough to work with a sketch artist?" McCord asked.

Meg shook her head. "Just the lower face isn't enough. That would throw the suspect pool too wide and would waste resources needlessly." She turned to the woman in the bed. "Let's look at how he knew things about you. He knew you volunteered on Wednesday mornings. He knew you were Wiccan. How would he know about that?"

"That's certainly an open book. We're not a cult that meets in secret so no one knows about our dirty second lives."

"That's not what I was implying."

"I know. But that's how some people think we should treat it. It's our faith, and it's based on purity, truth, and the goodness of Mother Earth. We're out in the community doing good works when we can. We hold open meetings, and we talk to the curious. We've been on the news and in the newspapers. So that part of my life is anything but secret."

"He tried to kill you based on your faith," McCord said.

"No, he tried to kill me based on the historical prejudices of a group of ultraconservative, late-seventeenth-century Christians. The Witch Trials of Salem played off the fears of Europe's Burning Times. A bunch of bored teenage girls took advantage of people's real fears and innocents died. Including Giles Corey." The eyes that met Meg's were hard with anger. "I know what he tried to do to me and why. But only because he doesn't understand anything about Wiccans at all."

"I don't think he wants to understand. He wants to make a point and get my attention. You're simply a pawn in his game. And he's going to pay for that. That's my promise to you."

" 'So mote it be.' " Her face colored and she sank into herself. "And that was a very un-Wiccan response. 'Do harm to none' is how we live our lives."

"Didn't you just say that everything you do will be returned threefold? Well, we'll be his deliverance of that. None of this is on you. And your faith aside, it's a pretty human thing to want to see justice for a wrong done to you. You've had a pretty horrible day, so take it easy on yourself. Now we have one more question that won't be in the article because it's all very specific to you and not to the greater public. We're working on the theory he's not only tying the method of death to the victim, but also to the location. Is there any reason the Choate Mine would be linked to you in any way?"

Cat was silent for a moment as she considered the question. "Not the mine, which I didn't even know existed, but the area. Soldiers Delight is an area high in the mineral serpentine."

"That's what's found in the serpentinite," McCord clarified. "The actual rock itself."

"Yes. We believe crystals are power objects that contain elemental energy, be it protection against evil, assistance in healing, good fortune, meditation, or in many other aspects of life. Serpentine is said to enhance the emotion of love, but also to bring peace. For decades, perhaps longer, the local Wiccans have used a site in the forest near Soldiers Delight for our handfasting ceremonies. To commit to your life partner surrounded by the stone that will enhance your love."

McCord sat back in his chair, laying his pen down on the pad of paper. " 'Handfasting'? Is that some sort of marriage?"

"It's our marriage."

"It's legal?"

"It can be. We're lucky to have a clergy member who is also a legal officiant. Our handfastings are legally binding ceremonies. But instead of Scripture readings and homilies in a church setting, we stand in a circle under Father Sky, blessed by the bounties of Mother Earth, as we invoke the four elements. We bind together the hands of the couple, we bless the loving cup, exchange vows and jewelry, and sometimes the couple even jumps over a broomstick, as was done in the old ways. It's a lovely ceremony." She gave McCord a pointed look. "Where do you think the phrase 'tying the knot' comes from?"

"I had no idea. You learn something new every day. So this place is near the mine?"

"I could show you on a map, but I'd bet it was within a mile of where you found me."

"So we're three for three then," Meg said. "The victims are related to the site."

"Has this been helpful?" The hope in Cat's voice was tangible.

"Very. If he takes another woman, we have a second investigative avenue to follow." Meg looked over to McCord. "Have you got everything you need?"

"I do. I can get this done ASAP and over to my waiting editor. It will be online tonight and front page for the six AM edition tomorrow."

"Perfect. Cat, give me a minute, I'm going to make some calls and find out where Lachlan is." Rising, Meg pulled out her cell phone and walked to the window to stare out over the rooftops of the surrounding neighborhood. Within minutes, she had her answer and could turn back, with a smile, to the woman in the bed. "He's safely at your parents'. He arrived there about a half hour ago."

Cat laid a hand—carefully—over her breast in relief. "Thank you. I'd prefer he was here with me, but I feel better knowing he's with people he loves."

McCord flipped his pad of paper closed and stood, holding out his hand. "We're grateful for your assistance, especially right now. I'm so sorry you went through what you did, but this could very well help another woman stay alive."

They said their good-byes and hurried out to Meg's SUV. "I'll drop you off and then I'm picking up Cara and the dogs and we're headed out to our parents."

"To explain all of this to them?"

"This isn't something to handle on the phone. And before you ask, yes, I'll make sure it's clear to Cara what the risks are. I'm not going to let that son of a bitch touch my family."

CHAPTER 10

Soldiers Rest: The Soldiers Rest in Alexandria, Virginia, was built as a temporary layover and rest stop for Union soldiers in transit. Occasionally, it also housed captured Confederate deserters who pledged an oath of loyalty to the Union. The complex consisted of sleeping quarters, bathhouse, a library and reading rooms, medical facilities, a kitchen and mess hall, perimeter fencing, and a guard-house. It was briefly used as a hospital during the summer of 1864, and after the war, some of the United States Colored Troops were quartered there. It was closed and sold at public auction in 1866.

Wednesday, May 24, 6:50 PM
Cold Spring Haven Animal Rescue
Cold Spring Hollow, Virginia

"God, I've missed this place." Meg turned off Cold Spring Road and into the long, winding driveway that led to both their parents' home and the rescue. "It's been too long."

"We've been busy. But we need to make a concerted effort to get down here more often. Even if it's just for the day." Cara sat back in the passenger seat, and took a deep breath of country air through the open window. Spring had given way to the warmth of oncoming summer and the air was rich with the scents of grass and flowers. The miles that sped by, once out of the city, were filled with the vibrant greens of verdant forest and farmers' fields.

Hawk gave a whine from the back and Meg glanced at him through the mesh. Saki and Blink shared the K-9 compartment with him, but they were both curled up, asleep. Hawk sat straight upright, his nose pressed against the grill of the K-9 compartment, taking in all the scents of the country from the cracked window, his eyes bright.

"Look at him. He totally knows," Cara said.

"He always does."

"How long since they've seen each other?"

"Must be over two months by now. Think she'll have forgotten him?"

"Ha! Never. They were inseparable for too long for that to happen."

The driveway wound up the hill through the woods until they broke out into fields and pastures. At the bottom of the sloped driveway, a pretty ranch-style house, fronted by fieldstone with a white wraparound porch, sat in front of a bright red barn and several well-tended outbuildings. Out over the rolling hills, neat wooden fences streamed in straight lines, the fields inside dotted with animals.

Meg spotted the bay mare in the paddock nearest the house and laughed. "Leave it to Dad. He put her out already. Hawk, look who's there!" Another whine was the only response.

"I think you'd better hurry to let him out," Cara said dryly. "He's vibrating back there, he's so excited."

Meg pulled up in front of the house, and she and Cara climbed out. Meg opened the back door on the driver's side. "Hawk, down." Hawk obediently jumped down and then simply stood at her side, vibrating, as Cara had so succinctly put it, in anticipation. Meg couldn't stand to torture him any longer and released him. "Hawk, go see Auria." And just like that, he was off like a shot.

The horse on the far side of the drive saw the dog streaking toward her. She gave a happy whinny of greeting and then the two of them were sniffing each other and rubbing noses ecstatically.

"I thought I'd save us a step and have Auria already out to greet Hawk." Jake Jennings strolled down the porch steps, with his wife, Eda, right behind him. The sisters marched right into their parents' waiting arms for hugs, then switched to greet the other parent. They broke apart, laughing.

"I see Blink is having his usual reaction to the rescue," Eda said, peering over Meg's shoulder.

As one, they all looked back at the SUV. Saki had jumped down and meandered in the direction of Hawk and Auria, but Blink still stood inside the SUV, quivering, his ears pressed flat against his head, his big brown eyes seeming even more oversized than usual.

"I've come to the conclusion he's never going to get over his nerves." Cara walked back to the SUV and stood outside the open car door, patting her thighs. "Come on, Blink, get down."

Blink jumped, but it was abrupt, the landing truncated, so he stayed as close to the vehicle as possible. He pressed close to Cara, his tail between his legs.

"Oh, Blink. Come here, you big baby. Remember me?" Eda crouched down in front of him, letting him sniff her, then running her strong, capable hands over him. The greyhound visibly relaxed under her touch.

"He just loves you," Cara said. "Sometimes I think you're the only thing that gets him through these visits."

"He had a hard life at the racetrack—the kind of life that leaves scars. It takes time and love to heal those wounds." Eda straightened. "Let's go see how Hawk and Saki are doing. Come on, Blink. You stick with me."

As a group, they wandered over to the paddock where Hawk was standing tall on his hind legs, his front paws braced on the top rail of the fence, nose to nose with the mare. Auria swung her massive head toward Meg when she stepped close.

Meg remembered Hawk's early days and her initial terror at his fascination with the mare. He'd been a tiny, sick scrap of a puppy when someone had left him on the front porch of the rescue. Meg had been living with her parents, licking her wounds after the traumatic loss of Deuce. She and Hawk had bonded almost on sight. She'd nursed him back to health, and the tiny dog started to bloom under her loving care, growing like a weed. One morning, Meg couldn't find him and started to panic, thinking he'd gotten outside and was lost or picked off by a mountain lion or coyote. She finally found him curled up in the corner of Auria's stall, fast asleep, while her father curried the horse. Back then, Auria was brand-new to the rescue, having been surrendered as practically skin and bones by an older woman who loved her, but couldn't afford to feed herself, let alone her horse. Auria was a nervous and skittish beast in her new surroundings, her stall bearing the marks of her tendency to kick, but Hawk's presence seemed to calm her. After that, anytime the stall door was open, Hawk could be found inside. At first, Meg was terrified the mare would kill him with her massive hooves, but Auria always seemed to take special care around Hawk. When the weather was good, Hawk would hang out with Auria and the two would play, chasing each other around the paddock. Early on, Hawk's short puppy legs and Auria's slow and weak gait were evenly matched. However, as she gained weight and strength, Auria began to outpace Hawk and would have to adjust her stride to allow him to catch up. During

Hawk's time at the rescue, they were inseparable. Both animals had shown signs of a funk when they'd been separated after Meg's move to DC, but frequent visits had helped alleviate some of the depression. Already too old to be adopted out when she was surrendered, the Jenningses knew they'd have Auria for life. Seeing as they'd all grown fond of her, everyone was happy with the arrangement.

Meg stroked a hand down Auria's neck and crooned to her as she studied her front legs. "She's looking good, and seems to be moving without pain. No problems since the treatment?"

"Nothing. We caught the osselets early and got them treated. The old girl is practically new again. She's a little stiff in the mornings, but aren't we all?" He rubbed his back for dramatic effect and earned a light smack from his wife.

"Don't let him fool you," Eda chided. "He's in better shape now than he was in his twenties when he spent all his time behind a desk." She turned around, her gaze searching. "Where's Saki?"

"She went into the barn." Cara pointed to the open barn door. "Is that okay?"

"Sure is. Clementine is in there with her litter, but Saki won't bother them."

"How old are the kittens now?"

"Five weeks. They're keeping Clemmy busy, let me tell you. Now I've got a pitcher of lemonade chilling. Come up to the porch and take a load off. If the animals need us, they'll let us know. But it sounds like you girls have something that needs discussing."

"I'll say," Meg muttered. "Hawk, you hang out with Auria. We'll be nearby if you need us." She unlatched the wide paddock gate, cracking it open, and Hawk shot through, racing in circles around the horse before taking off over the grass. Auria followed at a canter. Meg relatched the gate and stood for a moment, her hand resting on the smooth wood rail, watching dog and horse frolicking.

Her father's hand rested on her shoulder. "Good to see that kind of innocent joy, isn't it?"

"Sure is. It's been a bad couple of days. This is balm for the soul."

"You can drop by anytime. The door is always open for my girls."

She reached up to squeeze his hand. "I know. And I'm grateful for it. Now we'd better go. We're keeping Mom and Cara waiting."

The group wandered to the porch, slowly climbing the steps to settle in comfortably cushioned wicker chairs. Blink flopped down on the porch floor at Eda's feet. They made small talk, catching up on the happenings at the rescue and Cara's training school, while studiously avoiding anything having to do with Meg's job. Eda disappeared into the house, returning shortly with a pitcher of iced lemonade and a large plate of chocolate chip cookies, which she set in the middle of the table within everyone's reach.

"Mom, you didn't have to bake just because we were coming," Cara said.

"She absolutely didn't," Jake said, helping himself to a cookie. "But did you seriously think I'd stop her?"

Meg laughed as she reached for a cookie. "There are too many chocoholics in this family for that to happen. Including the cook." She took a bite and sat back, humming with satisfaction. "That really hits the spot."

"I thought it might." Eda poured a large glass of lemonade and handed it to Meg. "Now, chitchat aside, Dad tells me there might be a threat to the rescue."

"I just . . ." Words bubbled to the surface, too many words all at once; so, in the end, nothing came out. Meg forced herself to stop and breathe. To take a sip of lemonade and gather herself under the shrewd eyes of her parents. She could read in their eyes that they were already preparing for bad news. "I just don't know. But neither of us is willing to take any chances. Let me back up and tell you about this case and how it started two nights ago."

She explained everything to her parents from the taking of the first victim to that day's interview with the third.

"That poor girl," Eda said. "But she's got some steel in her and that will get her through. And the one who didn't make it . . . well, that's almost beyond bearing. When you think about what she went through—"

"I try not to," Meg said flatly. At her mother's curious look, she clarified, "It's not that I'm being insensitive, but it distracts me from what I really need to do."

"To catch the son of a bitch who's responsible for this," Jake said.

"Yes. But at least two of the three are still alive. For now."

Jake reached for another cookie, but didn't take a bite. "So we get the gist of the case. But that doesn't explain why my younger daughter calls me in a panic this afternoon and why both of my daughters show up in the evening. Not that we don't love seeing you, but clearly something else is going on. So what is it?"

Meg looked at Cara, who simply shrugged. "We always were open books to dear old dad."

"And dear old mom," their mother said. "Something happened this afternoon, something case-related, that has you concerned, not just for anyone else who might be taken, but for us."

Meg took a sip of lemonade to wet her suddenly dry mouth, and forced herself to shift the rock of security on which her parents stood. Not because of the threat to them—that they'd take in stride—but because of the threat to their daughters. "I seem to be directly linked to this case.

The coded messages that are coming in with each kidnapping, they're addressed to me personally."

Her father's eyes went dead cold. "He's specifically challenging *you* to find the missing women?"

"Yes. Now, of course, it's not a one-woman, one-dog show. Brian, Lauren, and Scott are all helping, as are any agents we need in the investigation. But there's something else. That first night, it was Brian and me together standing over that grave. And we both saw it."

"Saw what?" Caution and suspicion mixed in her mother's voice.

"The victim. She looked like me. I thought it might be a fluke, until the second and third victims also turned out to look like me." She turned to Cara. "Like us."

Cara stared at her for a moment, head slightly tilted as she took it all in. Then she sat back and blew out a breath. "Which means I might be on his list."

"You think he's targeting both of you?" Jake looked from one daughter to the other.

"He's targeting me." Meg's tone was sure, with no room for doubt. "But I think we're all somehow involved. Cara, tell them about the code."

Cara set down her own lemonade on the table. "The FBI cryptanalysts deciphered the first message on their own, but it took them some time because they didn't know what kind of code it was. In the end, it was a substitution code called a Vigenère cipher. To make a long story short, to solve the code, you need a key. If you don't have it, you can figure it out based on alphabetic frequency. That's what the professionals are doing with their computers."

"Which means you're doing something differently," Eda said. "You've always been a whiz at puzzles. What did you figure out that works better?"

"I noticed the key for the first cipher not only told us

how to solve the cipher, it also spelled out a word in its own right. The word was 'Deuce.' "

Meg felt the gazes of both parents snap to her, but she kept her eyes down and said nothing, letting Cara continue.

"The second key spelled out the word 'Hawk.' Once I knew that not only the message itself was addressed to Meg, but that the cipher key was a message for her as well, I started to work the new key backward to find out what the word might be and use that to solve the code. I beat the cryptanalysts and their computers today because of it."

"That was this afternoon, wasn't it?" Eda asked.

"It was. The word was 'Haven.' "

Jake muttered a curse under his breath. "So you think we're in danger because they used part of the rescue's name as one of the keys."

"We don't know," Meg said, stress making her voice pitch higher than usual. "But do you honestly think we'd risk you for a single second?"

"Of course you wouldn't." Eda reached over and folded Meg's limp hand into hers, where it dangled over the arm of the wicker chair. "And forewarned is forearmed."

"Damn straight." Jake leaned forward so Meg couldn't escape his gaze. "We'll take every precaution necessary. We'll make sure we're armed at all times, if that would make you feel better."

Meg blew out a long breath. "It really would. For now anyway. Are the security cameras still on?"

"Of course, and the trail cameras too. They're for the protection of the animals and to dissuade anyone who might try to harm or take one, but in this case, they'll be extra protection for us too. You know where all the recordings are, and you know the password, in case you need access. None of that has changed."

"You'll make sure the volunteers know? And no new volunteers in the short term?"

"I'll tell them the rescue has received a threat against the animals. That will be enough for them to be watchful. And no one new for now. You know most of the workers who come in. It's the same team we've had for a while. We can trust them. Meg, they're good people."

Meg blew out a breath, trying to dispel some of the stress with it. "I know they are. We just can't afford to take any chances."

"And we won't. We'll even make sure neither your mother nor I am alone with anyone coming in to adopt, so nothing will get past us. No one is going to hoodwink us."

Pounding hoofbeats sounded in the paddock and Auria whipped past, mane and tail streaming behind her, Hawk running full out at her side, barking happily.

Their antics broke the tension and everyone laughed.

"Okay, enough about that. You know what to do and rehashing it is only going to stress Cara and me out more. So tell us about the rescue. It's kitten season, so are you overrun?"

"Of course we are, just like every year. But we've got an attractive adoption price and are hopeful of finding homes for them, as well as some of the older, longer-term residents. Did Dad tell you about the two orphaned baby deer we took in a few days ago? Their mother was hit by a car. You have to come see them before you go. They're in a stall in the barn to make the regular feedings easier, and are just the cutest babies."

Meg let her mother ramble on about the day-to-day goings-on at the rescue, letting her gentle voice and the reminder of the good people out in the world soothe some of her worry.

CHAPTER 11

Attrition Warfare: Attrition warfare is the attempt to wear down an opposing force by inflicting unacceptable or unsustainable losses. Ulysses S. Grant chose to engage in attritional warfare and accept high casualty rates to his own forces in order to overcome the Confederate Army's advantages of mobility and independent unit tactics.

Thursday, May 25, 9:08 AM
Forensic Canine Unit, J. Edgar Hoover Building
Washington, DC

Meg stepped into the bullpen to find Brian, Lauren, Scott, and their dogs already there. "Craig's not here?"

"Not yet." Brian pointed to the covered coffee on Meg's desk. "Which means he's hung up somewhere. Sit down and have your coffee."

"You are the very best of men." Meg collapsed into her desk chair and reached gratefully for the coffee.

"I keep trying to get Ryan to tell me that, but I have yet to hear those blessed words pass his lips. Maybe you could teach him?"

"You married a Smithsonian archivist. I'm pretty sure I couldn't teach him a damned thing because he already knows it all."

Brian grinned. "Yeah, he is kind of a walking encyclopedia." He studied her. "How late did you get in last night?"

"Look that good, do I? Actually, I got to bed at a reasonable time last night. It was leaving my parents' place in Virginia at six AM that was the killer. They didn't want Cara and me to drive home last night after a long and stressful day. I dropped Cara, Blink, and Saki off at home and then came straight in." She toasted him with the coffee cup. "Bless you for this, because the cup I had in the car at six-thirty after hitting a drive-through has well and truly worn off."

"I live to serve."

"Good morning." Craig came through the door, carrying a file folder in one hand and a stainless-steel travel mug of coffee in the other. He set both down on the corner of Lauren's desk and pulled a chair around to join the group. "My office is too small for meetings. Someday we're going to invest in a conference room for this unit, I tell you."

"You run that by Peters and let us know what he thinks," Lauren said, a twinkle in her eye. "I'm guessing he'll tell you there are enough other conference rooms in this building."

"Who wants a five-minute walk to start an impromptu meeting?" He sat down and tossed back some of the coffee before putting the cup back down. Rocco meandered by, sniffing at his pants, and Craig gave him a distracted stroke. "Hey, boy."

"Rocco, stop being nosy. Come. Down." Lauren pointed at the floor beside her chair. The dog came and flopped on the floor with a dramatic sigh. "Honestly, I think he's a teenager some days. So, Craig, what do we know?"

"I've been down in the lab, hassling the techs again." He looked up and gave an evil grin. "They love me."

"I think they're scared of you," Scott said. "No one gets early results quite like you do."

"Peters does, and always did." Again with the slightly maniacal smile. "I learned everything from him."

"I need to come with you the next time you visit the lab," Brian quipped. "This sounds like a useful skill. So what did the useful skill win for us this time?"

"Early toxicological reports on the deceased victim." Craig opened the file and scanned the contents. "We've got a combination of two anesthetics being reported here. One was easy to find, the other not so much. Isoflurane was used initially. In the reports from Ms. Baldwin yesterday, she reported something cold and wet pressed over her mouth and nose. That was the isoflurane. It's a short-acting, inhaled anesthetic, with a generally short half-life, but they were able to find minute traces of it in the"—Craig leaned in and squinted at the word—"alveolar tissues of the lungs. It apparently disappears from the bloodstream quickly, but takes a little longer to get broken down in the tissues. The longer lasting anesthetic was ketamine. That was delivered by injection, right into the vein, as witnessed by marks inside both victims' elbows."

"So . . . fast-acting inhaled anesthetic to subdue the victim, then a longer acting anesthetic in the van to keep her quiet while he restrained and then moved the victim to the kill site," Lauren hypothesized. "Once the victim was in place, he likely wanted her awake and aware and terrified. He clearly planned on Michelle regaining consciousness, so he gagged her so she couldn't call for help."

"If she could draw enough breath to even manage it," Brian said.

"Doubtful he took the time to properly weigh and dose the victims," Scott said. "More than likely, speed was the important aspect. He'd have had a syringe ready to go in the van. The isoflurane would stop working as soon as the anesthetic-soaked cloth was removed, so he needed to have the second dose ready to go, overlapping them to make sure the victim stayed unconscious." Scott shrugged when Craig stared at him in surprise. "All those years volunteering at the local vet clinic are paying off."

"Are those typical veterinary anesthetics?" Craig asked.

"Not exclusively. But they're used in vet practices for surgery and the like. Pair that with the Animal Control aspect of the kidnappings and you have to wonder about the background of the perp."

"Would Animal Control have something like that?"

"They would. Ketamine is used for euthanasia, but the job is usually done by only one worker and it's a direct vein injection. So a second anesthetic is usually used to calm the animal enough to allow for the lethal injection."

"So the perp could be anyone in the small animal world?" Brian asked. "A vet, a vet tech, or Animal Control officer?"

"Could be a hospital orderly or a nurse also," Meg suggested. "I'm pretty sure those anesthetics are used in people too. But aren't they controlled substances? You can't just order a bottle from the pharmacy for your own use. You can't even just use the open bottle at your vet clinic. To the best of my knowledge, those drugs are tightly regulated and monitored down to a fraction of an ounce."

"That, in itself, tells us something," Lauren said. "The only thing is, you have to make sure there is no black market for it. There certainly is for ketamine. You can buy that stuff on the street as 'Special K.' "

"No market for isoflurane though." Meg sat back in her chair, cradling her coffee cup. "That wouldn't make a good street drug. No high, just one whiff and you're out for the count, until you're breathing air again. No draw there."

"One wouldn't think so," Craig said. "But it gives agents

a place to start. They're looking into any thefts at local hospitals, clinics, and veterinary hospitals." He shot back his cuff and looked at his watch. "Rutherford is coming in from Quantico at nine-thirty and has booked the big departmental conference room on four. I let him know about yesterday's victim and he stopped by to get all the information so he could work on the profile." He looked at Meg and cocked his head toward his office door. "Can I have a word with you?"

Foreboding rose like a tide. Truthfully, at the back of her mind, she'd been wondering when this shoe was going to drop. Might as well get this over with, because she sure as hell wasn't going to obediently agree to the suggestion she saw coming. "Sure. Hawk, stay." She stood and pushed in her desk chair, meeting Brian's eyes and clearly reading the question in them. She hoped the look she returned clearly spoke of her suspicion.

She followed Craig into his office, but purposely left the door wide open, hoping that would limit Craig slightly. He wasn't a yeller, but he did raise his voice occasionally when he was passionate about an issue, and she really didn't want to wade into an argument if she could help it. "What's up?"

Craig sat down in his chair and loosened his tie. He looked tired, the lines carved a little more deeply around his eyes. "I want you to think about removing yourself from this case."

And there it was, the size-thirteen Salvatore Ferragamos crashing to the floor. Meg didn't bother to beat around the bush. "Why?"

"Because it's getting too personal to you. The messages are directed at you. The victims resemble you. I can't afford to have any handler on the case who is distracted by what's going on."

You don't even know the half of it. "I'm not distracted. I'm completely on my game."

"You're going to tell me losing the first victim didn't bother you?"

"Of course she bothered me." As her voice rose, Meg watched Craig glance at the open door behind her, but she didn't modulate her words. "She died waiting for us. She died horribly, alone and terrified, trying to claw her way out. If that didn't bother me, I'd be a robot. If it didn't bother any of us, you should throw us all off the team." She studied his clenched jaw. "But it's not all of us, is it? It's just me."

"No one else is involved in the same way. And while you're a very valuable part of this team, the distraction from the stress of the perp doing this for you, hell, maybe *to* you, is a risk the team can't take."

"With all due respect, sir, I disagree." Brian came through the door, his face slightly flushed because he'd obviously been eavesdropping. "Meg is a crucial part of this team, and I'd argue it's her involvement in the case that makes the team stronger."

Craig shot him a furious glare. "Foster, I don't recall inviting you to this meeting."

"You didn't. But I couldn't help overhearing. You can't take Meg off this case. You'll only be damaging our chances of stopping this guy. Don't you get it? The answer is in here." Reaching over, he tapped Meg's temple. "This guy can't be completely unknown to her. She's working it all out, and he's somewhere in there, but she doesn't know who he is yet. You have to give her time to work the case and work through the possibilities. Send her home and we not only lose the contribution of a top-of-their-game team, but you block her from access to aspects of the case that might trigger a suspect in her mind. Remove Meg, and you'll be possibly irrevocably tying our hands, and more women may die as a result."

Meg felt it was time to cut in before Brian buried himself. Or he kept tapping on her skull like it was a wall and he was searching for studs. "I understand your position, sir, and respect it. But I agree with Brian—we need to catch this guy. And to do so, you need all hands on deck, and I need access to the case. Somehow I know, or knew, this person. And at some point, he is going to do something to give himself away. But we have to wait for that to happen. And if I'm in the dark, I can't help. Don't forget, I'm not alone in this. I'm paired with someone at all times on this case, and I've got Hawk. Don't underestimate him. Remember how he took Mannew down last month. Not to mention we also have Lacey and Rocco on the team. We all look out for each other, all the time. And this is no exception."

Craig heaved out a frustrated sigh. "You piss me off when you gang up on me. You piss me off more when you may be right. Jennings, I don't want anyone on my team getting injured or into a dangerous situation, do you hear me?"

"Loud and clear, sir."

"Good, keep it that way." He swiveled to face his computer. "We're done here."

"Yes, sir. Thank you, sir."

They retreated from Craig's office, this time pulling the door closed behind them.

Brian sank into his desk chair. "Oh, thank God. I wasn't sure that would work. You left that door open on purpose, didn't you?"

Meg stepped over Hawk and sat down, tipping her chair back to stare at the ceiling. "Damn straight. I suspected I might need help. He doesn't really have a right to pull me off the case, nothing that could be considered conflict of interest or anything, but he could still make things difficult." She picked up the stress ball on her desk—one that looked like a shrieking baby—and tossed it at Brian, who smoothly caught it. "Thanks for eavesdropping. I'm not sure I could have swayed him on my own."

"Happy to help. I don't want to do this without you, so I considered it well worth walking into the lion's den." Brian glanced at his watch. "We'd better head to the conference room. Rutherford will be here in five." He stood and rubbed his hands together in anticipation. "Let's see who the profiler thinks we're looking at. Then you can see if you know anyone who fits the bill to nail this guy."

CHAPTER 12

Crisis Planning: Unlike strategic planning, planning during a crisis refines or replaces the assumptions underpinning strategic planning and is based upon new intelligence and actual events.

Thursday, May 25, 9:32 AM
Fourth floor conference room, J. Edgar Hoover Building
Washington, DC

The conference room filled quickly. Not just the Human Scent Evidence Team and their dogs, but all the field agents associated with the case. Rutherford stood at the head of the table, leafing through the file folder he'd brought with him. Craig came through the door, studiously avoiding the eyes of his team, and took a chair at the end of the table.

Rutherford snapped the file closed and straightened. A tall, distinguished African American, with silver at his temples, he towered over most of the men in the room even when they were on their feet. Dressed in a black suit, softened by an aqua tie, he commanded the room simply by his presence. When he spoke, his words were clearly chosen with care, and the intelligence behind the power quickly became the most notable thing about him.

"Thank you all for coming." At the sound of the door,

his gaze shot to the back of the room, his eyebrows shooting skyward as Executive Assistant Director Peters slipped in, choosing to stand against the wall at the back of the room, rather than join the group around the table. Rutherford gave him a short nod, then continued. His eyes scanned the table, finally coming to rest on Meg. "Ms. Jennings."

"Agent Rutherford."

He studied her critically for a moment, his dark eyes assessing. "Please excuse being treated as a detail of this case. I know that's not how it is for you, that you're involved in this case, and, more so, personally impacted by it. But your connection to the victims is a crucial part of the investigation."

Meg tipped her head in assent. "I understand the methods and what's at stake. Please continue."

"Thank you." Rutherford removed two 8-inch by 10-inch photos from the folder and tacked them up on the board behind him on the wall, one under the other. "This is the first victim, Sandra Holmes. Better known as Sandy to friends and family." The first picture showed a death mask, the face pale and waxen, the expression lifeless. As horrible as that image was, the second picture in some ways was much harder to look at—a picture of life and health, a woman with dark hair, light skin, and blue eyes, smiling and waving to the camera. Rutherford tapped the first picture. "This was taken by the ME's staff at the time of autopsy." His index finger rested on the second photograph. "This photo was supplied by Sandy's parents. Sandy was taken from Glencarlyn Park at dusk. She was thirty-six, single, an Iraq War vet, and the owner of a PTSD service dog named Ruby. She was a loving daughter, worked as a bookkeeper out of her own home, and had a passion for backgammon and romance novels."

Meg noted that while Rutherford referred to her as "Ms. Jennings," he constantly referred to the victim by her first name to strengthen the image of the victim in the minds of the investigating agents. She knew from years of cop work that any investigator who connects personally with a victim will go the extra mile to find that victim justice.

"But none of that was important to our unsub," Rutherford continued, using the common shorthand jargon for "unknown subject." He pulled another photo from the file and added it to the board. "This was all that was important."

Meg found herself looking at an eight-by-ten reproduction of her FBI identification photo.

"Somehow Meg Jennings is the key. As you know, the first message came in attached to Ruby's leash, encoded, with the only part of the message that was instantly readable being Ms. Jennings's name and designation within the FBI. So this is someone who knew how to get our attention."

"And mine," Meg mumbled under her breath, earning a sideways glance from Brian sitting beside her.

"The clue itself was not related to Ms. Jennings, but instead to two aspects of the case that will likely continue through it—the American Civil War and the victim herself. The kill site chosen was one directly related to Sandy, who, as a veteran, would have been eligible for inurnment at Arlington Cemetery. She is still eligible, but her parents have opted to bury their only daughter somewhere other than the site of her murder, which is entirely understandable."

He slid another color image from the folder and placed it next to Meg's photo. Michelle Wilson smiled out from the photo in what was clearly a professional headshot. "This is Michelle Wilson, who was the first victim to be abducted, but, due to an oversight in the initial investigation, wasn't connected to this case for nearly forty-eight hours and was found as the second victim. Michelle is forty-two, widowed, and works in real estate. She is an elected officer of the Daughters of Union Veterans of the Civil War and is related to Corporal George Wilson, who died on Belle Isle in the Confederate prison camp there. She was out walking her beagle on the beach in Cape Charles when she was abducted after dark. Once the connection was made, linking her to this case, a similar coded message was found addressed to Ms. Jennings. Fortunately, even with the delay in identifying Michelle as a related victim, and in decoding the message, the Human Scent Evidence Team successfully found her alive on Belle Isle. She had been restrained specifically in a position that would cause asphyxiation, given enough time. I think the link between victim and method of death here comes back to the Confederate prison camp. Torture was common at most, if not all, Civil War prison camps. There was a particular method called 'tying on the spare wheel,' which was used for discipline of soldiers and prisoners alike. It was a position similar to a spread-eagled crucifixion and it could lead to positional asphyxiation if the prisoner was left too long. He picked a simpler position for Michelle, but one that was equally effective. She is still in critical condition, but doctors are hopeful she will make a full recovery. Now, assuming the unsub intended us to discover Michelle's disappearance first, he expected her to be found first, and likely alive, given the expected time frame. So she was his first foray into the abductions and either he meant her as a warning shot, or he's escalating. Personally, I believe he meant for her to survive so you would always believe you had a chance in the game."

Rutherford pulled out a photo of the third victim and tacked it up so Meg's face was surrounded by a living image of each of the victims.

Seeing the faces there in color was like a fist to the gut

for Meg. They weren't carbon copies of her, but they were more than close enough. Two thoughts tumbled over each other in her brain in a race to float to the top.

He's killing me, over and over.

Cara's in danger.

"Sweet Jesus," Brian muttered, turning to her. "You okay?"

"I knew it. *We* knew it. But it suddenly got a whole lot more real, didn't it?"

"Sure as hell did." Brian squeezed her hand under the table.

"This is Catriona Baldwin. Catriona was taken right off the street after leaving an AIDS hospice, where she and her therapy dog, Lachlan, volunteer on a weekly basis. She was walking to her car at the time. A coded message was found, once again addressed to Ms. Jennings. Catriona had the good fortune of being found by the Human Scent Evidence Team before the unsub managed to kill her. Catriona is a florist who owns her own shop, which is apparently very popular and a recognizable brand, according to my wife. She's known in the community as someone who gives back and is big into fund-raising and helping the local neighborhood. More notable and more important to this case, she is Wiccan by faith."

"*Witchcraft?*" One of the agents closer to Rutherford spit out the word like it left a foul taste in his mouth. "Like the Wicked Witch of the West?"

"*Wiccan.*" Rutherford stressed the single word. "They'd say they were white witches. They believe in peace and harmony and helping your fellow man. It's called 'research,' Brody, and I suggest you give it a try sometime before you scoff." Rutherford turned back to the table at large. "This explains the method of attempted killing—pressing, or compression asphyxiation. One of the victims of the Salem Witch Trials was killed this way. So for the third time, we have a tie to the victim through the method of execution. As discovered by Mr. McCord and printed in the *Washington Post* this morning, the location is also connected to the victim, as it has historically been used as a location for Wiccan handfastings, or weddings. A pattern is emerging." He started ticking off the fingers of his right hand. "One, the victims resemble Ms. Jennings in appearance. The victims are otherwise unrelated. Two, the victims had their dogs with them at the time of the abduction, and the dogs were used to convey the coded message. Three, the kill spot is related to the victim. Four, the specific method of death is related to the victim. Five, the coded message used to initiate the game is a Vigenère cipher, a code used during the Civil War by the Confederacy. Six, the death sites have also had a Civil War connection of some kind. Seven, the method of death is oriented around asphyxia, but that doesn't narrow it down much for us. So far, we have suffocation in an enclosed space, positional asphyxiation, and pressing. The question is whether he might repeat methods, or will he find other ways to asphyxiate his victims? That remains to be seen, as does his motivation for this particular kind of death.

"One other aspect of this case that has become very clear is the unsub's level of organization. In a fairly short period of time, he has found at least three potential targets—and quite likely more—and researched them to the point that he knows how to apprehend them in a predictable location. He knows enough about their backgrounds that he can choose a kill spot and a killing method related to them. This shows a meticulous, precise organization that will work against us. Organized killers like this are harder to catch because the discipline in their method keeps them grounded, and each successful cycle strengthens that resolve. The best thing we could do is interrupt that process, but until we know who is missing and solve the riddle to intercept him, that's not going to work reliably. If we can pull that off, if we could strand him with a victim, but no available place to take her, he will be shaken and should start to devolve."

"Wouldn't that put the victim at risk?"

"She would possibly be at less risk than from the original plan. A killer like this has a mental picture of how the killing must proceed, and there is usually no wiggle room. It's like *Clue,* with this victim, with that method of death, in that location. How it's supposed to go down is all set in his mind. If we can break his cycle, he'll be shaken enough that he might not know which steps to take next. But this is a methodical thinker. His first reaction won't be to slit her throat and throw her body into a ditch. I believe he'd attempt to salvage the situation first."

"But who do you think he is?" Craig asked from the end of the table. "What's your feeling on the man himself? We need to zero in on a suspect before we can start to look at his mental abilities."

"Down to basics, sure. What does all of this tell us about the suspect himself? I believe the unsub is a white male in his late twenties to midthirties, likely an oldest son. He is of above-average intelligence and has been trained for skilled work. He believes he is worthy of great things. He may try for something important and substantial, and likely has, but would fail in the attempt. Being left as an average worker would infuriate him, since he feels he deserves better. He won't recognize any deficiencies in his own performance—that's not the mind-set of this kind of unsub. He feels that the world is against him, and it or someone must pay for what are actually his own shortcomings. In this case, it's clear that the one who needs to pay is Ms. Jennings, although the reasons for this remain unclear at this time. Due to the types of anesthetics used in the crimes, I believe he is or was involved in some aspect of the medical profession, be it human or animal. He could be an orderly in a hospital or he could work as a veterinary technician. In my opinion, he is absolutely not in a position of power, like a vet or a doctor, or he'd use that power to his advantage. He takes the suspects from public places at times when the act could easily be witnessed, which highlights a significant level of bravado, and is indicative of his level of organization and confidence that he can blend in. For Catriona, he knew when she worked at the AIDS hospice, where she parked her car, and positioned himself so she would walk right past him. The van was ready, and he had her subdued and tossed inside within ten to fifteen seconds in broad daylight. It's a very cocky show of confidence."

"How do you think he's doing his research to find his victims?" Brian asked.

"This kind of planning and preparation substantiates the fact that he's an organized killer. More specifically, he's what we call a 'mission killer.' He kills, or tries to kill, because he sees it as a personal quest, something he gains his own personal satisfaction from as part of his end goal. As far as how he found the women, this is conjecture on my part, but I'd bet social media did a lot of the job for him. These days, everyone documents everything and posts it to Facebook, Twitter, and Instagram. Use the right filters and put in some time and patience, and you can sort through thousands of faces to narrow it down to a specific look over a wide geographic area. He likely would have zeroed in on a larger pool and then narrowed it down. And people don't realize how much of their personal information is captured in these places. You think you're just a name on the Internet, but you give away where you live, what your hobbies are, who your family is, and even sometimes what your day-to-day routine is. But that raises another point. Most organized killers have partners, a spouse or live-in, but my gut says this one is solo. He's spending way too much time working on this to successfully hide it from a partner.

"Now, serial killers like this have a stressor, an incident that sets them off and transforms what is likely a vibrant fantasy life into reality. I believe the stressor in this case was Meg Jennings's involvement in the Daniel Mannew case and the notoriety engendered there. Considering the timing, it gave the unsub approximately four weeks to formulate his plan, and select the players and locations. This gives him the freedom now to act quickly, moving from victim to victim with a minimal cooling-off period. By doing so, he shortens our investigative time, making it harder to concentrate on any one victim before the next is taken—and there will be another. McCord's article shines a very bright spotlight on his failure."

"Will he see it as a failure?" Meg asked. "Or is losing a round still part of the game to him?"

Rutherford looked at her thoughtfully. "You're absolutely right there. He does see it as a game. It's too early for me to predict how he'll take that. The best indicator of that will be his next note. If it's business as usual, then he's willing to concede he lost that round. Which means he's got a bigger endgame in mind. It's like playing chess—sacrificing a player on the way to checkmate is often a winning strategy."

"And if Meg is his endgame?" Brian asked. "His checkmate? If all these women are stand-ins to the fury he seems to feel for Meg, is she a target?"

The gaze Rutherford settled on Meg was cool and slightly detached. She could imagine his only way to distance himself from the hellish minds he had to climb inside was to separate his own psyche from them. Either that or succumb to their terror and darkness. By stepping back, he protected himself. "I think there's a very good chance of that. For him, that would be the final move in the game. All of this is a warm-up. It's practice and maneuvering. Ms. Jennings would be the real deal and likely would be his final kill. So we will do everything in our power to ensure that doesn't happen." Rutherford flipped the file closed. "That's all I have for now. As the case progresses, the profile will be amended and expanded upon, and you will all be kept up to date of any changes."

The door *whooshed* closed behind Meg and she turned. The back of the room was empty. Peters had disappeared like the shadow he was known to be.

CHAPTER 13

Wet-Plate Photography: Prior to the Civil War, painters often accompanied armies on the battlefield. Photographers like Alexander Gardner and Mathew Brady—who was a student of telegrapher Samuel Morse—developed wet-plate photography, which allowed the unlimited printing of larger pictures. Their artistic vision gave the media access to never-before-seen images of wounded soldiers, battlefield casualties, and an intimate portrait of soldiers' lives.

Thursday, May 25, 7:15 PM
Jennings residence
Arlington, Virginia

Meg opened the door to find Webb standing on the doorstep. "Why is it every time we try to make plans, I get in the way of them?"

"Because you have an unpredictable job. My job is unpredictable too, just on a predictable schedule. But thank you for trusting me with some of what you're going through. I realize you're taking a chance doing it. As I said on the phone, nothing goes past me. And if I can help in any way . . ."

"We'll start with tonight and see where it goes." She shut the door behind him and turned to find him holding out a brown-paper-wrapped bundle. "What's that?"

"Some guys try to win women over with flowers. I'm a bit different."

She opened the brown paper bag to find three nylon dog bones with sturdy center-wrapped ridges. "Are those Nylabones?"

"The one and only."

She continued to stare into the bag unblinkingly. "You brought my dog a bone. You brought all the dogs their own bones."

"Don't want them fighting over just one bone. That's no fun."

She studied him for a moment; then she pushed up on her toes to kiss him on the cheek. "I like your different approach."

He simply grinned back at her.

A bark interrupted them.

Meg leaned around Webb to stare into the living-room doorway in befuddlement. "Blink?"

The greyhound was standing in the doorway, tail wagging, his eyes fixed on Webb. Webb crouched down, patting his thighs. "Come here, buddy."

Blink pranced over, his body shaking with excitement to be met with praise and strokes.

Meg stared at them, her brows drawn together and her jaw hanging slack, until Webb finally looked up.

He glanced from her to the dog and then back again. "What?"

"He likes you."

"And . . . ?"

"He not only likes you, he's comfortable with you. That *never* happens."

"We had lots of time to get to know each other on Monday night, when we were waiting for you to get back. He was a little standoffish at first, but kept inching closer and closer until he finally introduced himself. Didn't you, buddy?" Blink's answer was a long tongue slurp over Webb's cheek, followed by Webb's rolling laugh. He stood up and reached into the bag in Meg's hands, pulling out a bone. Blink went stock-still, his gaze laser-focused on the toy.

"We train them to wait until they are released to take a treat or a toy, so he won't go for it until you give him permission. Hold it down in front of him." Meg waited as Webb positioned the bone in front of the quivering greyhound. "Now use his name and tell him to take it."

"Blink, take it. Take the bone."

Blink reached out and took one end of the bone gently from Webb's fingers and turned around and trotted through the doorway into the living room.

"That was really nice of you. Thank you."

"The way to a girl's heart is through her dog?"

Meg laughed, feeling lighter at that moment than she had all day. "You may have stumbled onto something. Come on in. Let's go treat the other dogs too."

After Hawk and Saki received their bones, the three dogs settled down in a happy group by the open screen door, where the mild evening breeze spilled into the house.

Meg sat down on the couch. "You're sure you don't mind staying in this evening?"

Webb settled beside her, casually laying one arm over the top of the sofa and crossing one ankle over the opposite knee. "Not at all. It sounds like you need to sit down and try to figure a few things out."

Cara walked into the living room, her head bent over a large scrapbook. "God bless Mom, I found it. Haven't seen this thing in years." She turned a page. "I wonder if she's still doing this." She looked up and stopped dead, seeing Webb on the couch. "Oh, hello. Sorry, I didn't know you were already here."

"Just a few minutes ago."

"He brought bones for the dogs. So they'll be busy with them for a while and won't be underfoot."

"You're a prince among men." Cara patted him on the shoulder as she walked behind the couch, and then threw herself down into the overstuffed armchair, laying the book down on the ottoman.

"What's that?" Webb asked.

"It's a scrapbook. Mom kept a record of every time we made the news, in print or online. She'd cut it out, or print it out, and put it in our scrapbook. When it was full, she gave it to us. That one is Meg's, and I have one to match."

"She's probably working on the next one," Meg said. "We should ask her about that. But I thought going back to look through this might be a good idea while we try to make up a list of who I might have pissed off so much, they have to kill other people who look like me to make me pay for it." Meg could hear the bitterness in her own words, but made no effort to tone it down.

Webb didn't say anything; he simply took her hand and squeezed it in silent sympathy.

"We met with the profiler today," Meg continued. "It's early still, but this is their current working theory." She reviewed the suspect characteristics outlined in the BAU profile. "So how far back does that scrapbook go?" Meg asked. "I don't think we need to go back to high school or anything like that. That's too far back. And the university years." Closing her eyes, Meg thought back to her years at the University of Virginia. "Honestly, I can't think of any one there. I was in with a group of kids who all wanted to study and do well. There was no significant conflict."

"You got a degree before going to the police academy?"

"Yes. You don't have to have one, but you can't get into the academy until you're twenty-one or older, so it's like they're making time for you to get one. Also, if you want to move up the ranks, you have to have one."

"So you got a criminal justice degree?"

"Actually, no. They like to see other backgrounds to make their officers more diverse. You'll be immersed in criminal justice while you're on the force, so they like to see other skills brought to the table. My B.A. is in cognitive science—a little cognitive psychology, some computer skills, some philosophy, linguistics, and neuroscience. I thought it was a good mix, and understanding psychology has been invaluable when dealing with perps, many of whom are on the mental health spectrum. Anyway, I was with a bunch of mostly geeks through my university days. No one there stands out at all, but the police academy . . ."

"Female firefighters have been known to have a hard time in training," Webb stated. "I assume it's a similar hard row to hoe for female cops?"

"Probably not as bad as it was twenty or thirty years ago, but there are still guys who consider us the weaker sex and believe we have no place on any force."

Cara held out the book. "Your academy graduation picture is there. Anyone stand out? Let's start thinking of names and I'll get a list going."

Meg took the spiral-bound scrapbook, laying it across her lap. Webb leaned in over her shoulder to study the rows of students in the graduation photo. She tapped on the face of the only other woman in the class: a shorter, blond-haired woman, with a wide smile. "That's Valerie Dunning. Val and I were the only women in the twenty-three-person basic recruit class that session. Most of the guys were okay, but there were a couple who definitely tried to give us a hard time." She tapped her index finger beside the head of a man on the end of the second row. "That's Tony Waters. If anyone in the class didn't like me, it was Tony. Didn't start out that way. He started off trying to come on to me. But when it became clear I didn't welcome his advances—to the tune of my knee in his balls when he tried to pin me against the wall in an attempt to convince me—he turned on me full blast. There wasn't an activity I did where he didn't try to make me look bad."

"I remember," Cara said. "You were royally pissed at him. He knew you were single, so the fact you turned him down for no one dented his fragile male ego." She grinned sheepishly at Webb. "Sorry. Present company's ego excepted."

Webb quirked a brow. "Many thanks on behalf of my ego."

"Definitely put Tony down on the list. He was a thorn in my side for the entire class. When we graduated, we were assigned to different precincts. And I always wondered if the head instructor, who knew a little of what was going on—because how could you miss it?—made a recommendation to keep us apart. Then I didn't stay on patrol very long before making the move over to K-9. And from that point on, I almost never saw him."

Cara looked up from jotting his name down. "Was he the only student who gave you trouble in the academy?"

"The main one. Some of the other guys gave Val and me kind of a hard time at first, but we won them over by working twice as hard as they did and showing some of them up. That won their grudging respect. Sometimes I'd run into those guys on cases when Deuce and I got called in, but they were always friendly. When you go through boot camp with someone, you have a connection with them forever after."

"Trial by fire." Webb nodded his understanding. "Yeah, I know what that's like."

"For you guys, it was literal fire. We, at least, were spared that." Meg turned the page in the scrapbook. "But . . . I guess I can't just look at the students. There was one instructor who was a throwback to earlier times and he didn't like women in his class."

"What one was that?"

"Sergeant Collins, the firing-range instructor."

Cara made a sound that was half groan, half growl. "I remember him. Wasn't he the one who was always calling you 'little lady'?"

"Condescending son of a bitch. Yeah, that was him. He'd stand beside me when I was shooting at the range, trying to make me nervous. Worse, when we were out doing sniper rifle training, he'd lie beside me in the grass, bellowing instructions to throw me off. You're stretched out, trying not to move a fraction of an inch, aiming at a target five hundred yards away, steadying your breathing, then taking the shot at the end of the exhale, maintaining constant pressure on the trigger up to and through the shot itself. All while some sixty-five-year-old fossil is screaming in your ear to break your concentration. The guys thought it was hilarious."

The laugh that burst from Cara carried an edge of triumph. "Or at least they did until you hit the target dead on, even with all that chaos going on around you."

"Wow!" Webb gave Meg a slow handclap. "Color me impressed. That would have been incredibly tough to pull off."

Meg shrugged. "It was, but I have a good eye and a very steady hand. I could have gone into SWAT with my ability to shoot, but that just wasn't my path. But I learned one thing that day. If I wanted Collins to shut the hell up, that was the way to do it." She looked over at Cara. "Add Collins to the list, but I can't believe it's him. He'd no doubt love for me to look bad, but he's too old to manage the kidnappings at this point, and I don't think he ever gave me or Val a thought since we've graduated. He just turned his attention to the next 'little lady' to come into his sights."

Meg turned the page in the scrapbook, scanning down the pages, considering each entry thoughtfully.

Blink wandered back toward them, his bone still firmly

locked in his jaws, staring at the corner of the couch and
then at Webb and back again. He put one paw up on the
cushion and whined.

Meg looked up from the book. "He wants up. Actually,
that's a significant sign from him. He normally hides from
visitors, but when he wants to join you on the couch,
you're his new best friend."

Webb shifted sideways, closer to Meg, and patted the
freed slice of couch. "Come on up."

Blink needed no further encouragement and leapt up on
the couch, somehow managing to turn around three times
without toppling off the cushion before flopping down
with a contented sigh. Only then did he let go of the bone,
tucking it between his paws, and put his head down, his
skull pressed along the edge of Webb's thigh and closed his
eyes.

Webb ran a hand down the dog's back, earning two
hearty tail thumps. "Is he normally that protective of his
toys?"

"He came from a stable of racing dogs, where he was
neglected, overtrained, and underfed, and where he spent
about twenty hours a day muzzled in a cage. He's much
better than when Cara first got him. She's worked with
him for years to get him to the minimal level of neurosis he
has now."

"He was really damaged goods, but we can see through
that damage to the dog underneath." Cara smiled over at
her dog. "You've turned out okay, haven't you, Blinky?"

Blink's eyes opened and fixed on Cara, his tail thumping
again.

"He certainly has a good life here. They all do. Sometimes when we're out on calls, we see . . . situations. Animals in bad spots, but we can't just walk in and take them
out. Same thing with kids. We've got a little more power
there, and can call in Child and Family Services, but

they're usually so understaffed that any new kids can be a burden. But animals . . . Sometimes you can't prove cruelty so Animal Care and Control can remove them. You know in your gut it's happening, but even if you could get them out, where can you take them?"

"That's where people like our parents come in," Meg said. "They're not only a rescue, but are also a registered wildlife sanctuary. They'll take the animal no matter what it is, or at least help place it. They currently have an emu because one was seized by a local PD, and then the cops had no idea what to do with it. They didn't want to have it put down, but the local shelter wouldn't take it. So Mom and Dad took it. He lives in one of the pastures and is as happy as a clam."

"What do you do with an emu?"

"People farm them for their meat, but our emu will never go to slaughter. He leads a pretty charmed existence, right where he is."

"Lucky guy."

"He sure is." Meg paused suddenly. "Speaking of rescues, Cara, what about Madeline Sutherland?"

Cara looked up sharply. "From Clover Leaf Rescue? Oh yeah, she didn't like you at all."

"I could have made her life a lot harder. I could have had her brought up on charges."

"For what?" Webb asked.

"For keeping her animals in terrible conditions. I had an idea how much money she was bringing in because I knew some of the rescue's corporate donors. But you never would have guessed it from her facility. The animals were underfed, filthy, and vets weren't called until it was sometimes too late, because she didn't want to spend money on them. But I bet her books didn't show that."

"You were sure she was skimming off the top."

"It was the only thing that made sense." Meg turned to Webb. "So I called her on it."

"You turned her in to the authorities?"

"No, worse from a rescue point of view. I told her if I didn't see improvement in the conditions, and if there weren't regular vet visits, I'd let her sponsors know their money should be spent elsewhere. The director of a rescue can be brought up on charges, even go away for them, but as long as the money keeps coming in, the rescue keeps going. But cut off that money and it's game over."

"You wanted her rescue to fail?"

"I wanted it to succeed. The way we work best is if we all work together. Even if we do, there are still not enough places for animals in need. But I wouldn't condemn an animal to that kind of mistreatment. Mom and Dad were totally in support. And in the end, it worked. The rescue cleaned up its act."

"That little bug you put in the ear of one of the board members didn't hurt either. Once they were aware—and horrified—by what they'd been ignoring up to that point, it got better."

"Madeline hates me, so we should add her. I know the profile is for a man, and one younger than Sergeant Collins, but at this point, I'm trying to list everyone who could be involved. What if the profile is wrong or if it changes a bit with more information? Let's make it a complete list now, and then we can pare it down later."

Over the next hour, they added more names to the list:

Ian Ross—a fellow K-9 handler on the Richmond PD, against whom Meg lodged a formal complaint after witnessing him leaving his dog in his patrol vehicle without the air conditioner running on a hot day in July.

Evan Prince, Max Bennet, Janet Sellers, and Levi Wood—criminals who had been apprehended by Meg and Deuce, but who were now out on parole.

Jimmy York—apprehended after a particular brutal "jumpin' in" gang ritual that left the initiate permanently paralyzed.

Kyle McKenzie—a hoarder who had all his animals seized and removed from the premises over his screams of revenge.

Meg sat back against the couch and closed the scrapbook with a snap, shaking her head.

"What's wrong?" Webb asked.

"I don't know. None of them feel right to me. I understand people being angry, but do any of these seem like they'd be so insane with rage they'd kill to make me pay?"

"But you're only seeing the surface."

"What do you mean?"

"You're only seeing the parts of their lives you came into contact with. What if you were just the catalyst that started them off to a life of misery and crime? Take that rescue lady, for example."

"Madeline?"

"Yeah, her. What's she doing now?"

"I admit I have no idea."

"What if your exposing her behavior eventually led to her leaving the rescue, taking away her identify as a do-gooder, someone who was a hero. Then she couldn't find a new position in the rescue world, because even though they're always looking for volunteers, the word was out on her on social media from her last position and no one wanted to work with her. Now she's lost that part of her life completely. It was never a paying job, so she hasn't lost her livelihood, but she's lost a major part of her identity, which could be worse from her point of view."

"Meg, he's got a point," Cara said. "This list might not seem like anything to you, but what if something you did changed someone's life irrevocably? What if you just can't see it?"

"Or what if I'm overlooking someone? What if it's as you say, what I did was something so minor, I can't see it or simply don't remember it? What if the person I need to identify is the one I can't see?"

"Give yourself a break," Webb said. "In some ways, this is the hardest way to do it. You're trying to think of who might be responsible. It's the person who springs to mind at three in the morning who may be the key. Sometimes turning off your brain or distracting it is when you remember something crucial. Give your subconscious time to work through this. Give your brain time to catch up."

Meg nodded, grateful for the support. But the knot forming in her stomach told her she was missing something. Something important.

Something that could save a life.

CHAPTER 14

Mobile Telegraph Wagons: The northern states laid more than fifteen thousand miles of telegraph cable along the eastern seaboard for purely military purposes during the Civil War. Invented by Samuel Morse in 1844, the telegraph provided rapid communications between the battlefield and Washington, DC, and mobile telegraph wagons allowed reporting from the cable nearest the battlefield.

Saturday, May 27, 7:54 AM
Jennings residence
Arlington, Virginia

The cell phone blaring in her ear roused Meg from a restless sleep. *It's Saturday morning, for God's sake. Is nothing sacred?* Rolling over, she reached for the phone on her bedside table, fumbling and nearly dropping it in the process. She cracked her eyes open just enough to accept the call, then squeezed them shut again as she rolled over, her phone pressed to her ear. "Jennings." Her voice was husky with sleep.

"Meg, I'm sorry, it's Craig."

Her eyes shot open, her body suddenly awake as if Craig had poked her with an electric cattle prod, her heart pounding. She pushed up on one elbow. "What's happened?"

The voice that answered was bone tired, not just exhausted from this case, but from the weight of years of cases. "He's taken another one."

"Who?"

"We don't know yet. A quartet of dogs was found this morning, just after seven AM, running through Green Park in Gaithersburg, Maryland. It looks like the target may have been a dog walker by trade, because all four dogs were found running free, but they all had collars with different contact information. Agents are calling all those numbers right now to find out who owned the dogs, and who was caring for them."

Meg pushed back the blankets and swung her feet to the floor. Hawk looked up from where he stretched out on his dog bed against the wall nearby, his head tilted questioningly. "Did they find a note?"

"Yes."

"Can you send it to me?"

"Already done. Meg, I don't know how long it will take them to solve this. The CRRU boys have weekend shifts, but it's so early, we had to call them into the office. It's going to slow us down."

It won't slow Cara down.

"Let me know when the CRRU boys have a direction for us. We'll be ready to go at a moment's notice."

"Done. Wait for my call." Craig ended the call.

"Cara!" Jumping out of bed and jogging down the hall, Meg headed for her sister's room, pulling up in the doorway at the sight of the neatly made bed.

Think, Meg, it's Saturday. She must have headed into the school for her nine AM class early.

She dialed the phone still clutched in one hand and Cara picked up after the first ring. "Are you at the school already?"

"I came in an hour early to do a one-on-one with Clay and Cody before their class starts," Cara said. "What's going on?"

"We just got another message and the CRRU guys aren't in the office, so they're being called in. That's going to put us behind."

"If you've got it, send it to me now. Clay just arrived, so we can work from here."

"Hold on." Keeping her sister on the phone, Meg switched over to her e-mail and read the newest messages, and forwarded Craig's e-mail to Cara. "Just sent it."

"I'm logging into my computer. Give me a minute. So, there's another one missing? Someone who looks like you?"

"I can only assume she does. They don't know who she is yet. Evidence, so far, says she's a dog walker because it was four dogs this time, none of which have the same contact information."

Keys clicked in the background; then Cara said, "Got it. I'm hanging up on you now so I can work on it. Keep your phone with you and be ready to roll, once we figure this out."

Meg clicked off and sprinted for the bathroom to shower and dress.

Saturday, May 27, 8:19 AM
Jennings residence
Arlington, Virginia

Meg was tying her wet hair into a ponytail when her phone rang. She snatched it off the counter before it had even completed the first ring. "What've you got?"

"I've got the message, but Clay is still trying to figure out the meaning."

"One thing at a time." Meg reached for paper and pen. "Let's start with the bad news. What's the keyword?"

Cara sighed. "I was hoping you weren't going to ask that. It's 'Marlowe.'"

Meg had to clamp her lips shut to keep the obscenity from slipping out. Now the perp was getting personal *past* the point of newspaper articles about her life and family. She was 99 percent sure she'd never mentioned her childhood dog in any of them. The image of the bouncy, energetic golden retriever filled her mind. Her first dog in so many ways—her first experience with the overwhelming loyalty and trust of a dog, her first efforts at training, her first personal experience of loss when Marlowe died at fourteen from cancer.

Her gaze dropped to the far side of the kitchen, where Hawk contentedly sprawled in a sunbeam with Blink and Saki. The first dog of the many the sisters would own and train and love over the years. And lose.

"Meg? You there still?"

"Yeah, I'm here." Meg's tone was unbending. "We'll deal with that later. What's the message itself? Slowly, I need to get this down."

"Here it is. 'Stonewall looks over the tops to the den. But she is at home with the pike and cemetery. Years of craftsmanship gone in a second, like a puff of smoke. The timer is running.'" Cara spoke the words a phrase at a time, giving Meg time to catch up. "Hold on, I'm putting this on speaker so Clay can talk to you too." There was a *click,* as if the phone was set down on the desk; then her voice came back sounding much farther away. "Can you hear me?"

"Yes. McCord, what does this say to you? 'Stonewall' is Stonewall Jackson, right?"

"That's the theory I'm running with," McCord agreed. "It's a pretty obvious first jump for a Civil War–related clue."

"So what locations are we looking at? And what's he looking over the top of? Trees? Buildings?"

"There are a lot of locations associated with ol' Stonewall if you want to get down to individual battle-fields, and that's considering he was only alive for half the war. He was accidentally shot by one of his own men and died of complications of the injury days later. But he was notable for the Battles of Bull Run at Manassas, both the one in 1861 and then again in 1862. He's also known for Fredericksburg and Antietam, and then there's Chancellorsville, where he was fatally wounded. But that's a really short list. There's a longer list of battles he also took part in, smaller skirmishes he was involved in as part of various Confederate campaigns under Robert E. Lee."

"He wants us to have a chance to find her, so I don't think he's going to give us something so obscure we don't have a chance of tracking her down in time. Bull Run was two battles in the same place, and Chancellorsville is where he died, so maybe one of those because they are notable. Does the rest of the message narrow it down at all?"

"Not really. When you look at . . ." His voice trailed off.

"What?" Cara asked.

"Hold on, hold on."

Meg could hear McCord repeating, over and over, the first line of the message: " 'Stonewall looks over the tops to the den.' "

"There's no spacing or punctuation in these messages, is there?" he asked.

"Who are you asking?" Meg asked.

"Cara. No spacing or punctuation, just groups of letters that aren't even representative of the words."

"Correct," Cara said. "No capitals to mark the start of a sentence either, because it's in all caps. Letters clustered in groups of five."

"You son of a bitch, I almost missed it," McCord growled. "And that would have meant her death."

"Missed what?" Meg was getting impatient. *This isn't moving fast enough.* "McCord, you're not making sense."

"It's not 'Stonewall.' That's what we're supposed to assume. It's 'stone wall.'" He paused between the two words, making it clear it wasn't a single name. "It's literally what it means—a wall constructed of stone."

"What does that tell us? There must have been thousands of walls like that at the time of the Civil War."

"But only one that pairs with the other clues in that first sentence. 'Stone wall looks over the tops to the den.' He's talking about the goddamn Battle of Gettysburg."

"Gettysburg, Pennsylvania?"

"The one and only. It's 'Tops,' not 'top,' as in looking over the top of something. In this case, the Tops he's referring to are the Big and Little Round Tops. The den is the Devil's Den. All three geographical locations played major parts in the three-day battle."

"What's with the stone wall?" Cara asked. "Why would that be notable?"

"On the last day of fighting, during Pickett's charge when the Confederate Army very briefly punched through the Union lines before internal reinforcements beat them back and then won the day, the Union set up behind a stone wall on Cemetery Ridge. That stone wall became the dividing line. The Union held firm and any Confederates who crossed the stone wall were either cut down or taken prisoner. So that's it. Put it all together and she's in Gettysburg."

"But where in Gettysburg? It's a small town, but a tourist mecca. We can't just toss Hawk into the middle of a National Battlefield of that size, with no trail to start with, and hope that he'll find our missing woman. He's good, but we have to be realistic."

"Fair enough. Give me a minute."

"Move fast, McCord. She's dying out there."

"You think I don't know that? But if I steer you wrong, she has no chance at all. Everything depends on this. It's worth the extra minute or two to make sure I'm not sending you to the wrong place."

"You said it's Gettysburg."

"Yeah, but where? I'll get this, just let me think." There was silence for a moment, except for the clicking of keys; then McCord spoke again. "Okay, let's look at this logically. The 'pike' was known as the Baltimore Pike back then and is known as the Baltimore Turnpike today. It's in the exact same location as it was one hundred and fifty years ago. So that likely makes the cemetery mentioned Cemetery Hill."

"I thought you said it was Cemetery Ridge."

"There is a Cemetery Ridge, but that's southwest of Cemetery Hill, and nowhere near the Pike. But the day before Pickett's Charge, there was significant fighting at Cemetery Hill and Culp's Hill, right beside the Baltimore Pike. It makes sense that she's somewhere in the area of Cemetery Hill."

"What's the last bit, then? 'Years of craftsmanship gone in a second, like a puff of smoke'? Is he setting some prized building on fire so the victim dies of smoke inhalation? Are there buildings like that on Cemetery Hill?" There were a few more seconds of silence. "McCord?"

"Hang on," said Cara. "He's looking at Google Maps for something."

Meg put the phone on speaker and set it on the counter while she continued packing her SAR bag with fresh supplies for the day's search—water; high-energy treats for Hawk, and energy bars for herself; Hawk's booties, in case the terrain got too rough for his feet; spare socks for herself, in case her feet got wet. She had just zipped up the bag and set it by the door beside Hawk's leash and FBI vest when she heard voices.

"Hang on," she called as she ran back into the kitchen. "Sorry, was packing our SAR bag and popped out of the room for a minute. What have you got?"

"I think I've got her location," McCord said. "It's not a fire. It's a demolition. The 'puff of smoke' is the dust cloud from a building coming down."

Meg's breath caught in her throat. "He's got her in a building that's going to be razed? So she'll be crushed?"

"It would be a new twist on the asphyxia angle. Anyway, there's an old furniture factory, Teller and Sons, that's been closed since the 1960s. It's a remnant of Gettysburg's furniture-manufacturing boom in the early twentieth century. It's a gorgeous old four-story brick building that's crumbling from neglect. Must be at least ten thousand square feet of space, small by today's standards, but no doubt huge back then. But that's the 'years of craftsmanship.' It's not the building that's art—it's what they made in it."

"And they're bringing the building down."

"Meg, it's scheduled to come down *today*."

She froze. Gettysburg was at least an hour and a half away and they had to gather the team first. "What time?"

"Ten-thirty this morning."

We aren't going to make it.

"I have to call Craig, and we have to move now."

"Go." Cara's voice was louder, as if she had leaned into the phone. "Call us if you need anything at all."

"Will do." Meg clicked off without a good-bye and immediately dialed Craig. She had no choice but to let the cat out of the bag. The newest victim's life was at stake.

Craig picked up so quickly, she suspected he hadn't put his phone down since talking to her earlier. "Beaumont."

"It's Meg. Craig, I know where she is."

"What? How?"

"You sent me the code. We cracked it and figured out the answer. She's in Gettysburg, Pennsylvania, being held in an abandoned historic furniture factory scheduled for demolition at ten-thirty this morning. Teller and Sons. We have to move now or we're going to lose her. Gettysburg is too far away."

"Hold on, back up. What do you mean 'we cracked it'?"

Damn. She'd been hoping he'd gloss over that until later. "My sister, Cara, is an amazing puzzle solver. I gave it to her and she figured out the code based on how the first code was solved. Clay McCord from the *Washington Post* figured out the rest. He's a Civil War buff, and can ferret out information like you wouldn't believe."

"We'll go over his qualifications at another time. God-damn it, Meg. You can't involve outsiders in a case like this."

"I know. But at some point, urgency has to outweigh FBI regulations. Craig, the only thing that matters is getting to her. We're running out of time. It's at least ninety minutes away, and that's if I walk out the door right now and hit zero traffic."

"We can't risk that kind of margin. Head for Ronald Reagan Airport. I'll arrange for a quick flight for you and the team. Gettysburg has a small airport, and I'll have cars waiting for you when you get there."

"You do that, and I'll call the team. Brian, Lauren, and Scott again?"

"Yes. I'll call you with more details when I have them. And I'll find out what demolition company is bringing it down and call them off. Now go. And, Meg?"

"Yes?"

"We're not finished with this conversation."

Meg closed her eyes at the sinking feeling in her stomach. Of course they weren't. "I'm on my way to the airport. Call me when you have more." She ended the call, and took two seconds to curse under her breath. Then with a call to Hawk, they were running out the door.

CHAPTER 15

Union Army Balloon Corps: On June 16, 1861, Professor Thaddeus Lowe demonstrated the usefulness of hot-air balloons for President Lincoln by lifting off from the Washington Mall, near the site of the future National Air & Space Museum. Aware of Lincoln's penchant for visiting the Telegraph Office, Lowe took a telegraph with him onboard the gas-inflated aerostat *Enterprise* and sent the president the first aerial telegram.

Saturday, May 27, 10:06 AM
Teller and Sons furniture factory
Gettysburg, Pennsylvania

The FBI handlers and their dogs poured from the Gettysburg PD SUVs, once the vehicles screeched to a halt just off the Baltimore Turnpike. On one side of the road, a crumbling factory could be seen through the chain-link fence surrounding the structure. Four stories in height, the building was constructed of rough red clay bricks, with rows of tall windows wrapping every floor. In the years before electric lights were commonplace, natural light was a workplace necessity, and this building was constructed to allow in the maximum light possible. Now, however, the windows were devoid of glass, and multicolored, spray-painted graffiti marred the lower story of the factory. The structure was topped by a black shingle roof that showed significant bare patches. A large faded sign, TELLER AND SONS, was situated over the gaping hole that was once the front entrance to the building.

One of the Gettysburg PD officers waved the teams to follow him through the chain-link gate. "Come on. The site foreman is waiting for us inside."

The four teams jogged after him through the gate. Meg glanced at her watch, fretting at the time. If anything went wrong, the site was set to blow in less than twenty-five minutes.

A tall man, wearing a white hardhat with DUNCAN DE-MOLITION stamped on the front, met them halfway to the gate. "Hey, Phil. Thanks for bringing them in." He held out his hand to Brian, who was closest to him. "Fred Duncan, owner of Duncan Demolition." He shook hands with Brian, then the other three handlers. "Officer Carmichael filled me in about the threat you reported. We've put the demolition on hold until you've had a chance to review the site, but we'd like to proceed later today, if possible."

"If we can clear the site and prove no one is inside," Brian said, "then you're free to proceed. Has anyone been inside the factory this morning?"

"No. We normally would have done a full review of the charges by now, but the directions were to keep everyone out until you arrived. I'm telling you, no one has gotten in here. Ever since we installed the charges yesterday afternoon, the site has been guarded and off-limits to make sure no idiot kids broke in and got hurt."

"How many people patrolled the site last night?" Lauren asked.

"Two, which is normal for a site this size. Honestly, sometimes kids try to come by in the evening just to say they got in, but once you scare them off, that's the end of it. This isn't New York City. Teenagers dare each other to pull this kind of stunt, but that's about it. Mostly, people want to be on the outside when it goes off, not inside beforehand. People love a good bang."

"Or they're watching for something to go badly wrong so they can say they were there when it happened," Brian said. "What time did you release the security guards?"

"When my crew and I arrived shortly after nine. I already had word to stay out, so I've been here since then, waiting with my men for you to arrive."

"We need to check out the site to see if it's been breached," Meg said. "We're going to take dogs in. Can you guarantee the charges you laid won't go off?"

"Sure can." Duncan pulled a small control box out of his pocket. "This is the box that controls the demolition. It's been disconnected from the wired explosives. The charges are placed strategically to bring down the internal weight-bearing columns so the building will basically fold in on itself. The explosives themselves are relatively inert until a charge is applied to the detonator to set off the reaction. No charge, no detonation. You're totally safe in there. Please don't mess with the wires though." He glanced down at the dogs, taking in the Labrador, German shepherd, border collie, and bloodhound. "Needless to say, don't let the dogs chew on the wires either."

"That would be about the last thing that would happen," Lauren said dryly. "They're working dogs. They know what to do and what not to do."

"Sorry. Wasn't trying to imply they aren't great dogs. We just don't want to have to rewire the whole mess later."

"Understood. Is there anything we need to know about the building? It's old and run-down, but is it safe? Are there any weak spots in the floor or stairways that we need to watch for?"

"There are a few problem areas, but we've very clearly marked them with fluorescent orange spray paint. The original construction was solid though, so the floor and stairs are in fair condition. They'll take everyone's weight, and then some. The problem areas are more upstairs where water has leaked through the roof, or in the basement, where the foundation is cracked. But the building is empty. Anything left behind, we've removed as part of preparation. It's mostly just an empty shell, so your search shouldn't be too hard. Just watch the yellow detonation cord that runs from all the columns out the front door. It's all over the building and you'll trip if you're not careful. Again though, it's inert. No charge, no boom."

"Good to know." Lauren looked around the group. "Ready?"

Meg pulled a small plastic case from her pack. "Ready."

"What's that?" Duncan asked, eyeing the case.

"A leash last held by Karen Teller, the woman we're looking for."

"Teller." Duncan's gaze darted up to the sign at the front of the building. "As in the family that owned this place?"

"That was confirmed for us on our way here. The leash is to give the dogs the scent so they can track her."

"Sounds like you know what you need to do. We'll get out of your way so you can start."

"Appreciate that. Let's go."

Meg led the way; Brian, Lauren, and Scott followed behind, the dogs all heeling next to their handlers. She pulled a flashlight out of her pocket, just before stepping into the cool interior of the building, carefully avoiding the thick bundles of yellow cord that ran through the doorway on one side. Meg stood for a moment, blinking, allowing her eyes to acclimatize to the lower light. She flipped on her flashlight, shining it into the deeper reaches of the factory, away from the row of windows.

The ground floor was essentially one giant room, with no internal dividing walls. The interior walls were the same rough brick as the outside. Solid squared timbers dotted the space at regular intervals, supporting the massive crossbeams carrying the floor above. Dotted throughout the space were heavy columns of brick, the weight-bearing supports for the building, to allow for the tons of equipment needed throughout the building in its heyday. The floor, made from thick wide planks of hardwood, was heavily scarred, but still intact.

"Okay, here we go. Unless they catch the scent right away on this floor, let's cover this space, then split up because this is a big building." Meg's voice echoed in the empty space, her words bouncing off the bare brick walls. "Lauren, you and Rocco take the basement. Scott, the second floor, Brian the third, and I'll take the fourth."

She unhooked Hawk's leash, coiling it, and jamming it in the pocket of her coat. She opened the box and offered it first to Hawk, then to the other dogs in succession. Slipping it back into her pack, she met Hawk's steady gaze. "Find her, Hawk. Find Karen." She followed him as he started down the long length of the room.

It was the tiny flash of red that caught her eye twenty feet down the room. A flash of color when there should have been nothing.

"Hawk, stop." The Labrador immediately halted, turning his head to look at her quizzically at the quick change in direction. "Everyone, hold!"

Commands from all the handlers had the other three dogs freezing.

"What is it?" Brian asked.

Meg shone her flashlight on the brick column a quarter of the way into the cavernous space. The column was wrapped in heavy black fabric tied into place with bright blue rope. Thick yellow cord ran in triplets from each column to the floor, where it joined up with cord from the other columns to run out the front door and across the dirt yard. But the beam of the flashlight moved higher, focusing on something duct-taped onto the black fabric.

"Holy shit, that's a cell phone," Scott breathed. "You can detonate explosives with the charge from a cell phone. Someone else is in control of this site."

"Fall back," Brian ordered. "Lacey, come."

The four teams hurried out the front door. Once free of the building, they sprinted over to the demolition team, the dogs racing with them.

Duncan stepped forward, his eyes wide and alarmed. "What happened?"

"Now we know your site has been compromised," Meg said.

"How?"

"One of your columns has a cell phone duct-taped to the fabric covering. Did you put that there?"

Duncan had gone pale, and a mist of sweat broke out on his upper lip. "No. Do any of the other columns have that?"

"Not that we saw," Brian said. "But we didn't stick around. This was scheduled to go off at ten-thirty?"

"Yes." Duncan pushed back his sleeve to reveal an ancient dial watch. "It's ten twenty-two. Maybe he hasn't tagged all the columns, but even just a couple could be disastrous. A few well-placed explosions going off could be enough for a sympathetic detonation—the shock wave from one explosion can detonate a nearby explosive, even if they're not connected. Only a few columns blowing could still bring the building down, but not in the order we planned. We've got to move back. We're now way too close and he could blow it any second."

Meg already had her phone out and was dialing Craig.

"We have to assume he's going to blow it on time. It's his insurance in case we found out and called off the demolition. As far as he's concerned, the clock is still ticking— that's all part of the game. Now I know, for sure, she's in there. Craig, it's Meg. We have a problem. I'm putting you on speaker." She hit the SPEAKER button and held the phone out as Brian, Lauren, and Scott gathered close. "Can you hear me?"

"Yes. What happened?" Craig's voice was slightly crackly, but his rapid-fire words highlighted his alarm.

"The site has been compromised. The demolition team had deactivated the explosives from their end, but we're seeing signs of tampering. Someone else is in control of the explosives, using cell phones for the electrical charge to set them off. We still need to get in there to find her."

"Absolutely not. He could blow the place as soon as you're inside."

"But that's not what he'll do, don't you see?" Meg didn't want to waste time arguing, but she needed to make Craig understand. She glanced at the clock in the system bar at the top of her screen. "It's ten twenty-three. We've got seven minutes. She's there, Craig. This proves it. And he won't blow it until ten-thirty."

"There is no guarantee of that," Craig barked. "And I'm not about to put the team at risk to prove your point."

Brian pushed forward. "Craig, Meg's right. There are four of us, we can do it. We can get in and out in time."

"You are out of your minds if you think I'm going to send my whole unit in there so you can all die together. Absolutely not. You're an important resource to the FBI and the country. You simply can't all go in there."

"I'll go alone." Meg's tone was backed by steel. "Craig, we have ten seconds to make this call. We can't just let some woman die in my place because we're cutting it too close. We're not that kind of coward."

"Jennings, stop pushing. I'm giving you all an order. Stand down."

Several beats of silence passed as Meg stared at the words "SSA Craig Beaumont" displayed on her screen. To disobey his direct order was to risk expulsion from the FBI. More than that, it was possibly a death sentence. But could she live with herself if she simply stood back and watched as the building imploded and an innocent woman died? Could she risk the life of her dog, because she sure as hell couldn't do this without him?

An image of Deuce filled her mind at that moment—huddled with him in the pouring rain in a dark alley, the blood from his gunshot wound warm on her hands as he bled out. As he died in her arms. Taking Hawk inside that building could mean his death as well.

She looked down at Hawk, who stood stock-still beside her, staring up at her with trust, loyalty, and love. As if sensing her thoughts, he gave a wag of his tail, as if to say, *Come on, we're wasting time.* That's when she knew she didn't have a choice. Not for either of them.

"I'm sorry, Craig. I can't live with your decision."

She pushed the phone into Brian's hands. He frantically fumbled at it before his fingers locked around it and he stared at her, all the fear he was feeling shining in his eyes. Because he knew her too well.

"Hawk, come."

They sprinted for the front door and toward the darkness of death.

CHAPTER 16

Remote Surveillance: On September 24, 1861, Professor Thaddeus Lowe ascended more than one thousand feet in a tethered balloon named the *Union,* near Arlington, Virginia. He was able to observe and provide intelligence on the position of Confederate troops near Falls Church several miles away. His information allowed the Union Army gun crews defending the Capital to aim and accurately fire at an enemy they could not see. Soaring over flat landscapes, balloons provided a surveillance and intelligence platform for military commanders. Although some balloons could ascend to five thousand feet, threats were often concealed by mountains or within buildings.

Saturday, May 27, 10:24 AM
Teller and Sons furniture factory
Gettysburg, Pennsylvania

"MEG!"

Even at a run, Meg could hear the tinny sound of Craig's shout exploding from the phone's speaker, but she ignored it. He'd made his choice and so had she; this was no longer in his hands. She paused for a moment in the factory doorway, looking back one last time. Brian was flanked by

Lauren and Scott, who had him in a death grip by both upper arms as Lacey frantically barked and tried to get between them as he struggled to free himself and follow.

It's not your place.

She raised one hand in farewell to him, heard his bellow of *"NO!"* and then she was through the doorway and into the dim interior. She yanked the leash out again, giving Hawk the scent one more time. "Find her, Hawk. Quickly find her. We can do this."

Hawk put his nose down, scenting the planks and then trotted across the floor, weaving back and forth around wooden pillars and explosive-wrapped columns, stepping carefully over yellow detonation cords, trying to find a single trace of that one particular odor. Another cell phone duct-taped to a column caught Meg's eye as she jogged past it. *Not the only one. When this place comes down, it's going to come down hard.* Her heart pounding so ferociously she could feel the frantic thump in her temples, she forced herself to take a breath, hold it for a moment, and then exhale. She needed to be calm for Hawk. Her fear would only transmit directly to him, throwing him off his game, and that would be the end for all of them.

She saw the moment he caught the scent trail as his tail curved high and his whole attitude suddenly intensified. "That's it, boy, that's her. Find Karen."

She followed him across the cavernous first floor, the scratch of his nails against the wood and the thump of her boots echoing in the empty space around them. Unerringly, he ran to the far end of the floor, where an ancient wooden staircase and banister led up to the second floor in one direction and down in the basement in the other. Hawk didn't hesitate, heading straight toward the basement. Meg pulled out her flashlight and shone it down into the inky darkness. The wide wooden steps showed their age, the middle of each step worn into a smooth curve by decades of work boots, but they looked solid. The construction was minimal—simply the steps and twin runners to support them between banisters buffed to a dull shine by the touch of thousands of hands. The second step was spray-painted orange, likely one of the weak spots Duncan had noted.

"Go on, Hawk. Find her." She shone the light down along the staircase to light their way and he gamely started down the stairs. She stepped onto the first tread, but then whipped back toward the factory door at the sound of shouting. She resolutely turned away from the sound. Her dog was nearly at the bottom of the steps and her place was with him. She skipped over the second step, and then ran down the rest of the stairway.

Unlike the factory floor above, the outer perimeter of the basement was constructed of less expensive local fieldstone. The air was suddenly heavy and damp, and a quick flash around showed moisture running in rivulets over stone and mortar to puddle on the floor, where patches of black mildew bloomed. Walls of mismatched brick partitioned the space into individual rooms, which would make the search longer. Some of the walls abutted heavy brick columns, identical to the ones upstairs, and Meg spotted a cell phone mounted on the nearest pillar.

Hawk was undaunted by the more complex search area, his nose down, letting the scent lead the way. He confidently started back toward the far end of the building, giving doorways a cursory sniff, but then moving on without a second glance. Meg had to assume the basement had the same footprint as the first floor, but the hallway before them melted into blackness at the edge of the flashlight's beam. It was a big area and time was running out.

"Karen? Karen, I'm from the FBI, we're here to help you. Can you hear me?"

The faintest of noises met her ears.

"Wait! Hawk, stop." They both stood stock-still. "Karen? Karen, if you can hear me, make a noise."

There was no mistaking it this time—the sound of a muffled female scream. Hawk's ears perked high and he took off at a run toward the sound, Meg right behind him, trying to angle the bobbing flashlight to light their way. Hawk cut abruptly into the last doorway on the left and pulled up so fast, Meg nearly fell over him.

A woman lay on her stomach at their feet. Her mouth was gagged and her wrists and ankles were zip-tied; even now as they stood over her, she was struggling, trying to pull her hands free of the restraints, leaving meaty gouges behind as blood rolled down her arms and soaked her sleeves. She rolled sideways to look up at them, blinking in the light, and Meg felt the blow above and beyond the additional signs of vicious abuse. *Blue eyes, pale skin, long black hair. She's me again.* She only had one eye open; the other was a deep charcoal-magenta and swollen shut, the lashes nearly lost in the puffy tissue. Her jaw sported a large misshapen lump, and the neckline of her shirt showed a long ragged tear, giving a glimpse of black bra beneath. Behind her, in the dirt floor, was a clear trail, at least twelve feet long: He'd beaten, bound, and gagged her, and left her to die. However, she wasn't about to go without a fight. She had dragged herself along the floor toward the scant light filtering down the stairs into the basement. She would never have been able to make it on her own, but she was going to die trying.

Not anymore.

Meg dropped to her knees beside her, dragging the pack from her shoulder and rooting quickly through a front pocket. She pulled out her folded knife, the blade popping free at the touch of a button. "Karen, we're going to get you out. Hold still so I can cut off the ties."

The woman instantly stilled, allowing Meg to slip the tip of the blade under the tie, a quick flip of the wrist slicing through it. She groaned, partly in relief, partly in agony, as she quickly grasped one bloody wrist with the other hand. Then, as Meg dealt with her ankles, Karen yanked the gag out of her mouth, spitting cloth bits into the dirt.

"Can you walk? We literally only have minutes before this place blows."

Karen formed the word "yes," but nothing came out of her parched throat. Meg jammed the knife into her pocket, shouldered the pack again, and held out her hand to Karen. The woman grabbed on tight, forearm to forearm, and let Meg haul her to her feet. She was unsteady and weaving almost drunkenly—likely the residual effects of the ketamine—but her jaw was set and determination flashed in her eyes. Meg slipped an arm around her waist, even as she shone the beam of the flashlight out the doorway. "Lean on me if you have to. We have to move fast. Hawk, out."

Hawk shot through the door and Meg half jogged after him, dragging Karen with her. The other woman was trying hard to help support her own weight; and with each step, she grew steadier, although the stiffness in her body told Meg she was in considerable pain. In less than thirty seconds, they reached the stairs and Karen half crawled up them, collapsing to her knees at the top, once more in daylight.

"Can't stop," Meg panted, hauling her back to her feet. "Any second, it's going to go. Come on!" She took her hand, grasping tight, and ran toward Hawk, who stood halfway down the floor, pointing toward the open door. "Talon, outside, *GO!*"

Hawk showed no hesitation—the use of his "don't mess with me" name was deeply ingrained in him for instant obedience. He galloped for the open doorway and sunlight.

Meg sprinted full out, Karen at her side, showing a burst of adrenaline that pushed her to match Meg stride for stride. Meg kept her eyes locked on her dog—*Come on, come on, faster!*—then losing sight of him as he burst out into sunlight. *Keep going, get clear of the building, can't stop.* The doorway was looming larger and larger; blinding sunlight was spilling into a path to guide them.

They burst out into fresh air, leaping over the threshold to land in the dirt of the yard. Karen stumbled and nearly toppled, but Meg yanked her upright and kept her moving. "Keep going." She could barely breathe, her lungs burning with lack of oxygen. "Have to . . . clear . . . perimeter."

Screams and shouts attracted her attention, and she focused on the sound to see Brian, Scott, and Lauren a good two hundred feet away, waving their arms. "Hawk, go to Brian!" The words were meant to be a shout, but came out half strangled. But Hawk, thirty feet in front of them, angled toward the group, Meg and Karen following.

The deafening *boom!* of the explosion suddenly rocked the building behind them, rolling the ground under their feet. Meg had a microsecond to think, *Not enough time,* before the shock wave hit, sweeping them all off their feet to carelessly toss them into a maelstrom of heat and light and chaos.

CHAPTER 17

Emergency Medical Services: The first documented use of specialized, dedicated ambulances by the military occurred after the Battle of Spires (French Revolutionary Wars) in the late 1790s. Unfortunately, the concept of professional, dedicated ambulance services was not in place at the start of the American Civil War. After the first Battle of Bull Run on July 21, 1861, more than one thousand wounded Union soldiers were left to fend for themselves on the battlefield as empty ambulances led the retreat to Washington, D.C.

Saturday, May 27, 10:32 AM
Teller and Sons furniture factory
Gettysburg, Pennsylvania

Meg woke to light behind her closed eyelids and a frantic voice in her ear. "Meg! Wake up! Meg!" A hand slapped her cheek, then incongruously pushed hair back from her face tenderly. "Goddamn it, Meg. I'll let you win all the races we run for the next year if you wake up." The voice broke to a whisper. "Please wake up."

"I'm so going to hold you to that, because loser buys coffee." The words were a hoarse croak, but Meg heard Brian's sharply indrawn breath at the sound of her voice. With difficulty, she cracked open her eyes. Brian loomed over her on his knees in the dirt. Behind him was all blue sky and fluffy clouds.

So bright. Meg closed her eyes again for a moment, trying to clear her head of the cobwebs and pain.

But Brian wouldn't let her go back into the dark. He tapped her cheek again. "No, stay with me."

"Would you stop knocking on my head?" Meg growled. "I have a headache and I'm feeling a little dizzy, but I'm fine."

"No wonder. You escaped that explosion with just seconds to spare, but you were close enough to the blast zone to get tossed a good twenty feet by the shock wave."

With that, memory flooded back in a rush. She jerked upright, trying to raise herself up on her elbows. "Hawk!" The sudden change in position made her head spin and she clamped her eyes shut, fighting nausea.

Brian grasped her shoulders, steadying her. "Whoa, whoa, slow down. Hawk's okay. He got thrown too, but he was farther away, so he fared better. He's over with Lauren and Lacey. Rocco and Theo are with him too. Right there." He pointed to her right and she carefully turned her head to find her dog surrounded by the loving concern of his team. He was covered in gray dust, but was on his feet, standing under his own power. His tail was low and motionless, and he kept trying to look over his shoulder, no doubt searching for her. Lauren held him still as she ran her hands over him, looking for any sign of injury. "Give Lauren a chance to check him out. We don't want him bolting over here on a broken leg."

Meg lowered herself back down to lie on the ground again in exhaustion. "No, we don't." Then another memory struck and she started to struggle upright again. "What about Karen?"

Brian pushed a hand against her shoulder to keep her flat on her back. "Give yourself a minute. Karen is fine—

well, fine considering what she went through. He beat her pretty bad. Scott's with her now and the ambulances are on their way."

Meg glared up at him. "Ambulances? Plural?"

"You both need one." When she tried to push up again, Brian foiled her attempt by pinning her shoulder with a single index finger. "See what I mean? You'd normally clean my clock if I tried that, and now you can't even sit up. You've probably got a concussion from the blast, and the ambulance team will want to check out your neck and back, so stay down, for God's sake." He let go of her shoulder and collapsed into the dirt beside her. He yanked off his jacket, balled it up, and slipped it under her head so she was somewhat cushioned against the packed dirt. "You really had me scared. The way that explosion just tossed you into the air. You landed like a puppet with all its strings cut, totally limp. I was sure you were dead."

"It would take more than that to kill someone as ornery as me."

"You know, you'd think I'd remember that with all the times you get into these life-or-death situations. But no, every time it's all new."

She reached for his hand and squeezed it. "I'm sorry I scared you. I'm sorry I left you behind. But it wasn't your fight and it wasn't your time. You understand why I did it? That I couldn't leave her there to die?"

Brian loosed a tired breath, his body sagging as the air left his lungs. "Yeah, I get it. But you know I would have gladly gone with you."

"I know," she said simply. "But I wouldn't ask that of you. That's not a sacrifice you need to make. Neither does Ryan." She turned her head sideways to look at Karen. She was sitting up, partially supported by Scott, who sat with her in the dirt, holding her hands, keeping her bloody, mangled wrists out of the worst of the dust.

"You should have seen her—she was magnificent. He met his match this time. I think that's why he beat her, because she fought him. She was in the basement, in one of the farthest rooms. He zip-tied her ankles and wrists and left her there. She was dragging herself across the floor toward the light, struggling all the time to break the ties on her wrists."

"That's why they're such a mess. I shudder to think of how many stitches she's going to need."

"We'll leave that to the experts. But I bet she's going to carry the scars from it for the rest of her life."

"Not the kind of memory you want."

"I'm not so sure. She wasn't going to let him win. With more time, she would have freed herself. That kind of strength should be celebrated. We just helped at the end." She craned her neck a little farther to look at the remains of the building. The pile of rubble was a blow to her solar plexus, temporarily stealing her breath. "There's nothing left." The words came out as a shocked whisper. That could have been her grave.

Hawk's grave.

It was what she hadn't allowed herself to focus on before, couldn't have allowed herself to, because it would have paralyzed her.

"There really isn't. The demo crew made us pull back even farther than originally required. Duncan was really worried the building wouldn't come down as planned, since he no longer knew the setup."

"I saw several additional cell phones on other columns as I went farther in. And there was at least one down in the basement itself. If it set off a chain reaction, the building may still have come down in close to the original order." For a moment, all she could do was stare at the rubble, dust still floating in a cloud above it. "Shit, Brian."

"You're only figuring that out now? We had that nailed

down from the moment you shoved your phone into my hands and took off like you were trying to break the record in the hundred-meter dash."

"How wonderfully poetic. You really should try your hand at writing someday."

"On my 'to do' list, at approximately number 3,200,006. Being verbally poetic is good enough for me. Everyone loves a snappy handler after all."

"God knows I do."

"Back at you, babe." At the sound of Lauren calling his name, Brian looked up and a huge grin spread. "There's our boy. Come here, Hawk."

Ignoring Brian's previous instructions, Meg propped herself back up on her elbow and held out one hand to him. "Hey, Hawk. Come here, boy."

Already headed toward her, Hawk perked his ears at the sound of her voice, his tail wagging in happiness as he trotted even faster toward her. Reaching her, he danced around her before slurping two sloppy kisses over her cheek. "It's good to see you too," Meg said, laughing.

"Uh-oh." Brian's gaze was fixed on Lauren as she pulled herself from the dirt.

"What?" Meg followed his gaze and immediately understood his meaning. She hadn't seen it often, but the glint in Lauren's eyes spoke of pure rage as she stalked toward them.

"Hi, Lauren." Brian's tone was all bright cheer.

"Stay out of this, Brian." Lauren focused the full force of her fury on Meg. "What the hell are you doing?"

"I—"

But Lauren was beyond listening and ruthlessly cut her off. "You go over the head of the Bureau to bring in a reporter and your sister to help with the case, then you disobey a direct order from your superior. What gives you the right to make those decisions? It's called a chain of command for a reason."

Meg was exhausted and her head was pounding like it might explode, so she let the reins on her temper go. "Women are dying in my place, Lauren. I can't live with that. If it was you, would you be able to live with it?"

"I'd use the Bureau to help me. You're endangering lives with your rash actions, including your own and your dog's. He can't make these decisions. Are you really willing to get him killed over this?"

"This isn't about degrees. I can't be in this case, but only so far. I have to stop him, so no one else dies instead of me. So whatever it takes."

"Then you do what you need to do. But I'm glad you don't call the shots for me or my dog. Rocco, come!" She stalked off toward Scott and Karen.

Meg gave a low groan and collapsed back down onto Brian's coat.

Brian laid a hand on Meg's arm. "She doesn't mean it, at least not to that extent. There's more fear behind her words than anger. She knows we came within seconds of losing you and Hawk. It scared her. Give her some time to work it through in her own head. She'll come around."

"Maybe, but she's not wrong. I did go off on my own, just like she said. I did put Hawk's life at risk. Brian, I could have lost him, just like I lost Deuce."

"We could have lost both of you. Look, you made the only decision you could live with at the time, and that's the best you can do."

"You're the second person to say that to me in the last week."

"So, clearly, I know what I'm talking about," Brian said. Sirens sounded in the distance, growing louder. "Here comes the cavalry. And speaking of which, you have a phone call to make."

"Ugh. I know. What do you think he's going to do?"

"Suspend your ass is my guess."

"I'll be lucky if that's all he does."

Brian's smile was gone now. "You disobeyed a direct order."

Meg squinted up at him, the brightness of the sky back-lighting a halo around his dark head. "You disapprove."

"No, I totally understand, and I would have joined you in a heartbeat. But they can't allow their agents and handlers to just do their own thing. They'll have to make an example of you. He'll have no choice."

"Brian, I can't be cut out of this case."

"He'll say you should have thought of that before you ran into that building."

"But she would have died."

Brian held up both hands as if in surrender. "Again I get it. I'm just channeling what he's going to say. You knew the risks going in."

"Sure, I knew them. But the only risk that mattered was the weight of her life against mine and Hawk's. Promise me something?"

"Whatever you need."

"Keep me in the loop. If I'm blocked from the case, I still need to know what's going on."

"Because you're going to work it from the outside?"

"Did you expect anything else?"

"Not really."

Meg met his eyes so there was no way he could mistake her intent. "I need to know. So, if he sends any more messages, I need you to forward them to me so I can work them remotely. I'll never let anyone know I got the information from you."

"You won't need to. There's going to be a glorious neon arrow pointing right at me. Bring it on, I can take it." The wail of sirens entered the yard and paramedics jumped out of the ambulances as soon as they stopped. "How about I call Craig," Brian suggested, "and tell him you made it, you brought Karen out, and you're being treated. You'll call him as soon as they let you use a phone."

"That works for me. Thanks."

"I can deflect him for a little while. But after that, you're on your own in the lion's den. Take a spear and shield. You're going to need it."

CHAPTER 18

Between Scylla and Charybdis: In this Greek myth, Odysseus must navigate between two undesirable outcomes—sacrificing a few sailors or losing his ship. The Greek names are part of the title of a famous book by Henry S. Foote published in 1866 about the "causes, course, and consequences" of the American Civil War.

Monday, May 29, 9:57 AM
EAD Peters's Office, J. Edgar Hoover Building
Washington, DC

"I'm Meg Jennings. I'm here to see EAD Peters," Meg said to the young assistant sitting behind the desk in the outer office. Just beside his desk was a door with the nameplate EXECUTIVE ASSISTANT DIRECTOR ADAM PETERS—CRIMINAL, CYBER, RESPONSE, AND SERVICES.

"He's expecting you," said the young man, briefly looking up from his computer monitor. "Please have a seat and he'll be ready for you shortly."

"Thank you. Hawk, come." Meg turned and crossed the small office to take one of the three uncomfortable chairs against the opposite wall, signing Hawk the hand signal to sit. No doubt, the chairs were there to discourage people from wanting to take up too much of EAD Peters's time. She tugged at the collar of her blouse—she much preferred the casual wear the team sported for searches to actual office wear—then pulled her cell phone out of her blazer pocket to double-check she had it on vibrate, only to find a text from her sister sent ten minutes before: **Heading to the school for my private lesson with Mrs. Williams so I won't be here when you come back. Good luck! Stand your ground and make me proud. Let me know how it goes . . .**

A smile curved Meg's lips, her sister's support easing some of the tension locking her shoulders and squeezing her lungs. She was prepared to defend her position, but she knew it wasn't defensible. When push came to shove, she'd disobeyed a direct order. It may have been for the best possible reasons, but, in the end, that was exactly what she'd done. She'd walked the fine line between doing what she felt was necessary to save a life versus what the Bureau considered proper protocol for normal operations. The only question was how would Peters see it? As a man valuing a human life above all else, or as an administrator running a high-risk operation?

She slipped her cell phone back into her pocket and leaned her head back against a wall, ignoring its dull throbbing. Brian had stayed with her at the hospital on Saturday through all the various testing, including an MRI. The doctor proclaimed it a grade-three concussion, seeing as she'd actually lost consciousness following the blast, and told her to rest for the next seven days. When Meg reminded him she was an FBI handler on a crucial case, he said the jury was out on how long to rest and for her to be aware of her body and to take it easy as much as possible. She was feeling much better after resting yesterday, but the low-grade, nagging headache wouldn't go away, no matter what she took for it. *Just have to wait it out.*

The phone on the young man's desk rang and he picked

it up. "Yes, sir? Yes, sir." He put the phone down and looked over at Meg. "EAD Peters will see you now."

"Thank you." Meg stood and started for the door, Hawk at her side. Reaching the threshold, she squared her shoulders, opened the door, then walked through. "You wanted to see me, sir?"

"I did, Jennings. Come in and close the door."

Meg closed the door behind Hawk and turned back to the big desk in front of the wide window looking out over Pennsylvania Avenue NW toward the Department of Justice Building beyond. Peters sat behind the desk, his ice blue eyes watching her keenly from behind his glasses. Peters was one of the most average-looking people Meg had ever met, a trait he ruthlessly used against those who prejudged and often underestimated him based on his appearance. Behind the slight frame, glasses, and balding pate was one of the keenest minds in the FBI, as evidenced by his rise to executive assistant director at age forty-five. He was a force to be reckoned with.

It was only as Meg crossed the office that she realized Craig sat with his back to her in one of the two chairs facing the desk. Peters motioned to the other chair.

But Meg came to stand between them instead. "I'd prefer to stand, sir." Standing, at least, felt like a small release of the building tension. Sitting felt too much like giving up. But she gave Hawk the signal to sit and he did, head up, staring unblinkingly at Peters.

Peters eyed the dog for a moment before his gaze rose to Meg. "Suit yourself. Would you care to explain yourself, Jennings? It is my understanding you disobeyed a direct order from SSA Beaumont on Saturday."

Might as well bite the bullet. Peters will respect that more than dancing around. "Yes, sir. I did."

Peters's eyebrows shot upward. "That's it? You just admit to disobeying the order?"

"Well, there's more to it than that, sir. A lot more. But SSA Beaumont is telling the basic truth of what happened."

Peters's gaze flicked to Craig and then back to Meg again. "Well, you know me, Jennings, I'm not a 'basics' kind of guy. You tell me what happened, as you see it."

"Are you familiar with the case, sir?"

"I am."

"Then you know women who look very much like me are being kidnapped and their lives are put at risk in various situations. Messages addressed to me are coming in, coded messages, that have to be deciphered to even give us a search location. Then we go in with our dogs to find the victim before she suffocates, a different way each time. For most of them, it's set up to be a slow, horrific death. A torturous death."

"Why do you think he's choosing victims that look like you?"

His piercing blue gaze pinned her and she met that gaze openly with nothing to hide. "Because he's killing me, over and over. Because I've done something he considers so heinous I need to die, again and again. Well, sir, I won't allow that. No innocent woman should be forced to die in my place. We beat him on Catriona Baldwin and on Karen Teller. Only time will tell if we beat him on Michelle Wilson."

"Do you consider Sandy Holmes's death to be on your head?"

Meg gave a single sharp nod.

Peters sat back in his chair, his elbows on the arms, his fingers linked together as he studied her over them. "Even though you didn't know what you were dealing with at the time, and even though that put you and the entire team from the CRRU to the Canine Unit at a disadvantage."

"Yes, sir. We had a chance. We missed out by only thirty minutes." Her voice dropped to a hiss. *"Thirty minutes."*

"Tell me about Saturday. It sounds like there are a few things we need to discuss there. For starters, did you really share the encoded message with your sister and a *reporter?*" The last word was practically spit, as if made of acid.

"Yes, sir." *Time to go for broke.* "For starters, that reporter is Clay McCord from the *Washington Post,* someone I've come to trust, someone this office should realize has shown himself to be trustworthy. Have you seen a single story from him on this case not sanctioned by Director Clarkson or yourself?" Clarkson was head of the FBI—if the buck stopped somewhere, it stopped with him.

"I haven't."

"He also happens to be an unofficial expert on the Civil War. Remember the first clue, the one our boys reasoned out incorrectly?"

" 'Find her before she dies. Come to Washington's House in Alexandria. The clock is ticking on her life.' "

Meg blinked at him for a moment, at a loss for words. She knew he liked to stay on top of the cases in his office, but there were so many of them. She never thought he'd be so far inside this one. That could play to her advantage. "Yes, sir, that's correct. The clue about Alexandria split the team and lost us precious time. McCord got the correct answer the first time—in seconds. So as messages came in, I started to use him as a sounding board. He knew the subject matter and lives were at stake. When Craig called to tell me where the third victim was, we were already on the way. That's how we arrived so quickly. McCord had already figured it out."

"Based on what?" For the first time, Craig interjected. "You didn't have the code translation yet."

"Except I did. Sir, there's a part of this case I haven't told you about yet, for this exact reason. You were going to be angry I went outside the Bureau. I knew if I didn't withhold this information, you'd likely remove me from this case and I couldn't let that happen." She swayed slightly on her feet and Hawk gave a low, anxious whine.

Peters pointed at the empty chair. "You're recovering from a concussion. Stop being a hero, Jennings, and sit." He punctuated the command with an exacerbated finger stab. "That's an order. I assume you do follow those on occasion."

Meg sank into the chair. "Yes, sir." Hawk circled the chair to sit at her feet and she automatically stroked the back of his neck, just a quick touch to tell him to stay, but also for her own comfort and strength.

"Thank you. Now let's make this more of a discussion and less of a lynching. That means putting everything on the table. What haven't you told us?"

"I've been sharing the codes with my sister from the third victim onward." When Craig started to speak, she continued right over him, her eyes locked on Peters. "She's always been a crackerjack with puzzles and codes. I've used her before on Richmond PD cases, not that they ever knew either. She never breathed a word of it, no one ever knew, but cases were solved and lives were saved, and I considered it a fair trade-off."

"The ends justified the means?" Peters asked.

"Sometimes, yes. Do you consider a human life more important than following the letter of the law? Before you answer, I should qualify that question with the statement that I'm aware of your history with the department. Particularly with the Bannister case."

Peters's gaze narrowed on her, and Meg's heart rate kicked up a notch at the thought she'd just gone one step too far with him.

"Are you now?" Peters said in a conversational tone. *Too* conversational.

"I am. I know there have been occasions when you

haven't played exactly by the book because lives were at stake. That you've *only* done it in the most extreme circumstances, and when your back was to the wall and there was no other choice in your eyes. That's how I felt on Saturday."

Peters's fingers unlinked, their tips tapping together in sequential rhythm. "I do consider human life more important than following the letter of the law. But never the spirit of the law." The words were a slow drawl.

The knot in Meg's belly unraveled slightly. She hadn't just ended her career; he was giving her the leeway to make her case. "Exactly. Yes, Cara should never have seen those messages. And there was no way she could beat the CRRU boys with their big computers. But she had something they didn't, and because of it, she figured out something I haven't shared with anyone in the Bureau yet."

"And what is that?"

"We know the messages are coming to me. We know the victims look like me. But the codes have all been linked to me as well. Each keyword for the Vigenère code has been a coded message in itself. The CRRU boys never saw it, but Cara did from the very first message. The numbers in the first keyword spelled the word 'Deuce.'"

Craig stiffened in the chair beside her.

Peters saw the reaction, his head cocked slightly in confusion. "That doesn't mean anything to me. Beaumont?"

"It's the name of her first K-9 partner who fell in the line of duty when she was with the Richmond PD."

"Son of a bitch." Peters's attention turned back to Meg. "That must have been a kick in the gut."

"Yes, sir. The second keyword spelled 'Hawk,' so she knew it was a pattern and not a coincidence. From that point on, Cara would figure out the length of the keyword and then go through words of that length she could think of having any relation to me. Meanwhile, the CRRU analysts were trying to work it backward based on letter frequency in the English language. Cara's good, and she always got there first because of her personal knowledge of me. The third code, the keyword was 'Haven,' part of the name of my parents' rescue near Charlottesville, Virginia. While we're putting our cards on the table, I have to tell you, I have already informed them about the case." Her voice went hard. "If he touches my parents . . ."

Peters held up a hand. "I get it, Jennings. I may be in charge of this branch, but I have parents of my own. I can assign agents to protect them."

Meg sagged slightly in the chair. "Thank you, sir. I hope we won't need that, but if we do, I'll gladly take you up on it. For now, they're watchful and prepared. They always have security in place to protect their animals. Now they're using it for themselves." She took a breath, and prepared to lay the rest of the story out. "Because she had the keyword, Cara figured out the second clue at home, with McCord and me looking on."

"That's why you left the office so quickly that day," Craig said.

"Yes, sir."

"You should have said something. We could have worked something out, brought it to EAD Peters even then."

Shame warmed Meg's cheeks. "And that was my error, sir. I should have trusted you both."

"So Cara worked out the ciphertext and then McCord figured out the location." Peters steered them back onto the topic at hand.

"Yes. So we were ahead of the teams. I don't know if that saved Cat's life, but it might have. Could she have held on for another fifteen or twenty minutes? Maybe, I don't know. And thank God we didn't have to find out."

"So, then, with the last message, you finally had to tell

me," Craig said. "The CRRU cryptanalysts were just getting started while Cara already had it solved and McCord had already figured out the kill site and the time limit. Faking it at that point wasn't an option."

"No, sir. The only thing that mattered at that point was saving Karen, and you made that happen. You got us there."

"What was the fourth keyword?" Peters asked.

" 'Marlowe,' the name of my childhood dog."

Craig swore quietly. "Now it's getting even more personal."

"Yes," Meg agreed. "My current K-9, my late K-9, the name of my parents' animal rescue, that's all public knowledge. The name of the golden retriever I had at five, not so much. But I couldn't let that stop me." She swiveled to face Craig. "So when we got there and found the site wasn't in our control, I couldn't obey your order to stand down." She turned back to Peters. "Yes, I disobeyed a direct order, but it was because of the stakes involved. A woman was going to die—because of me. I had to try to save her or die in the attempt."

"You took an asset valuable to the FBI in with you," Peters said flatly, his gaze dropped down to where Hawk sat at her side.

Meg smiled down at her dog, then ran a hand over the back of his head. "I know." Her gaze snapped back to Peters, the smile gone and iron backing her words. "Although I'll remind you, the FBI doesn't own Hawk—I do. I came into the Bureau with him. And no one loves him more than me. It almost stopped me from going, the fact his life would be in the balance. But he's got too much heart, and I know he wouldn't hesitate to risk his life if it meant the chance to save someone else. I couldn't go without him—he'd disobey my order to stay, like I disobeyed the order to stand down. In the end, he saved all our lives—by guiding me in, and then Karen and me out as quickly as possible. It came down to seconds making the difference. He gave us those seconds. A concussion is nothing compared to what could have happened."

"I've seen the site photos. It could have been catastrophic." Peters stared at handler and dog for long seconds, the silence only broken by the rhythmic tapping of his index finger on the desk beside his keyboard. "You're putting me in a hard position, Jennings. You've involved people in the case from outside the Bureau without permission, hidden evidence from your supervising agent, and then disobeyed a direct order from him."

Meg's heart sank at the condemnation in his tone and her gaze sank to her dog. *Damn it, it wasn't enough.*

"But I can't say I wouldn't have done exactly the same thing if I had been in your position," Peters continued.

Meg looked up, her heart suddenly full of hope.

"However, you understand the Bureau has to be run under a hierarchy, or there would be chaos."

"Yes, sir, I understand."

"I hear from SSA Beaumont that you've been told by the ER doc that you should be off work for up to a week following the actual injury."

"Yes, sir."

"Then, Jennings, it is my decision that you be suspended with pay for the duration of this week." When she opened her mouth to question his decision, he held up a hand in a clear *stop.* "That's my final decision. Nothing you say will make me change my mind."

I'm not being fired. Meg fought to keep a smile from curving her lips. "Yes, sir. Thank you, sir."

"Also, just so you know, Karen Teller worked with one of our sketch artists yesterday and we have some good preliminary sketches on the unsub."

Hope rose like a wave. "I need to see them. I might recognize him."

"I'll arrange for it as soon as possible. But otherwise, Jennings, you are off this case. Is that clear?"

"Yes, sir, but—"

"No 'but.' Don't push it. Given some time to consider, I think you'll see that I'm being extremely lenient, and this could have had a much different, much more permanent outcome. Don't try to work this case from the sidelines. Don't try to bring any of your team into it behind Beaumont's back. If I get wind of that, you're all going to be on the unemployment line. *Is that clear?*"

"Yes, sir."

Her phone vibrated in her pocket, once, twice, but she ignored it.

"If he strikes again, it will come into this office and we will handle it. As of now, you will have to trust we can get it done, and also trust your team can do its job without you."

"Of course, sir."

"In the meantime, remember that you're a target. Stay alert and stay safe. I don't want our teams to be looking for *you* in the next few days."

Her phone vibrated again. "No, sir. Thank you, sir."

"Dismissed."

"Yes, sir. Hawk, come."

Meg left the office with Hawk at her side, closing the office door quietly behind her. She threw Peters's assistant a wan smile and led Hawk into the busy main hallway. Only then, did she let out the pent-up breath she'd been holding.

She'd been lucky. He could have had her job. He'd never have her dog, but she could have lost her livelihood. More than that, she could have lost her calling. No decent law enforcement organization would—or should—rightfully take on a renegade who disregarded orders, no matter what the reason behind the decision. If a week off was the worst outcome, she'd gotten off lucky. Granted, she knew sitting at home, waiting, at a time like this would be a killer. But she knew her team would do whatever it took to catch this guy.

She also knew Brian would never leave her in the dark at a time like this. Maybe she couldn't be involved, but she would know how the case progressed. And if it was still active next week, she'd be back with them.

Her cell phone vibrated again and she pulled Hawk into a smaller, deserted side corridor. She pulled her phone out of her pocket to find out who needed her so badly that he or she was sending a constant stream of text messages. She unlocked her phone to find the notification splashed across her screen, indicating a number of texts from Cara.

What on earth? Cara knew she was in a meeting. Had something happened on the way to the school? Was she in an accident?

She opened her text message and just about went to her knees at the first message. Not a message, per se, but an image. One that would remain seared into her mind for as long as she lived.

Cara lay on a diamond-textured metal floor, her body limp, her eyes closed, her face colorless. Duct tape covered her mouth, and her arms were bound behind her back.

For a moment, all Meg tried to do was suck air into her lungs, but her body had forgotten how to carry out its basic functions. There was a strident buzzing in her ears and she couldn't feel the phone cradled in her hand.

Beside her, Hawk pushed at her with his head and pawed at her leg. He clearly knew something was wrong. She let her knees buckle and sank down to crouch on the floor beside him, forcing her blurry vision to focus on the words beneath the picture: **Do exactly as I say or else.**

Her first impulse was to call for help from the agents in the building around her, but she held her tongue. Her brain belatedly acknowledged she needed to know what was going on before taking any steps.

She closed her eyes for a moment, drawing up the strength that shock had temporarily beaten down. She could do this. Whatever her sister needed, she could do. Would do.

He had her sister, and he was talking to her directly through her sister's phone. Maybe there was a chance it could be traced and they could find him.

Time to end this.

She turned back to the phone, even as it vibrated again with a new incoming message: **Tell no one of this message. We've played enough games. Now it's just you and me. I've taken your sister, but I've also taken another. You must choose who lives and who dies.**

Meg dropped her head down against Hawk's shoulder.

Do not tell the authorities. If the FBI hears of it, then you told them. If the police know, then you told them. If law enforcement comes, they might live, but your parents will not. I will make sure of it. The only way to win the game is by my rules. Here are your clues.

Two separate messages of five-letter clusters were delivered next.

She shot to her feet. No authorities. But Clay McCord was not the authorities. She and Cara needed him, and they needed him now.

Hawk at her side, she sprinted from the building as if pursued by the hounds of hell.

CHAPTER 19

Blockade Runners: The blockade runners were a group of Confederate sailors, naval officers, and private entrepreneurs who attempted to evade the Union blockade of Southern ports deployed as part of the North's Anaconda Plan to "strangle" the Confederacy with minimal bloodshed. More than three hundred steamers made over thirteen hundred sorties out of Confederate ports from the Chesapeake Capes to the Rio Grande. Voyages were planned based upon natural constraints like high tides, moonless nights, and weather. These voyages allowed the Confederacy to export cotton, to import food, machinery, gunpowder, and to accumulate millions of dollars in foreign exchange.

Monday, May 29, 10:48 AM
Jennings residence
Arlington, Virginia

Meg didn't remember most of the drive home. She'd called McCord first from the car as she frantically wove through downtown DC traffic. He'd asked no questions, had simply said he was on his way and hung up. Webb was her next call. At this point, she wanted all the skilled manpower she could get her hands on; and while he was a first responder, he wasn't law enforcement. If she was being forced to play this game, she was going to take advantage of whatever leeway she could find. Webb might not have McCord's history background, but as both fire-fighter and paramedic, she needed his talents and strength because she didn't know what she was walking into. She didn't even know if he was on shift today—his "twenty-four hours on/seventy-two hours off" schedule was hard to remember when she was this rattled—and by the third ring, she was sure he wasn't available. Then he picked up. The story fell out of her as a garbled mess, but it was enough for him to understand the gist. He was also on the way. They would all meet at her house.

She screeched into the driveway, jumped out of the SUV, and let Hawk out. They hurried into the house, and were met at the door by Saki and Blink, both of whom instantly sensed her anxiety. Meg quickly calmed them, as best she could, then hurried into the house. She changed into search clothes, gathered up all their SAR gear and added in extras. If they were going to do two consecutive searches, they'd need extra supplies. The mudroom door banged open and her name was called. "In here."

Webb stopped on his way in for a cursory greeting with the dogs, who clustered around his legs. "Where are we?"

Meg didn't even look up, just continued jamming items in her pack. "I forwarded the messages to McCord so he can deal with it as soon as he gets here. In the meantime—"

The door slammed open and shut a second time and McCord ran in. "I'm here. I got your e-mail." He was al-ready pulling his laptop from his messenger bag as he headed for the couch to set up on the coffee table.

"You know what to do with the messages?"

"I've seen Cara do it from start to finish once and have gone through the process with her a couple more times. The first thing she does is run the code through a Vigenère analysis site. Give me a minute to find it—I think I'll recognize it when I see it. Then I'm going to need your help with the keywords, assuming each one is something different. We'll have to do this one message at a time." For the first time, he seemed to take in the presence of another man and thrust out his hand. "Clay McCord, the *Washington Post*. I think we met briefly in Jill Cahill's hospital room after the Mannew case."

"We did." Webb shook his hand. "Todd Webb, DCFEMS."

"Emergency response. Excellent. That could be handy." McCord hunched over his laptop and started Googling, flipping through websites, muttering in the negative, and flipping back to the search.

Meg turned away from him and went to let the dogs outside; watching him work only made her more nervous.

Webb stepped forward and took her by both shoulders. "We're going to get her back. We'll get them both back."

"I can barely think right now. I know I should have it more together than this, but I just keep going over and over in my mind what his next kill method might be. Hanging? A plastic bag over her head? Or what about—"

"Whoa." Webb gave her a little shake, stopping her words. "Stay with me. I know this is going to be hard, but you have to concentrate on one thing at a time. Right now, it's deciphering the codes and then solving the riddles. Then we can figure out what to do and how to handle two searches at the same time. This is the hardest part, because all we can do is watch McCord work. From what you've said about him, he's been a huge help. So give him some time, he'll get there. Has he let you down yet?"

"No."

"And he won't now."

As if on cue, McCord opened another site and said,

"Bingo! Got you." Switching to the other window, he ran the first block of text through the analysis. "This is going to look for repeated sequences and will give us an estimate of the possible length of the key. Okay, so it's giving us a couple of options, but it looks like it's most likely eleven characters long." He turned in the chair. "Meg, I need you to come up with a word that is meaningful in your life that's eleven letters long. Give me that and then I'll apply it to the code and see if it makes sense working backward." He picked up Cara's pad of paper and pen from the corner of the table and handed it to Meg. "Jot down any ideas. Nothing is too outlandish. The more possibilities, the better. I'll try them all. While you're doing that, I'll get going on the second code."

Meg took the pen and paper and perched on the edge of the sofa.

Webb gave her shoulder a squeeze and then stepped back. "I won't hang over your shoulder. Just take a minute and think."

I can do this. Meg took a deep breath and cleared her mind to concentrate. *What would Cara do?* Putting pen to paper, she started a list. She jotted down words, tapped over the letters with a pen, counting, and either kept it or crossed it out.

Richmond PD. Ten letters. A line slashed through the word.

Search-and-rescue. Fifteen. No.

Human Scent Evidence Team. Twenty-two. Way *too long.*

The list continued.

After a minute or two, Webb came back to see how she was doing. The list crawled down the page on her lap, each word followed by a number, each word then neatly struck out, or, as the words covered the page, raggedly scratched out. He crouched down beside her, catching her hand as she scribbled a word out so hard the paper tore under her pen. "Stop for a second."

Her eyes rose to his. "I can't find it. I can't find the word. Cara's the one who's a master at puzzles. I've never been as good at it."

He wrapped both his hands around hers and just held on. "You can do this. If you weren't under pressure like this, you might have it already. But this is what we have to work with." He scanned down the page. "Can I offer some advice?"

She nodded.

"The clues have been getting more and more personal as the case has progressed. You, your parents, your childhood. It's not going to be something like the 'Human Scent Evidence Team.' That may be what you do, but it's not who you are. The clues are all about *who* you are. Think personal." He released her hands and then started to rise.

She pressed a hand to his shoulder, halting his motion. "Stay?"

"Sure." He shifted sideways to sit beside her on the couch.

She started the list again, pausing between each rejected word to consider other options.

Mrs. Panabaker. My favorite elementary-school teacher. Twelve.

Roseland Park. Where Cara and I used to play after school. Also twelve.

Marty Garber. The boy next door, before his family moved away. Eleven?

"Try 'Marty Garber,'" she said. "He was the kid who lived next door to us in Charlottesville for years. That's eleven letters."

"Give me a second." McCord picked up Cara's print-

out of the twenty-six by twenty-six block of letters, a spare
pad of paper and a pen, and started scribbling. Thirty seconds passed then. "No, that's not it. All I'm getting out of
that is gibberish."

"Good first try." Webb's voice was low. "You haven't
hit on it yet, but you're on the right track. Keep going."

Angelina. The first cat at my parent's rescue. Eight.

Scott Patterson. My first preteen crush. Fourteen.

"*It's who you are. . . .*"

*Journey's End. The name of my grandparents' seaside
cottage on Nantucket.*

Eleven.

" 'Journeys end in lovers meeting—Every wise man's
son doth know.' "

"What?" McCord stared at her. "Did you just quote
Shakespeare?"

"Yes. *Twelfth Night,* to be specific. Try 'Journey's
End.' "

"What's that?" Webb asked, with his gaze glued to Mc-
Cord's pen.

"The name of my grandparents' cottage on Nantucket.
It's old, been passed down through the family for genera-
tions. Was an actual full-time mariner's house back in the
day, complete with a widow's walk, where wives would
stand, looking out to sea, waiting for their husbands' ships
to come in. Or not. Luckily, in my family, it truly was
'journeys end in lovers meeting'—all the husbands returned. My great-grandmother loved literature and she officially named the cottage. We don't use it full-time
anymore—winters on Nantucket can be brutal—but it's a
wonderful escape during the summer." Meg knew she was
rambling, but talking focused her mind on something
while they waited. "They're on the northern shore. Some
people on the island have sold to buyers who renovated

their cottages into these monster houses, with pools and a tennis court, but our cottage is still the charming saltbox it was back in 18—"

"I've got English!" McCord slammed his pen down on the paper in triumph. "Better than that, I've got English that makes sense. The first few words are 'The landing point kept.' Give me a few minutes. I'll have it all." He picked up the pen again, bent his head over the letter key, and began writing.

Meg collapsed back onto the couch.

Webb took one of her hands in both of his. "Knew you could do it."

"It's only the first step. The first step of the first message."

"The first of several, but it's one step closer. The bastard doesn't stand a chance and we're going to pull this off. You just watch. Let's solve this one, and then we'll tackle the next. Once we know both locations, we'll make a plan."

"It's two victims. What if we don't make it simply because of the time?"

"This guy's a psycho, but the game actually seems to matter to him. If it didn't, he'd just kill the vics for you to find later. But part of the fun for him seems to be the chance you might actually succeed. It's a competition, and it's no fun if he stacks the deck against you so high you have no chance to win. So there has to be a way to win here. And we're going to find it."

She covered the back of his hand with hers. "Are you always this positive?"

"Always this stubborn. In my line of work, you're always playing against the odds. The trick is finding a way to beat them." He flashed her a wide grin, which was more steely determination than joy. "I'm very good at beating the odds."

Meg was just sitting down again, after letting the dogs back in, when McCord put the pen down again and swung around to face them, the pad of paper in his hands. "Okay, I've got it all now." He looked down and read. " 'The landing point kept the secret and saved ten thousand. Below are the skeletons of those gone before. And those to come.' " He frowned down at the message and then set the pad of paper down on the coffee table. "This one makes me wish for the specificity of the first victim's clue. That one was easy. This one, not so much. But I guess that's the point. We've beat him multiple times, so he's making it harder for us." He slowly read the message aloud again.

"It sounds to me like the 'below are the skeletons' is referring to where Cara is," Webb said. "So what's that, a Civil War graveyard? And does the reference to the ten thousand represent the size of the graveyard?"

"Most of them aren't that big." McCord pulled up his browser and started typing. "I mean, we've got Arlington, but we've already done that once, and it's much bigger than ten thousand. Try about four hundred thousand. You've also done Gettysburg, which is about thirty-five hundred. There's Antietam, which is larger, with just under five thousand, if I remember correctly, but that's only half of the ten thousand." He rubbed his hand over his chin, staring at something on his monitor, his gaze then switching back to the message on the pad. "I think the 'landing point' is the key. The skeletons are related to the landing point. Below it."

"But isn't a 'landing point' basically a port?" Meg asked. "So we're looking at something directly on the eastern seaboard?"

"Could be a port. Could also be something as simple as a jetty used to off-load passengers and bring on supplies. However . . ." McCord paused, tapping his index finger over the words. "Also important is the phrase 'kept the secret.' "

"It was war," Webb said. "Most things were secret. War strategies, camp locations, sympathizers, spies. Hell, even the Underground Railroad."

McCord looked up sharply, his blue eyes fixed on Webb. "Wait a second. You may have something there."

"Which part?"

"The Railroad. What else would be a secret that saved ten thousand lives? Hang on." He crouched over his laptop, first typing, then frantically clicking, his eyes darting back and forth over the screen, the light washing his face alternatively with white and then various pastel shades. As he worked, he kept up a constant low mumble. "Cumberland. Philly. Portsmouth? No, too busy. Fredericksburg. Fredericksburg!" He looked up. "I may have something. Fredericksburg, Virginia."

"That's pretty close. Less than an hour away. That's the 'landing point'?"

"No, but a port close to it might be. It fits the bill. It's relatively local, and it was a part of the Underground Railroad. Fredericksburg is on the Rappahannock River. But the Richmond, Fredericksburg and Potomac Railroad was already twenty years old at the time of the Civil War. It was part of a major link between DC and Richmond, Virginia. You could steamboat from DC to the shore of the Potomac River, get off at the Aquia Creek Landing"—he looked up meaningfully at Meg and Webb—"and train from there to Richmond. Or you could do the reverse, train to the landing and then get on a steamboat headed north."

"And that's what the slaves did?" Meg asked.

"I didn't know the exact number for this particular location, but according to this site, ten thousand slaves escaped this way during the period of April to September

1862, from the time the Union took control of the area to when they lost it. Okay, so Aquia Creek Landing is right on the Potomac River. So define 'below.' South?"

"Fredericksburg isn't south though. More like southwest," Webb said.

" 'Below,' as in altitude?" Meg suggested.

"That's a good idea, but that close to the Potomac and the Atlantic, it's basically already at sea level. To get any lower, you'd have to be under . . ." His voice petered out, his eyes going wide.

Fear was like an ice spike piercing right to Meg's soul. "Water," she finished for him. "He's drowning her? Whoever 'she' is?"

Webb's voice was calm, a man used to dealing with urgent situations. "There's no way he's even there yet. If that's his plan for Cara, he's still in motion."

Meg couldn't sit still any longer, and she shot to her feet to prowl the living room. "The ocean, it's an angle we haven't thought of before. When is high tide today? He could leave her somewhere, clear out, and then wait for high tide to come in for her to drown."

"We aren't going to let that happen." McCord's fingers were flying over the keys. "High tide at Aquia is at twelve forty-nine. But we have to be careful here. After you're south of Alexandria, there's no crossing point over the Potomac until Route 303. If this is where we're going first, we need to think this through or we're not going to be able to get there in time, because we're on the wrong side of the river. And then losing the second victim will be a foregone conclusion. 'Below are the skeletons.' So what does that mean? The remains of people lost on sunken ships? Are we looking for the location of a major shipwreck or a Civil War battle? Okay, Google, make me some magic. 'Sunken ships Potomac River.' Go." He clicked his mouse and then scanned the search results. "Sweet baby Jesus, I've got it.

The entire first page of results is all the same site. Mallows Bay. 'Skeletons' doesn't refer to human bones. It's the bones of ships." He looked up at Meg. "We need to figure out which victim this relates to, and then we'll know who one of them is. So what's special about this spot? Every site has been related to the victim. Every killing method"— McCord grimaced, but went on—"has been related to the victim. This is an area with sunken ships and our theory says his method is drowning. How does that relate?"

"I'm pretty sure it's Cara, because of our great-grandfather Arthur Jennings." Meg sat back on the couch, but swept her fingertips over Hawk's fur, knowing he was helping her stay calm. "He was a midshipman on board the *USS San Diego* when the Germans sank it in 1918."

"I'm not familiar with the *San Diego*. Was it torpedoed by a U-boat?"

"No, it was a mine. A German U-boat had laid mines along the south shore of Long Island. It hit one and sank in twenty-eight minutes. My great-grandfather was one of six men who died. He was trapped in the crow's nest and drowned. He was just twenty-eight and left behind my great-grandmother and two sons under three years of age, one of whom was my grandfather. A child he never met, because when he went to war, my great-grandmother was six months pregnant."

"That makes me feel better and worse at the same time." The set of McCord's jaw was rock solid and anger shone in his eyes. "I'm sure the site is right, but now we really know what we're looking at."

"It all makes sense," Meg said softly.

"It also means this guy had access to details about your family that go way back," Webb said.

"It's a matter of public record. Anyone with an Internet connection who wants to shell out to Ancestry.com could have figured this out. But it takes a special kind of cruel and crazy to reenact it."

"Speaking of 'cruel and crazy,' how the hell are we supposed to get to her and someone else when the tide is essentially calling the order of the rescues?" McCord's eyes were fixed on his screen, but he was shaking his head at the impossibility of the situation. "What kind of crackpot is this?"

"We already knew he's nuts," Webb said. "Okay, time's wasting. What's the second keyword length?"

"Eight." McCord pulled up the other message. "I'm ready to go as soon as you've got something for me to try."

"Okay, take two. Eight." Meg settled back on the couch and scanned the top sheet of paper. "I've got one here already with eight letters. 'Angelina.' Try that."

"Give me a sec." Head down, McCord started working the code. This time, he was faster. "Nada."

Meg ripped off the top sheet of paper, balling it and tossing it over her shoulder. "Worth a shot. Okay, let me try this again."

Buford. The middle school we attended. Six.

Clarinet. The instrument I played in middle school. Seven.

Briarcliffe. The street we grew up in, when we still lived in town. Eleven.

Meg was running out of ideas for herself. *Unless . . .*

Unless I'm going about this keyword the wrong way. This is about family. So far, there'd been clues related to me, a clue for our parents, one for our grandparents. Maybe this time it's about Cara.

Sudoku. One of Cara's favorite pastimes. Six.

Jenny Rae. Cara's best friend in high school. Eight?

"Try 'Jenny Rae,' " she said, spelling out the first and last names. "That's eight letters."

" 'Jenny Rae.' " A long pause, then, "Not it. Sorry."

"No need to apologize," Meg said. "You're not the son of a bitch who got us here."

Lola. The name Cara affectionately gave her first used car, a rust bucket held together by a half-dozen bolts, if she was lucky. Four.

And then it came to her, the word echoing in her mind in Maimeó's voice.

A Stóirín. Eight.

" '*A Stóirín.*' " The Gaelic endearment rolled off her tongue as *ah-store-een.*

McCord repeated the word back to her. "What language is that?"

"Gaelic. My paternal Irish grandmother had Gaelic pet names for us. That's Cara's." She spelled it out for him. "It's eight letters. Try that."

Again it didn't take McCord long. "That's it. Good job. Give me a second here. . . ." He went back to it, working out the code at top speed.

Meg sat back on the couch, and just let silence take over. She was exhausted, both emotionally and physically, and her head was pounding, making her feel vaguely nauseated and unbalanced, and the day's trial had yet to begin. And while they were spending time here, God only knew what torture her sister was enduring.

"Okay, this I don't get." McCord put down his pen. "After all those messages that just about broke my brain, this one is a gimme."

"What do you mean?" Webb leaned forward to stare at the writing on the pad of paper. " 'Blood and indecisiveness decreed the final campaign, but history was made nearby. Look to the man who deduced the treatment if you hope to save her.' How is that a gimme?"

"Look at how this clue is written—it feels more straightforward than some of the previous clues. And while you might jump to the conclusion that 'the final campaign' was the Appomattox Campaign that led to Lee's surrender, neither Lee nor Grant could have been called indecisive. Tie that to the reference to blood and it can only mean one thing—the bloodiest day in US military history—Antietam. Sharpsburg, Maryland. The indecisiveness is the fact the war could have been won then and there. Lee's army was beaten, but General McClellan, weak-minded fool that he was, didn't follow through and finish the Confederate Army off, once and for all. Lincoln commanded him to go after Lee, but it took him weeks to do it. Lincoln relieved him of duty, and the war went on for three more years because he let Lee get away and rebuild his shattered forces. It's a gimme. It's definitely Antietam."

"What about the rest of the message?" Meg asked. " 'The man who deduced the treatment'? What 'treatment'?"

"That's going to take a little more research." McCord clicked a few more times and slammed down the lid of the laptop before jamming it in his bag and pushing to his feet. "I'll hotspot into my cell and research while we drive. We can't waste any more time here."

"Hawk, come." Meg was already reaching for the packed-and-ready SAR bag and his vest.

"He's given us two locations. One is an hour south, with the tide rolling in. One is an hour and a half north, and we have no idea what scenario that is. What's your call?" McCord asked.

"You know what my call is."

"Good, because you'd have had a fight on your hands from me otherwise." Meg's dark expression had McCord reaching out to grab her arm. "Meg, this monster is telling you that you have a choice, but you don't. Don't let him make you suffer when he's forcing your hand. If Cara is out there, the tide is rolling in. If we go for the other one first, she will die, no question. If we go for Cara first, we have a chance to save both."

Webb pulled his keys from his pocket. "I'll drive. Where are we going?"

McCord slid the strap of his messenger bag over his shoulder. "Nanjemoy, Maryland. He's taken Cara to the Ghost Fleet."

" 'The Ghost Fleet'?"

"I'll explain on the way."

"You're okay with driving?" Meg asked Webb as they headed for the door.

"Totally. We won't all fit into your SUV and I've got gear in my truck, in case we need to stage a rescue."

Meg hoped to hell Webb was wrong, but her terrified gut was telling her this might be the hardest rescue yet.

CHAPTER 20

Triage: Triage is a system of sorting victims and rationing limited medical resources and supplies to a large number of casualties. Triage patients are divided into (1) those who are likely to survive even if untreated, (2) those who are unlikely to survive, no matter what care is available, and (3) those who are more likely to survive if they receive the best medical care possible. Typically, group-three patients are treated first, while groups one and two are offered palliative care. Dr. Jonathan Letterman—known as the "Father of Modern Battlefield Medicine"—introduced the concept of triage for the treatment of wounded Union soldiers.

Monday, May 29, 12:06 PM
MD-210 South
Oxon Hill, Maryland

Meg grabbed at the door handhold with one hand, and the dog at her feet with the other, as Webb sped through traffic, deftly weaving around anything in his way.

"You're pretty good behind the wheel," McCord said from where he sat in the passenger seat, his laptop open on his thighs. "Do they let you drive the fire truck?"

"Not on a regular basis, but I can in a pinch. Needless to say, it's a little harder to handle than this."

"I bet."

From the back of the king cab, Meg watched the forest flanking the eight-lane, divided highway fly by in a blur. Hawk made a small noise and she looked down at him, running her hand over his back where he lay on the floor behind Webb's seat. He wanted to sit up beside her, was used to watching the world go by through the mesh of his compartment as they drove. But Meg wasn't taking a chance that they'd get in an accident and knew the floor was the safest place for him. Her sister was at risk; she wasn't about to risk her dog as well.

"Keep going," Webb said, his eyes, never leaving the road. "I'd like to know what we're walking into. Where did this 'Ghost Fleet' come from, why is it there, and what's in it?"

"From what I'm reading, Uncle Sam is the reason it's there."

Webb's eyes quickly darted sideways and then back to the road. "The government purposely buried a fleet of ships in the Potomac." The tone of his statement clearly implied his disbelief. He switched lanes to pass a sedan nailing the speed limit, then signaled his way back.

"You make it sound like they built the ships to destroy them. That wasn't the intention at all. How's your history of World War One?"

"Not bad, but not to the level of knowing how many dead are buried in each graveyard."

"Guilty as charged," McCord quipped. "Then you know we didn't enter the war until 1917. At the time, Germany had the upper hand on the seas, sinking about half of all boats launched against them. The U-boats were killing machines. So America joined the fray and set about building one thousand ships in only eighteen months. That was the window normally reserved to build a single ship, but President Wilson put a million men to work building steamships. But when the war ended in 1919, only four hundred warships were completed and none of them ever saw action."

"So then we were left with a fleet of ships and nothing to do with them?"

"Sort of. Some of them were sold off, but these weren't pleasure vessels or even good transatlantic freighters, because they were too small. So most of them were never used, and, in the end, were sold as salvage and eventually scrapped."

Meg had been listening quietly from the back, but finally spoke up. "Why on earth would they sink them in the middle of the Potomac? That seems like a bad idea."

McCord turned around in his seat to speak to her directly. "It's not exactly in the middle, but I understand your point. The Potomac has always been a busy waterway. The problem is they were never meant to stay there. The salvage company moved them to a bay just off the Potomac that put the ships out of the main waterway, but was still easily accessible thirty miles south of DC. Their plan was to just keep them there, short-term. Except they went bankrupt during the Depression and the ships have been there ever since. Some of the ships were lined up and burned to destroy them faster, but you can't burn what's underwater, so that was never going to work. There are over one hundred and eighty-five wooden ships in the bay and a couple of latter-day metal additions, all just slowly falling apart and returning to nature. And when I say 'returning to nature,' I *really* mean it. The metal ships are rusting, but are still mostly intact, while the wooden ships are disintegrating from the water and the weather. Most of them are totally underwater at high tide, but those ships closer to the shore have become nesting islands for waterbirds, herons, osprey, and bald eagles. In fact, the site was proposed for national marine status in 2015."

"So where will she be? Where would he put her? She could be on any one of those ships."

"It looks like some of them are submerged all the time, so it won't be there, but other than that, any of the others could be fair game. What I'd like to know is how he's getting her out there."

"That one is easy," Webb said as they bulleted past a pickup truck overloaded with building supplies. "There are a ton of boat rental places up and down the Potomac where you can rent a boat by the day or even for only a few hours. I've done it myself. All he would need to do is rent a two-person kayak and then keep her sedated and drop a blanket or tarp over her while he's on the water and no one would be the wiser. The river can be busy on the weekends, but on a Monday morning, I bet he could slip around, unseen, while everyone is off at their day jobs. As far as where she is, don't forget we've got a secret weapon," Webb said. "Do you trust your dog?"

There was no doubt in Meg's mind. "Always."

"Then I think we need to leave it to Hawk," Webb said. "He'll know, and he'll get us there. He's a Lab, and he can probably swim better than us anyway. The rest is on us to get Cara to safety, and then we've got to run for Antietam." He glanced in the rearview mirror at Meg. "There isn't any way we can pull in anyone else? Someone to search for this other victim on the QT?"

"Do you know how many times I've nearly called Brian?" Meg could hear the edge of hysteria in her own voice and tried to curb it, pushing down the panic rising inside, not only for Cara, but for some unknown woman, another mirror image of herself, dying terrified and alone. "He threatened my parents. Sure, I could call them and tell them to keep an eye out for a maniac, but what if he just waits? Maybe he doesn't strike this week, but he'll do it next week, or the week after that. They can be as careful as they want, but he's already proven himself to be deadly. And it wouldn't be a game this time. There would be no clues. Just two executions." She swallowed hard, steadied herself. "No, this has to be us. In his mind, both women are going to die because he thinks the CRRU has been cracking the code and solving the riddles. He doesn't know it's been us for half the case."

"So we'll save them both." Webb's statement didn't allow for any alternative outcome. "That should make him go off the deep end. McCord, do we have any idea of what the second site might be?"

"Working on it. Okay, the first part of the clue was 'history was made nearby.' We know we're looking at Antietam, but this says not on the battlefield itself. Tie that in with the reference to 'treatment' and I think I've got a good idea for the location." He looked over his shoulder to see Meg peering at his monitor. He tapped a small square just to the east of the long, sprawling battlefield on the map, filled with red and blue bars and arrows indicating troop lines and movement. "The Pry House Field Hospital. Back in September of 1862 it was used by the Union Army as General McClellan's headquarters, but today it's a museum."

"There's no way he's got a victim stashed in a museum," Webb scoffed. "What happens when someone trips over her on a tour and sounds the alarm?"

"I'd be with you on that logic, except this museum is only open Thursday to Sunday."

"And today's Monday," Meg said. "The place would be locked up tight. And it's away from the main battlefield. No one would be going in or would be anywhere near the place."

"The worst that might happen is the cleaning crew

found her, but chances of that are pretty small. They'd probably either be going in Sunday night after closing or Wednesday before opening. If he got in earlier today, either by breaking a window or picking a lock, no one would even know she was there."

"Why is this place significant?"

"Because besides being McClellan's headquarters, it was also the emergency medical center run by Dr. Jonathan Letterman, the Union Medical Director. According to this website, it's considered the birthplace of battlefield and emergency medicine. But now we're into your area of expertise, Webb, not mine."

"Trauma response?"

"Right. We know we're going to be looking at something having to do with suffocation. And based on the location and the background, it's going to be some sort of battle injury that could lead to death by suffocation. So what could it be?"

Webb did a quick shoulder check and then darted around a bus lumbering along under the speed limit. "A couple of things. You could have crush injuries, like a horse falling on you after it was shot. But considering the Wiccan victim, I think we've been there, done that. Or you could have any number of injuries that breach the pleural space."

"What's that?"

"It's really a cavity, but in emergency medicine, we tend to think of it as the fluid-filled space between the two membranes that surround the lungs and separate the lungs from the chest wall. It maintains negative pressure in the chest—meaning less than atmospheric pressure—and this allows the lungs to expand and contract during normal breathing. But anything penetrating that space is catastrophic. If there is blunt-force trauma—say if you're hit by a nearly spent cannon ball—and your ribs are broken and pierce the pleural membrane, that negative pressure will go positive. Or if there is sharp-force trauma—maybe a shallow thrust of a bayonet—that breaks the membrane and lets in air, that's a pneumothorax. Or penetrating trauma—let's say a musket ball this time that not only pierces the pleural space, but also hits blood vessels—then there will be a buildup of blood. That's a hemothorax and that puts pressure on the space as well. The end result for all three is the same: the lung on the side of the injury collapses and you can't inhale and exhale, your oxygen level drops, and in severe or prolonged cases you suffocate."

"Nasty," McCord muttered.

"Definitely. There's also one other thing it could be. Those battles were fought in the woods and in the cornfields. There were hundreds or thousands of troops stomping through those areas. If they marched through a hornet's nest and stirred up a few hundred angry yellow jackets, anaphylaxis is also a possibility from an extreme allergic reaction. No EpiPens for a speedy save back then."

McCord was muttering and typing madly, clicking, searching. "Not anaphylaxis. Too early. Nobel prize for that research given in 1913." More searching and muttering. "Hemothorax standard practice of intercostal incision came about in the 1870s."

" 'Standard practice,' " Webb repeated. "Which means they were experimenting with it earlier. Given the time frame, we could be looking at early innovations during the Civil War. Believe me, with battlefield injuries, there were a lot of men to practice a new technique on."

"Okay, so that's one to keep in mind." More typing. Then he held very still. "Wait a second. I may have something here. Something better than the hemothorax. Dr. Benjamin Howard."

"Who is Dr. Howard?" Meg asked, leaning between the

front seats to look at the picture on McCord's laptop of a solemn man in a Union Army uniform, with a full beard and dark, wavy hair.

"Dr. Howard was the assistant surgeon who came up with the technique of hermetically sealing chest wounds to stabilize a pneumothorax."

"Smart guy," said Webb. "The number of deaths from pneumothorax dropped astronomically, once it was figured out that resealing the wound with an airtight dressing could reestablish the proper pressure and reinflate the lung. So, is this guy related to either Antietam or this field hospital?"

"Both. He served with the Nineteenth New York Volunteer Infantry Regiment as an assistant surgeon and was with them at Antietam. In fact, when their commanding officer, General Hooker, was shot in the foot, he treated him and got him back to active duty within only a couple of weeks."

Impatience was steadily building in Meg. She knew there was nothing they could do right now while Webb got them to Mallows Bay as fast as possible, but all this talking just made her want to *do* something. "Maybe I'm not following, but what does General Hooker's foot have to do with a suffocation injury?"

"Dr. Howard was the guy who figured out a way to treat the 'sucking chest wounds' killing so many Union soldiers. The injuries themselves might not be that serious, but men were dying anyway. He figured out that closing the wound with metal sutures, then bandaging the wound with alternating layers of linen drenched in thick syrup, which dried to become an adhesive film and created an airtight seal. He saw survival rates quadruple with this treatment. Think of the clue. 'Look to the man who deduced the treatment to save her.' That's our guy, Dr. Howard. He's telling us where to go, once we get to Antietam. That's how I got to the Pry House Field Hospital Museum. It all fits."

"If we're looking at a pneumothorax, you could be looking at someone who takes hours to die slowly. It would be exactly what this guy would need if he has to take two vics and hide them in separate, distant locations." Webb's eyes narrowed on the road, and Meg could tell his mind was somewhere else.

"What are you thinking?"

"I'm thinking I'm going to need some basic supplies on hand. Leave it with me." He glanced at the clock on the dash and pressed down harder on the accelerator, pushing them all back into their seats.

"You trying to get us pulled over?" McCord asked.

"A firefighter and an FBI K-9 handler on the way to an emergency? I could talk us out of a ticket and into an escort in about twenty seconds. I'd rather not waste time stopping, but if it happens, we'll use it to our advantage."

Meg met Webb's eyes in the rearview mirror, knowing all the worry swirling inside her was there for him to see.

"Hang in there," he said. "We'll be there before you know it."

Monday, May 29, 12:33 PM
MD-224 South
Nanjemoy, Maryland

"That's it—the dirt road to the right." McCord pointed at what looked like a double-rutted cart path about twenty feet ahead, mostly engulfed by trees and tall brush.

Webb hit the brakes, the back of the truck fishtailing slightly in response. A honk sounded behind them as he wrestled the truck around the sharp turn and into the lane. "Sorry," he muttered, raising a hand in apology to the driver behind him who was caught off guard by the sudden turn. He had to bring their speed way down on the bumpy, narrow road. "You're sure this is it? We meet another vehicle on this road and I'm not sure I'd be able to pass it."

"There's a paved road farther along that leads to a boat landing, but it's set back into an inlet that's the mouth of Mallows Creek and is surrounded by marsh. I've been studying Google Maps as we drove, trying to find the fastest way to get us there. This will take us almost all the way to something called Sandy Point. It's a little farther north of Mallows Bay than the boat launch, but this road will take us almost all the way to the shore. We can then run along the beach to the ships. I figured we'd make better time on foot over land than swimming through the inlet and out into the bay."

"Unless we're very wrong," Meg said, "we're going to be swimming no matter what. Water is the key to his plan."

"But the less we have to do, the better. The fleet goes a fair way out and we have no idea of where Cara is or what we'll need to do, once we get there, so we need to save our strength for when we really need it. I like to work out at the gym as much as the next guy—" He cut himself off to glance at Webb. "Okay, you're the wrong person to be sitting next to because you firefighters work out *a lot,* so let's compare me to the next *normal* guy. But I don't swim that much. Running, I'm your guy. If you go to Iraq and don't have the stamina to run like hell for long distances when needed, it's game over."

"You've probably got me beat there," Webb said. "But I could bench-press circles around you."

"Really? Want to put your money where your mouth is, fireboy?"

Meg studied the two men in the front seat, knowing their whole performance was to keep her distracted during a drive where she couldn't do anything other than focus on being helpless. "Hey." The men stopped comparing gym routines. "Thank you, both. No matter what happens, I owe you everything for trying. It's just . . ." She broke off, not even sure how to put the maelstrom of fear swirling inside her into words.

"No thanks required." McCord's tone was edged with something she hadn't heard before, and, for the first time, Meg had an idea of how terrified he was. He'd gotten to know Cara over the past month—had become friends with her—not as Meg's sister, but as a smart, independent woman who ran her own business and was working one-on-one with him and his beloved, and still slightly nuts, puppy. He had his own personal connection to Cara—maybe more of one than Meg suspected before now.

A connection she was more than willing to use because the only thing that mattered was Cara.

Webb slowed the truck as the road in front of them ended in a small clearing. He pulled off to one edge, the truck lurching slightly sideways on the uneven ground. "This is as far as we can go. Time to let Hawk lead us the rest of the way." He glanced at the dash. "Twelve thirty-five. We've got fourteen minutes to high tide. Let's move."

They jumped from the truck, Hawk leaping down behind Meg. She glanced back at the vest still lying on the seat of the truck, then slammed the door, leaving it inside. If she was right, and water was going to be their way in, he didn't need anything extra weighing him down. When they hit the beach, she'd even remove his collar. They were going into waters full of disintegrating wood and rusting ironwork. She couldn't chance him going in with anything that could catch his collar or pull him under.

She pulled on her SAR pack and turned to find Webb in the bed of the truck, a compartment open, pulling out items he was tossing to McCord. "What's that?"

"Anything we can carry that can withstand water and might be useful out there and not weigh us down too much." Webb eyed the pack on her shoulders. "Take that with you in case we need closer access to it, but leave it on the beach. You'll want to pull out anything useful you have. Small tools, a knife. Have you got pockets?"

"Would never go on a search without them. I buy these yoga pants specifically because I can move in them and they've got two big zippered thigh pockets."

Webb jumped down from the truck and slammed the tailgate back into place. He took a few items back from McCord to split the load, jamming them in his jeans pockets. "Do you need to give him her scent?"

"For Cara? No." She hunched down in front of her dog. "Hawk, we need to find Cara. Find Cara." She gave him the direction toward the beach and then followed as he broke into a run, his nose high in the air. The men fell into an easy jog behind her.

They worked their way toward the beach for the first few minutes. The call of gulls and the scent of river water drew them toward the shore, Hawk unerringly leading them through trees and underbrush toward sunlight flashing off water before them. They broke through the trees just as a *whomp-whomp-whomp* overhead heralded a double-rotor Sea Knight helicopter shooting into view to sail overhead across the Potomac, headed for Marine Corps Air Facility Quantico on the other side of the river. Hawk didn't give it even a glance as he stopped briefly to scent the air, and then headed south, toward the Ghost Fleet.

"Do you think he has her scent?" McCord puffed, jogging beside Meg. "Is it possible with this kind of breeze coming off the river and all the other smells?"

"You'd be surprised," Meg said simply, and left it at that. She trusted her dog. The scent he was looking for was one he knew intimately. All he needed was a single trace of her scent and he'd be after her. That he drove forward without hesitation gave her hope.

The beach below their feet had once been fine sand, but now was littered with shards of weathered, sun-grayed wood and strewn with denuded trees toppled from the forest, turning what could have been an easy jog into an obstacle course. Fronds of feathery seaweed, dotted with bright yellow starflowers, danced at the water's edge, swaying back and forth with the current. The fronds rolled perilously close to the smooth line in the sand clearly marked at high tide.

Cara's running out of time. Meg couldn't stop the thought from forming. She furiously pushed it away before it broke her concentration and swamped her with fear. *Just concentrate on finding and saving her. That's the only thing that matters.*

Hawk ran along the beach, staying just clear of the water, leaping over anything in his path. Balanced on four feet, he did better than the humans following him, who clambered less gracefully over any challenges blocking their path.

As they rounded a curve in the beach, the land before them split as the forest rose above their heads, the sharp edge of the eroded land forming a cliff, which fell vertically down to the water. The going became more difficult here, with only mere feet of beach as their path. But as they continued along the curve of the beach, the bay and the fleet came into view.

Meg's steps slowed for just a moment as she took in the area, trying to calculate all the possibilities at once. McCord's analysis of the bay was correct. It was only about a square mile in size, but the hulls of the ships were sandwiched together from shore all the way out to the Potomac proper. At the water's edge, the hulls of several beached ships sat five or six feet above the water even as high tide approached. The wood planks curving from bow to stern were weathered and warped, but still held firmly in place by hundreds of rusting nails. Nature was reclaiming her own with these ships, and the top of each was a lush mass of bushes with even the occasional tree standing tall over the water. At least a half-dozen ships scattered along the shore were their own individual ecosystems. Farther out into the water, just the tops of most of the vessels showed, but dotted above the water were spots of growth, bushes seemingly springing whole and hearty straight from the river. In the distance, the long hulking form of a metal ferry stretched across the far side of the bay.

Cara was out there somewhere.

With a sudden burst of speed, Meg recovered the few lost steps, falling back in with the group to follow Hawk as he cut right to tear down a narrow strip of beach projecting into the bay. The tiny spit of land was only about forty feet long; they were about to run out of beach.

The loud, clear whistle of a raptor sounded to their left, and Meg looked up sharply at what she could only describe as a warning. Piled in the prow of the boat sitting perpendicular to their path was what looked like a compact pile of sticks. Atop the sticks perched an osprey, sitting easily two full feet higher, her striking yellow eyes watching their every move as she guarded her nest.

Don't worry, Mama, we're not here for your babies.

She turned back in time to see Hawk run to the edge of the river and stop, his nose high, scenting the breeze.

Meg knew this posture; knew he was about to spring. "Hawk, stop. Come." She dropped her SAR bag on top of a sun-bleached pile of flotsam just beyond the high watermark on the beach. As Hawk returned to her, she unbuckled his collar and dropped it beside her bag. "Nothing on you for this swim, buddy. There's too much out there."

Straightening, she toed off her hiking boots to see Webb
and McCord pulling off boots and socks and dropping
their electronics onto the discarded clothes. Webb pulled
off his Henley for the simple white T-shirt underneath.

Meg dropped to her knees, rooting through her pack to
pull out her spring-loaded knife, a thick twist of cord, and a
couple of carabiner clips. She pushed the items into her
pockets, making them bulge, then turned back to her pack,
pulling out her waterproof cell phone. She made a quick call
to the Coast Guard, giving her FBI designation and re-
questing immediate assistance with a possible medical rescue at their location. She pushed her phone into one
pocket and then zipped them both shut. She glanced at the
men. They were ready.

"Be careful out there," she warned. "There's a lot of
metal and it's going to be rough and rusted. Chances of
getting sliced are high."

"I'm up to date on my tetanus shot," McCord said.
"Let's go."

Meg pointed out over the surf and out to the ships visible beyond. "Hawk, find Cara."

With a bound, Hawk ran to the river's edge and with a
leap of shining fur and outstretched paws, he hit deeper
water and started to swim. Meg and the men waded out
after him, quickly taking his lead to get their unprotected
feet off the rough, bolt-strewn river bottom. The cold
water was a shock to systems already overheated from a
sprint along the beach. Perhaps not cold enough to require
a wet suit, but for a moment, it took Meg's breath away.

"Son of a—" McCord's truncated oath came from behind, the splash of his strong strokes covering up whatever
else he might have said.

But Hawk never paused, seemingly oblivious to any discomfort in his drive to find Cara. He swam steadily, his
nose in the air, his breath coming harder with the addi-

tional exertion of swimming. He paddled across the bay, angled for the far shore, his path between shipwrecks narrow and treacherous. Iron bolts thrust into the air from wooden bases of ships resting on the bottom of the bay, double and sometimes triple parallel strips of long, lethal nails jutting above the water's surface. Partially intact hulls lurked just beneath the surface, the massive two-foot spikes used to hold the layers of planking together now reaching down into the water, ready to stab the unwary swimmer.

Depending on the location, swimming wasn't allowed in the Potomac under normal conditions, but in a place like this, an area that not only bordered on being designated a nature sanctuary, but was also a minefield of hazards to a soft-skinned human, it was simply banned. Obviously, with a sanctioned boat launch, canoeing and kayaking around the wrecks was allowed and encouraged, but the Maryland Parks Department would have something to say about this excursion after they found out.

Meg paused in the water for a moment, treading in place, scanning the terrain ahead. Hawk was about twenty feet in front of them. Beyond him, a forest of metal spikes and nails speared from the river into the air. Amid the spikes, a great blue heron seemed to stand directly on the water, its long, pointed beak angled toward them as they approached. Then it spread its magnificent wings wide as it launched into the air, away from the interlopers interrupting its fishing.

"You okay?" Webb asked, drawing up to tread water beside her.

"Yeah. Just trying to get the lay of the land. Let's go."

Webb stayed at her side as they swam, McCord right behind them, easily keeping up.

Meg kept her eye on Hawk the whole time. They'd performed water rescues before, but not one this far out in a large body of water, or with this level of hazard. But Hawk stayed strong. She could hear his panting breaths even this far behind, but considering the way her lungs were burning with exertion, she suspected hers were just as loud. They were easily five hundred feet from shore, and while most of the boats this far out were completely submerged at high tide, there were still several that rose above the river.

It was then that Meg heard Hawk's gurgle—part whine, part bark, both sounding half submerged—and the hair on the back of her neck stood up. Hawk was swimming frantically toward a vessel twenty feet in front of him. The stern of the boat disappeared below water, but the bow rose several feet into the air, propped on the skeleton of another ship. Greenery sprang from the front of the boat, but the hull of the boat from the midsection down spread wide to fall into the water as if all stern support was long gone. Hawk was heading right for the spot where the wooden planks sank under the water. He was trying to swim, scent, and alert all at the same time and nearly went under. Hard kicks drove him back to the surface as he struggled to the boat.

Meg turned in the water to Webb, still right beside her. "He's trying to alert. She's there."

Webb pushed even harder, pulling in front of Meg to reach the side of the ship first. He got one knee up on the side of the hull and hauled himself up. Reaching down to grab the dog behind his shoulders, he pulled Hawk out of the water and onto the hull, a full eighteen inches across, where he balanced as he scanned his surroundings. Staring at the middle of the boat, Hawk barked furiously.

Webb hauled Meg onto the deck next, but the boat shifted suddenly under the additional weight and they both lurched sideways as the support gave way beneath their bare feet. As Meg nearly toppled off the slippery wood, she had a glimpse of something that made her heart go cold. Cara had been in the middle of the boat, struggling as the water nearly covered her, her neck extended, lips tipped toward the last of the air. But with their additional weight settling the wreck, she went completely under.

"Cara!" Meg screamed even as she used her lack of balance to throw herself into the water, where she'd seen her sister disappear.

"Where?" Webb leapt in after her.

"Somewhere in the middle here. I saw her, but when the boat shifted, she went under."

"We can find her." McCord was swimming beside them now. "Go under. We'll bring her up."

They all dove. The river water was murky, full of particulate silt and algae, making it mostly a task of feeling for Cara, rather than looking for her. Meg dove, her hands outstretched, her fingertips touching soft, slimy wood, or catching on rough, uneven metal until—*Yes!*—she felt cloth. Her sister's shoulder. Her very limp shoulder, which Meg pulled, trying to pry her upward, but to no avail. Her sister's body rose an inch or two and then sank again. She frantically pushed back to gasp air, just as Webb and McCord were also breaking the surface.

"She's tied down somehow. I need to cut her free."

Webb turned to McCord. "Breathe into her mouth, give her your air. I'll go first, give me ten seconds and you follow. We'll alternate, giving Meg time to find the ropes and cut Cara free." He took a huge breath and disappeared below the surface.

Meg dug into her pocket for her knife. Pulling it above the surface, she pressed the button, the wickedly sharp blade springing free. She found Hawk, standing right where she'd left him, but looking like he was tempted to jump in and join the fray, something she couldn't risk now with a knife in the mix. "Talon, stay."

She and McCord both took a big breath at the same time and went under. Below, it was a hazy jumble of sunlight filtering through turbid water to partially light the way. Meg could just barely see the pass-off between Webb and McCord, Webb pushing off, and McCord dropping in to breathe precious air into her sister's mouth. *Trust them.* She turned away to concentrate on her own job.

She ran her free hand over Cara's shoulder down to her arm, which disappeared under her body. Using her sister's body to keep herself anchored, Meg found the cause of the problem—Cara's wrists were wrapped with cord looped multiple times around a thick beam. Meg got a finger under one loop of the cord and pulled, but it didn't budge. Lungs burning, Meg pushed back to the surface.

McCord was waiting as her head broke the surface. "Do you know how she's secured?"

"Looks like mountain-climbing rope. Static cord because it has absolutely no stretch, probably seven-sixteenths inch. I'll have to cut her out."

"Do it." McCord took another breath and sank under the water.

Meg took a few extra seconds to get her breath back. Before she could go under, Webb surfaced. "Update?"

Meg repeated what she'd told McCord. "How's Cara?"

"She's unconscious. Move fast."

Meg didn't respond. She simply pushed the terror of losing her sister to the back of her mind, took a deep breath, and then went under.

It wasn't possible to cut Cara lose on the first try. Meg got below, found a place where the cord wrapped the beam and started to saw at it. But the cord was tough, meant to support considerable weight and constructed of bundles of slimmer woven cords wrapped in a tough outer layer. It took her three tries to finally slice through the cord, then one more dive to unwrap the cord from around the beam. Freeing Cara's hands could wait until she was breathing on her own.

Just before the last dive, she found Webb above water, breathing hard with the exertion of providing oxygen for two people. "How's it . . . going?" he panted.

"This should be it. Give me ten seconds and then try pulling her up." She folded the knife and thrust it back into her pocket to free both hands and went under.

Back in the murky depths, she found the free ends of the cord and fought with it, unwrapping and untangling it until she felt Cara's body suddenly shift. Reaching out, she pushed against the man breathing for her—she thought it was Webb—and together they pulled her sister up and out of the water.

Cara's head lolled to the side as they broke the surface.

"Let's pull her up here," Webb ordered.

With McCord's help, they dragged her out of the water and up onto dry planking toward the bow of the boat. They laid Cara down on her back, awkwardly arched over her bound hands, and Webb went to work, launching into classic CPR with artificial respiration. Tipping her head back, he gave two strong breaths and did thirty strong chest compressions, followed by two more breaths, before repeating the cycle.

An engine in the distance caught her attention. Help was nearly there. Meg reached for her cell phone and contacted the Coast Guard again, updating them with their exact position. She needed them to arrive quickly so they could pass Cara off to the paramedics; then they needed to move fast. A second life was at stake. As she talked, she gave Hawk the hand signal to come and he leapt onto the planks to stand beside her, watching Cara closely.

Meg was just hanging up, when Cara gasped, then started to cough violently. Webb smoothly rolled her over on her side as she vomited up the water trapped in her lungs. McCord crouched by her, holding her shoulders, steadying her, as her body was wracked with spasms.

"The Coast Guard will pick her up here in just a few minutes," Meg said to Webb, before circling her sister to crouch beside McCord. "Cara? It's going to be all right. We've got you now." She pulled the knife from her pocket again, and made quick work of the cord binding Cara's hands.

Her sister blinked up at her dazedly and tried to form Meg's name on lips that didn't move yet.

Meg pushed wet strands of hair from her face. "Shhhh. Don't speak. You're safe now. Clay and Todd are here with me. They helped rescue you. And the Coast Guard is on its way." When she saw the question in her sister's eyes, she smiled. "Hey, if you can't call in a favor now and then, what's the point of working for the FBI?"

But Cara kept trying to say something, so Meg leaned in closer.

"Surprised me from behind." Cara's words were a rasping whisper, but clear enough to Meg.

" 'From behind,' " Meg repeated. "That's a new MO. Did you see him?"

Cara shook her head.

"He's changing his strategy. He knows the word is out about an Animal Control officer, so he's abandoned that method. Where did he grab you? At the school?"

Another nod.

"Can't this wait until she's checked out?" McCord asked. "We just got her back."

Cara looked up at McCord, and tried to give him a small smile. He picked up her hand and held it in both of his before bending his head to touch his forehead to it.

Feeling suddenly weak, Meg collapsed back onto the

rough planks of the vessel. Her limbs felt unbearably heavy and her mind dull. But the sunlight felt deliciously warm on her skin as they huddled out of the river breeze.

Webb reached over to rub a cold hand over her equally cold arm. "You okay?"

"Just need a minute." She met his eyes and kept her voice low. "We're not done yet. That's only one of two."

"I know." His gaze shifted to over his shoulder and she turned to follow it. A Short Range Prosecutor was on the river, coming in quickly, and then slowing as it reached the outskirts of the Ghost Fleet. Three men were on board, dressed in Coast Guard navy blue, with bright orange life jackets.

Meg leaned over her sister, who stared up at her with blurry eyes. "The Coast Guard is here, Cara. And they're going to get you to safety." She gripped McCord's forearm. "I need you to stay with her. Can you do that for me?"

"Don't you need me for—"

Meg squeezed harder, cutting him off. "She needs someone right now, and it can't be me. I have to go." She gave him a look that carried more weight than the pressure of her hand.

He nodded, knowing exactly what they were up against. "You know what you need to do and where you're going. Good luck. Let me know what happened, when you can, though I'm not sure how, because my cell is on the beach and my computer is in Webb's truck."

"We'll find out where they're taking her and go from there. And we'll grab your things on our way back."

She stood as the sound of the motor grew louder and the boat drew up to them.

One down. One to go.

CHAPTER 21

Sawbones: During the Civil War, amputation was believed to prevent infection or gangrene and was the safest way to deal with gunshot wounds caused by the Minié ball. The majority of the fifty-thousand-plus amputations were performed using the "circular" method, with the attending physician using a modified chain saw to remove a limb in less than ten minutes—thus the origin of the nickname "sawbones."

Monday, May 29, 1:44 PM
Pry House Field Hospital Museum
Keedysville, Maryland

Webb took the turn into the museum driveway with only the slightest drop in speed, causing them to bounce over the grassy border before skidding sideways. Meg clutched at the dashboard, while Hawk scrabbled to halt his slide on the floor in the back.

"Sorry," Webb ground out through gritted teeth as he white-knuckled the truck back under control.

Meg felt the jolt all the way down her spine as they lurched back onto the driveway. "Don't apologize, just get us there."

Nearly a quarter of a mile ahead, they could see the

house, a majestic redbrick Federal-style two-story dwelling sitting on a small hill, wrapped round with a white picket fence. They bulleted down the drive, screeching to a shuddering halt less than fifteen seconds later.

Meg and Webb threw open their doors. Meg grabbed for the SAR bag at her feet, while Webb opened the cab door on his side and called for her dog. Hawk threw Meg a quick look and she gave him the hand signal to go. She pulled on the pack and ran around the back of the truck.

"Hawk, come!"

They tore across the narrow space to the low, decorative fence and didn't even confer. They simply vaulted over it, landing on the neatly trimmed grass, and bolted up the hill, not bothering to take the stairs.

Meg reached the door first and grabbed the knob, rattling it. Locked tight. "He may not have come in this way. He might have found another way in."

"Doesn't matter where he got in. We're going in here." Webb pulled his Henley off over his head and wrapped it around his left hand. "I'm a firefighter. We don't pick locks."

He rammed his padded fist into the decorative leaded glass window and it shattered, glass raining down in musical shards onto the floor inside. He pulled off the Henley, and carefully threaded his hand back through the jagged opening and flipped the deadbolt on the other side. He extracted his hand and then pushed open the heavy front door, standing out of the way. "Go!"

Meg stepped into the front foyer, sweeping the loose shards of glass off to the side with her boot to protect Hawk's bare paws, all while taking a quick scan of her surroundings. Antique oak planking covered the floors, and the walls were painted a pale cream. Doors opened up on either side of the foyer, both rooms and the foyer itself filled with exhibits, the spotlights over them dark. A single flight of steps hugged the right wall of the foyer, disappearing into the upper level of the house. Meg bent down to her dog, running a hand over fur slightly crusty from his swim through murky river water. "Find her, Hawk."

Hawk took all of two seconds to scent the air; then he lunged for the stairs, leaping up them, his nails clicking on the hardwood floor. Meg and Webb followed, taking the steps two at a time to keep up with him.

"How does he know who he's tracking?" Webb asked. "He doesn't know her, and you don't have anything of hers for him to get the scent from?"

"He'll go after the freshest scent, which will be hers. Look at him! He knows exactly which way to go."

Hawk rounded the landing and took the last four steps in two springs. Without hesitation, he took off down the hallway, passing open doorways, lit only by the light pouring in through the uncurtained windows. He half slid as he took the corner too fast and headed straight for a doorway on the far side of the house. Meg and Webb pounded after him as he shot through the door, disappearing from view. Webb slowed enough to let Meg go through first and then followed her inside. They both jolted to a stop inside the room.

The far end of the room was a tableau of a Civil War operating suite, with an old door balanced on piled crates serving as a makeshift surgical table. Under the table lay a bloody sock and a blood-soaked boot. An open divided crate of replica medical supplies sat next to the table and green glass bottles were close at hand. A metal jug and bowl sat nearby. The figure of a bearded man in a Union uniform stood at the bottom of the table, partially bent over, his hands held out as if to cradle something.

But the figure on the table was not the mannequin intended to be part of the tableau. It was a woman, with pale skin and dark hair, bound to the table with cord, her hands secured beneath the table. Duct tape covered her mouth, adhering to the stark white skin of her cheek. Only the faintest sounds of labored breathing came from her.

Webb sprang forward, pushing past the display cases and into the tableau, now not just a re-creation of a battle-field memory, but a living nightmare. He stepped over the inanimate form of a prone man with blood pouring from his foot, no doubt the missing part of the tableau. He ripped the duct tape from the woman's mouth, but she barely responded to the sharp pain.

Webb started a lightning-fast assessment. "She's in respiratory distress. Blood on her shirt over the left breast." He unceremoniously ripped open the placket on the blouse she wore, buttons flying off to *ping* onto the floor. "Small wound, looks like a small penknife or maybe an ice pick, likely just a few inches deep from the amount of blood. No major vessels hit." He pressed two fingers against her throat. "Pulse is weak and thready. And we've got jugular vein distention and tracheal deviation." He leaned in close. "Ma'am? Ma'am, can you hear me?" The woman's eyes stayed closed, her features slack. He glanced back at Meg. "Call 911. We need an ambulance. I can hold her, but I need help."

Meg quickly made the call, once again giving her designation and their location. "Done, what else can I do?"

"Stand back in case there's some spray." His unflinching gaze met her expression of confusion. "We're in agreement with McCord's assessment of the situation?"

"Yes."

"What I see are all the indications of a late-stage pneumothorax. She's suffocating to death, to the extent her blood vessels are blowing up." He reached into his pocket, struggling against the damp denim, and pulled out a sealed plastic bag. "I don't need your permission, but I'm just letting you know I'm going to perform an invasive technique to hopefully save her. What I'd really like is a chest X-ray, but that's simply not happening. Without this procedure, I don't think she'll survive until the ambulance arrives. She'll go into cardiac arrest first."

"I trust you. Do what you need to do." Meg stepped back several paces. "Hawk, come." She pointed at the ground at her feet. "Sit." Hawk sat, but watched Webb with his tilted head.

Webb ripped open the bag and pulled out a pair of latex gloves, quickly tugging them on. Small squares came out next and he ripped several open to reveal alcohol wipes. His gloved fingers found the woman's collarbone, then moved down, finding the second rib and then the sunken soft spot between it and the third rib. He used the wipes to quickly disinfect the skin, and then he pulled out a long, thin object in a sealed sleeve.

Meg only had a moment to wonder what it was before he stripped it out of the sleeve and then out of the plastic holder it came in. She had to hold back a gasp at the wicked three-and-a-half-inch needle he pulled free.

Webb bent over the woman, found the spot again, and quickly, without hesitation, pushed the needle slowly into her chest. It penetrated one inch, then two; then a great gust of air whistled from the open end of the needle and Webb froze. "Gotcha," he murmured. Grasping the shaft just below the hub of the needle, he pulled upward, extracting the needle itself and leaving behind a sheath Meg hadn't even spotted before. Webb dropped the needle into the nearby metal bowl with a *clang* and checked the sheath. "The catheter is in place."

He bent over the woman again, who suddenly seemed quieter, and the deadly white of her cheeks flushed ever so slightly. "Ma'am, can you hear me? You're going to be all right. Can you hear me?"

The woman's eyelashes fluttered slightly and she moaned.

"How's she doing?" Meg asked, still not moving an inch.

Webb slid his fingers against her throat and paused for a moment before answering. "Better. She's going to need real medical treatment, but her pulse is steadier and her breathing is easier."

"What did you just do?"

He threw her a quick glance. "The original wound opened up the pleural space, which I told you about earlier. Her chest cavity was filling with air, compressing her lungs. A wound like that is like a one-way valve. Air could get in, but couldn't get out, and was building up in the chest cavity. I let that air out to relieve the immediate pressure. I've done it before, and when it works, it's pretty much instantaneous. It's stabilized her in the short term."

"Where did that"—Meg pointed at the woman's chest—"come from?"

"The needle catheter? You were busy with the Coasties when they came for your sister, but I grabbed one of them, explained who I was, told him I needed a few items and why, and he slipped them to me. I had to hope McCord was right, because I otherwise might not have the right supplies. If I didn't have those few things, I'd be doing CPR on her right now, and I'm not sure I could have held her." The far-off sound of sirens wailing slipped in from the distance. "Although they're coming in pretty quickly. From Sharpsburg, I guess."

"I didn't ask, but I'd guess that's their home base. Hawk, stay." Meg moved to the table to look down into pale blue eyes and a face that was, once again, startlingly like her own. "Ma'am, I'm Meg Jennings from the FBI. You're safe now. Can you tell us your name?"

The woman took a shallow breath. "Julie . . ." Another breath. "Moore."

"Okay, Julie. Is there anyone we can call for you? Someone to meet you at the hospital?"

"My . . . husband." She slowly gave his name and a phone number, which Meg put into her phone.

"I'll contact him as soon as I know where you're going." The scream of the siren came closer and then abruptly died. "I'll go bring them up," Meg told Webb.

Ten minutes later, Julie was strapped onto a gurney and being carried down the stairs, with Meg, Webb, and Hawk following behind. They stood aside as the paramedics loaded her into the ambulance, and then set off for Frederick Memorial Hospital, nearly twenty miles away, with lights and sirens going.

"Two women. I can't believe we actually pulled that off." Suddenly feeling a little unsteady, Meg reached out to grab the top of the picket fence.

"You okay? You've gone gray." Webb caught at her arms, steadying her when she started to sway, and then backing her toward the front steps to lower her down to sit. He crouched down in front of her. "What's going on?"

"I kind of didn't tell you, but I got a concussion on Saturday. Grade-three."

"*What?*" Concern streaked across Webb's face and the look he gave her was suddenly clinical as he assessed her.

She braced a hand against his shoulder. "I'm fine. I made it through everything today okay, didn't I?"

"Only by pushing it way more than you should have. Any headache? Nausea? Blurry or double vision?"

"I currently have one hell of a headache, but other than that, I'm fine. I think the adrenaline rush kept me pumped up enough that I wasn't feeling any symptoms until now. I'll go home and take a nap, I promise. Once I've seen my sister. And Julie." She gave a groan. "And talked to my boss. And probably his boss." She dropped her head into her hands. "They may fire me for this. I was told that under no circumstances was I to work this case while I was suspended."

Webb's eyes went to slits. " 'Suspended'?"

"Saturday might not have been my best day. Although since we saved a victim, I take that back, it was a good day." She gave him a wan smile. "I guess I need to catch you up on a few things—from the explosion we got caught in on Saturday morning to my meeting with the executive assistant director this morning, when he suspended me for disobeying a direct order."

He simply raised one eyebrow.

"I know we're starting something here, you and me, but I don't really know where the lines are yet. So maybe you'll give me a break this time?"

"Maybe. As long as you keep me in the loop next time. When you have someone special in your life, you can't keep that person in the dark about stuff like that. That goes for me too."

"Fair enough."

"Are you going to be in trouble for this?"

Meg sighed and leaned back on the step, bracing her elbows on the tread above. "Quite likely. My only saving grace is that Cara and Julie survived. If they'd died, my career would be over for playing fast and loose with lives like that. There'd never be a way I could explain myself out of it. But now, Hawk and I have a leg to stand on." She reached out and ran her knuckles over the line of his jaw, the stubble rough under her skin. "Two saves today for you. Not bad, Mr. Firefighter."

"I wasn't so sure about that last one, but yeah, not bad. Rescues are always a crapshoot. You never know what you're going to get or whether you'll get the victim out alive." He grinned and echoed her sentiments. "Today's a good day."

"It is." But her smile melted away and her voice went rock hard as she looked over his shoulder, out at the farm fields that surrounded the Pry House. "You know, there's nothing I'd like more than for him to take a shot at me right now. No more substitutes. *Me.*"

"Hey." The steel in his voice drew her gaze. "I want you to promise me not to do anything stupid."

"Like take him down?" she said sweetly.

"Jesus Christ, Meg, I'm not kidding. The man is dangerous."

"You think I don't know that? Do you think I can ignore what he did to those women?" Her voice became dangerously quiet, but the fury behind her words was unmistakable. "What he did to my sister?"

"And I don't blame you for being pissed, not that 'pissed' can even come close to describing what you must be feeling. If that happened to someone in my family, I'd be murderous right now, and not feeling one bit of guilt over it."

"I'm glad you see it my way."

"So I'd expect one of my brothers to step in and set me goddamn straight. And since you don't have a sibling handy who isn't involved, I'm going to do it for you. You're not thinking straight, and that's entirely justified. You need to not do anything stupid right now, or he wins. You can handle this one of two ways—stupid or smart. Stupid lands you in jail, or worse. Smart lands *him* in jail."

"Or worse."

"Yeah, maybe. But you've got the smarts and you've got some time. And you've got people willing to help. Don't you think we can outsmart one measly lunatic? Let's be smart, and make him pay. Only then will there be justice for all the women he's hurt. Including Cara."

Meg considered his words for a moment, then slid him a sideways glance. "I like the way you think," she said. "Now we just need to figure out how to get him."

CHAPTER 22

USS Indianola: In early 1863, the new ironclad *USS Indianola* was damaged after running aground in the Mississippi River near Vicksburg and was captured by Confederate troops. Union naval commander David Dixon Porter had his men construct a mock-up of a giant ironclad, painted black, and flying the "Jolly Roger." The ship sailed past Confederate shore batteries unharmed, and as rumors of a giant, invincible warship swirled through Vicksburg, Rebel salvage crews abandoned the *Indianola* without destroying her.

Monday, May 29, 6:21 PM
Inova Urgent Care Center
Woodbridge, Virginia

"There she is." Meg came through the door, half hidden by an enormous bouquet of flowers, Hawk in his FBI vest at her side. Webb brought up the rear, his arms full with several large paper bags, and he balanced a tray of fast-food drinks in his hands and McCord's messenger bag over his shoulder. McCord's boots dangled from where they were tied to the bag's strap.

Cara lay propped up in the hospital bed, while McCord slouched in a stiff plastic visitor's chair by her side, his bare feet crossed on the edge of the mattress while they talked. As soon as he saw them, McCord straightened, his feet slapping to the floor as the chair screeched back an inch on the tile floor. "There you are. All I got was the message 'Two for two.' You were successful?"

"We were," Webb said.

Meg set the flowers down on a table beneath the window and rushed to Cara, sitting down on the edge of the bed to catch her up in a tight hug. She gave herself a moment to just hold on, rocking her sister back and forth, until the gentle pat of Cara's hand on her back caught her attention. She pulled away, laughing. "You're not the one who's supposed to be comforting me. It's supposed to be the other way around."

"Clay caught me up with everything he knew. With the day you've had, I'm not sure who needs comforting more." Cara let herself fall back onto the pillows and looked her sister over with an assessing eye. "You look terrible."

Meg rolled her eyes. "Just another day at the office. But a good day." She glanced at Webb, who flashed her a quick grin. "Look, we brought food."

"You're an angel." Cara's gaze fixed on the bags in Webb's hands. "You did not go to Five Guys."

"We absolutely did." Meg reached for one of the bags, opened it and peeked in. The tantalizing aroma of grilled meat and fresh fries drifted out. "Got you a cheeseburger, Cajun fries, and a salted-caramel milk shake. You are allowed to eat, right?"

"Oh, I'm allowed. There just hasn't been anything here actually worth eating."

"That's what I thought." Meg dove into the bag and started handing out food.

Webb reached into his bag and pulled out a foil-wrapped burger, which he extended to McCord, who had just finished putting his socks and boots back on. "Hope a bacon cheeseburger, fries, and a chocolate shake is okay. I figured, you're a guy and we like meat." His eyes narrowed suspiciously and he pulled the burger back a few inches. "Unless you're one of those New Age vegan types."

"God forbid. Hand it over. It's been a long time since breakfast and I could eat the whole cow right now." He snatched the burger from Webb's hand. "Thanks."

Webb dragged a chair over to the foot of the bed, set out fries and drinks for himself and McCord, pulled out his burger and dug in. For a few minutes, the room was quiet.

McCord finally couldn't take it anymore. "You guys are killing me. I need details. Was the location right?"

Meg blotted a smear of grease from her lips with a napkin. "Sure was."

McCord turned to Webb. "Pneumothorax?"

"Yup." Webb took another bite of burger.

McCord continued to stare at them, his gaze darting from one to the other, his burger held loosely between his hands. Then he exploded with questions. "So what happened? What shape was she in? Who was she? Did you find any new clues about the perp?"

"Patience, Grasshopper." Meg sent McCord a sharkish grin in response to his outraged expression. "Frustrating, isn't it?" She laughed when he sat back in his chair and took a long pull of milk shake, glaring at her from under his brows. "I'm sorry, I shouldn't be teasing you, but this is the first time today we've had anything lighthearted to enjoy." She lay her burger down on its wrapper and studied her sister. "Are you okay discussing this?"

"If you try to handle me like I'm made of glass, we're going to have words." Anger glinted in Cara's eyes and she struggled to keep it under control. "He hurt me, and tried to kill me, but I held on until you got there." Her voice wobbled. "I knew you'd come for me. It was just a matter of holding on."

Meg grabbed her hand, holding on tight. "I will always come for you. He knocked you back a step, and, God knows, he knocked me back. But we're a team and we're going to catch him."

"I'm still a part of that team. I want to know everything. And then I want to help catch this son of a bitch and get some of my own back."

"Deal." Meg turned to McCord, but didn't release her sister's hand. "Okay, all the cards on the table so the four of us are on the same page. Her name is Julie Moore, and, no surprise, she looks very much like me. She's a pulmonary care nurse working with lung cancer patients at Georgetown University Medical Center."

"And there's your tie-in to the site and the kill method," McCord said around a mouthful of fries. He chewed and then swallowed. "Goddamn, but he does his research. Where did he grab her? There wasn't a dog found running loose this time, was there?"

"She owns a dog, but the dog wasn't with her when she was grabbed. She and her husband live in Silver Spring. She said she got up this morning to go to the gym, like she usually does. Tries to get there about five-thirty in the morning. She was running a little late today. When she got to the gym, it was dark. Dawn was still twenty or so minutes away. She parked in her usual spot, got out of the car . . . and that's all she remembers."

"There's your anesthetics at work," Webb said. "And the same pattern Cara reported. No interaction with the victim, just a quick snatch and grab in a predictable, but mostly untraveled, spot."

"I parked behind the school, like I usually do, to leave the parking spots out front free for clients. No one was around to see him grab me. I don't even know where his truck was, but it must have been nearby. Maybe parked near the empty unit next door."

"I'd really like to talk to Agent Rutherford about the change in pattern—he's either escalating or devolving. Clearly, he's seen McCord's article in the *Washington Post* and he's changed his MO accordingly. And there's one other thing I haven't had a chance to tell any of you. Karen Teller, the victim from Saturday, got a look at him. A good-enough look for one of our artists to do a forensic sketch. When I had a meeting with Peters this morning"— Meg tossed a quick look at Cara—"he told me he'd arrange for me to see it, in case the sketch rang any bells. Needless to say, I haven't seen it yet. Been a little busy."

Cara gave her a long look, like she was afraid to ask the question. "Did your meeting go well?"

"I didn't get fired."

" 'Fired'?" McCord froze with his burger an inch from his open mouth. "Because of us working this case?"

"No, it's more than that. I told you we got the victim safely out on Saturday before the building blew. But I didn't tell you the whole story. I kind of disobeyed a direct order from my supervising agent to not go in, when it became clear the demolition team wasn't in control of the explosives anymore. We made it out of the building with only seconds to spare, and then got caught in the shock wave from the blast. And I got concussed." She shrugged, as if to say, *What can you do?*

"And your supervisor was pissed. Even though *you* nearly got blown up."

"Oh yeah. So his boss, the executive assistant director, called me in for a little chat this morning. That's where I was when Cara was grabbed. When I called you, I was on my way back from that meeting at the Hoover Building."

"And he didn't fire you," McCord stated.

"He suspended me for a week, but he didn't fire me. And since I was supposed to take a week off for the concussion, he was basically making sure the department took a hard stance that didn't really hurt me in the end. He did, however, tell me under no circumstances to work the case while I was suspended. He's going to have some pretty big problems with what happened today."

"He doesn't know yet?"

"He probably does by now. I had no choice but to call Craig when we were on our way back from Antietam and tell him what happened after I left Peters's office."

"How did that go?" McCord asked.

"Let's put it this way," Webb interjected. "I was on the other side of the truck and I could hear every word he bellowed for a full two minutes."

"He wasn't happy," Meg translated. "Not only had I involved myself in the case while suspended, I hadn't informed anyone else at the FBI and insisted on trying to carry the whole thing off without the assistance of law enforcement."

"You told him Clay and Todd were involved?" Cara asked.

"I wasn't about to try to hide anything this time, so yes. Then I told him the unsub threatened Mom and Dad."

Finished his burger, Webb started on his fries. "He got quieter after that."

"I think I made my case there. This may sound stupid, but I think I'm getting a feel for how the unsub thinks. We play along within the rules he's set, and he'll respect them as well. If I'd cheated, if I'd called in the team, our parents' lives would be in his hands—today, tomorrow, or next week. We played by his rules, so I think they're safe, at least for now."

"But what will the consequence be to you?" Cara asked. "Mom and Dad wouldn't want you to lose your job because of them. They'd argue they could take care of themselves."

Meg just stopped herself from snapping out an answer and made herself take a breath. Cara didn't deserve to be the victim of her blinding headache and short temper. "With what you know of the man, do you really think they'd manage to keep themselves safe?"

"Not a chance, because this guy is insane and has zero boundaries."

"Exactly."

Webb tossed his empty wrappers into the paper bag and sat back with his milk shake. "We've learned something important about this guy today."

"That he can be in two places at once?" McCord asked.

"That's not what I meant, but you're right, he's organized and can move fast. No, I mean he's got medical training of some kind. When we found Julie, she was tied to a table, and all he'd done to her was a single stab wound. A single extremely precise stab wound in exactly the right place, at exactly the right depth, and with exactly the kind of weapon needed for the results he wanted. He didn't want her to bleed out and die. He wanted to collapse her lung and for her to suffocate slowly. In fact, his game was dependent on the fact she would die slowly. He set it up so it would take hours, allowing him to drive back to Arlington, take Cara, and put her life in danger, all long before Julie's condition became critical. That kind of precision requires very specific knowledge."

"You could do it?" Meg asked.

"Yes. You're likely looking at someone within the medical field, or with medical training—a paramedic, nurse, doctor, or med student. That also ties into the use of anesthetics. Before, we just thought we were looking at someone who had some sort of access to anesthetics. But this is someone who also knows specifically about human anatomy."

"Keeping the profile in mind, Rutherford would disagree with the paramedic, doctor, or nurse," Meg said. "But maybe you have something with the student. Maybe someone who washed out, couldn't cut it, and then had to fall back on another career?"

"And then there's the keywords," McCord added. "The first two you were able to pass off as general knowledge that would be found online or in newspapers. But we've gone past this now, haven't we? I think we're looking at someone with a personal connection to you."

Cara frowned, her brow deeply furrowed. "I don't like how personal that connection is. Like inside-our-house kind of personal. Knowing what Maimeó called me, that's beyond any keyword we've had so far."

"I know. I need to totally reevaluate that list I made. No one on it seems right now."

"That was really solid work by all of you though. Real teamwork. Meg, you figured out the keywords and then you and Hawk found both your targets." Cara turned to McCord. "You solved the ciphertext and then the riddle—and were right both times—without having ever done it before. Amazing!"

McCord's cheeks flushed a ruddy red at her praise. "Couldn't have done it without watching you do it first. Though I'm sure I wasn't as fast as you."

"You were fast enough to save two lives. And Todd—" She met Webb's eyes from where he sat at the end of the bed. "I don't know how to thank you. Your quick thinking and skills saved my life. And Julie's."

"All in a day's work." But Webb bent his head in acknowledgment. "I'm just happy I could help. But that brings something else to mind. I think McCord is right—

this is someone you knew. But not necessarily someone you know now, or at least know well. I don't think he knows who you interact with now."

"Meaning someone with the kind of medical skills that could save someone from a life-threatening pneumothorax? No, I imagine not."

"I think he was counting on both women dying." Webb glanced at Cara. "Sorry."

"Don't apologize," she said. "We need to reason this out. So you think he was counting on it to wreck Meg?"

"Yeah." He pinned Meg with a laser-sharp look. "He takes two women, and one of them is your sister. He threatens to kill your parents if you bring in any official help, so you're between a rock and a hard place. Someone is going to die."

"You mean *may* die," Meg interjected.

"No, I mean *will die*. I'm trying to put myself in his perverted shoes. You're without your team at the FBI. So even if you can crack the code, you're going to be in over your head. Let's say you manage to get to your sister in time. Lots of people know CPR, and if you ever took lifesaving in swim class, you may even know how to deal with a drowning victim. In this fictional version of events, you get to your sister, save her from drowning, because you get there before she goes under, pass her off to the Coast Guard, and then get to Antietam. At that point, there's no way in hell you save that victim. Hell, if McCord hadn't figured out her condition before we got there, I wouldn't even have been able to save her without the ability to dart her."

" 'Dart'?" Meg asked. "Is that what you call that procedure?"

"That's what paramedics call it. Officially, it's a 'needle decompression of the chest.' "

"What on earth did you have to do to this woman?" McCord looked horrified.

Webb quickly outlined what he'd done to save Julie's life. "I got the supplies from the Coasties while they were picking up Cara. Without your call on the pneumo, I wouldn't have asked for the right equipment, and I'm not sure she would have made it. I could have done CPR to try to hold her, but I don't think it would have worked. And I'm a professional." He turned to Meg. "Julie would have died. And that would have torn you up, which was the whole point." His expression turned speculative. "I think I might know what he has in mind."

"Really?" McCord leaned forward. "Enlighten us."

"What if this whole thing today was to crush Meg? Working under the assumption that what he's been trying to do all along is get her off her game, what if this is the penultimate move? She's his final target, but unless he's an idiot—and I don't think he is—he knows she's smarter and stronger than he is. He's not going to win against her if she's at the top of her game." His gaze dropped to Hawk, lying on the floor with his ears perked, listening to every word. "He's especially not going to win against the team of Meg and Hawk. So he needs to boost himself on the playing field by putting her at a disadvantage. And what better way to do that than two women, two carbon copies of herself, dying because she failed to save them."

"You think he's ready to move on her," Cara stated. "That she's the next target. Or, more sensibly, that Hawk might be the next target just before he takes Meg out."

"Yes."

"Good." The cardboard sleeve that had held her fries crumpled under the force of Meg's clenched fist. "Bring it on. Not that I'd let him get within fifty feet of Hawk."

"We've already had this conversation today." Webb's tone held a warning.

"I know, I know. 'Smart, not stupid.' But I'm tired of playing his game and waiting. I'm ready for him."

"So why don't we force his hand?" When everyone stared at him, McCord continued. "Let's set up a sting. Make him think poor little ol' Meg is a shattered shell of her former self because Julie Moore died. Maybe she's even been fired from the FBI because she went rogue and tried to work the case on her own."

"Better still," said Cara, "what if her sister died? Then she'd really be a mess."

Meg leaned back in her chair, her lips twisted in a grimace of horror. "Don't even say that."

"But you would be. You'd be a mess. And vulnerable. In other words, the perfect target. But how do we get that message to him?"

"That's where I come in," McCord said. "What story do we want? I'll put it on the front page of the *Post* so he can't miss it."

"That would be perfect." Cara's smile was full of calculation. "He's been in control up to now. This time, we'll be calling the shots and setting it up." Her face clouded. "But what if he's been watching somehow and knows I survived?"

"That's easy," Webb said. "McCord's article will tell the story of your death tonight from secondary drowning. It's rare, but it does happen. You have a drowning, or near drowning, and you think the victim has come through with flying colors. But up to twenty-four hours later, there can be water still trapped in the lungs that causes pulmonary edema. If untreated, it can cause death. So the story is Meg tries to save both vics on her own and fails spectacularly. Julie dies on site. Even if he was watching at Antietam, all he'd have seen was a body on a stretcher rushed down the stairs and into a waiting ambulance. We can't call death at the scene, so you get to the hospital to be pronounced DOA. Then Cara dies after being rescued. She has one brief moment of hope that her sister made it, which then is cruelly crushed when Cara suddenly dies at the hospital. The FBI fires her, and then what does she do? Where does she go?"

"I can tell you the answer to that because it's happened before." Meg's voice was expressionless. "I tuck my tail between my legs and go home to my parents' rescue."

"Hey!" Webb's tone was sharp with rebuke. "We've had this conversation before too. You didn't tuck your tail between your legs. You lost a partner violently and you needed to get your balance back. There's a difference."

Cara nodded, but McCord simply looked confused, his gaze jerking from Meg to Webb and back again.

Meg took pity on him. "He's referring to when my K-9 Deuce was killed on the job with the Richmond PD. I resigned from the force and went home." She turned to smile down at her dog. "To you, as it turned out."

Hawk's tail thumped happily on the floor.

"Maybe we can use that. With your permission, of course," McCord added quickly. "What if the story is that you're suspended and under review, so you quit in retaliation? You've done it before, so you do it again, that kind of thing. We tell him exactly where you've gone, maybe through a quote from one of your team members, and then we wait for him to show up."

"How exactly are you going to convince your bosses to do this?" Meg asked.

"Am I going to get an exclusive and be able to talk about my own part in this case as soon as it's all over?"

"You know I have to get Bureau approval for it, but I think we can swing it."

"Then I won't have any problems selling it to my editor. He lights up like a Christmas tree whenever the word 'exclusive' is uttered."

"I need to call a meeting tomorrow." Meg picked up her milk shake from Cara's side table, fiddled distractedly with the straw, and then set it down again, untasted. "Everyone needs to be in on this. The whole team, including Craig, Rutherford from the BAU, and any involved agents. And I'd really like Peters to be there."

"You don't think he'll just shoot the whole plan down?"

"Maybe? But he suspended me, so for me to attempt to do an end run around that suspension, even with the goal of saving other lives and trying to protect my own, I'm going to need his blessing if I have any hope in hell of keeping my job."

"And if he doesn't give you his blessing?"

"Then my life is worth more than my job and we're still going after him." She pulled out her cell phone. "I need that sketch. Hold on, I'm going to see if Brian has access to it." She shot him a quick text. The reply came back almost immediately. "He's got it. Craig sent it out to the team—well, the active members of the team—this afternoon. He'll forward it to me in a few minutes." She sat back in her chair, her phone in her hand, waiting for the e-mail to arrive. "Cara, let's think about this. Deuce, Hawk, and Haven, those are names that are easily accessible."

"It wasn't until Marlowe came up that we started to suspect someone with deeper access. I was about three-and-a-half when we got Marlowe."

"And I was five. But he lived to fourteen. So there are potentially a lot of people who came in and out of our lives during that window."

"You said Rutherford thinks the suspect is about the same age as us, right?"

"Late twenties to midthirties, so yeah."

Cara stared up at the ceiling, her eyes unfocused. "So we're talking about someone we may have met in elementary, middle, or high school."

"What about outside those circles?" Webb suggested. "Unless you hung with someone who gave you a weird vibe, I suspect this kid was something of a loner. Someone on the outside looking in. If he'd been a part of your group, there wouldn't be this kind of hostility."

"I just . . ." Meg struggled to put her reservations into words. "I just can't figure how I alienated someone this badly as a child or teenager that he'd need to kill me now."

"You may not have ever known you'd done it, which is why nothing is leaping out at you."

"When we sat down last week, I didn't put anyone from this period of my life on the suspect list. In fact, we specifically only looked at when I was an adult."

"Maybe that was our mistake," Webb said. "I'd suggest this person might have been older than you, maybe one of the adults you associated with, but that goes against the profile. How much faith do we have in the profile?"

"I'd put a healthy amount of stock in it. Rutherford and the BAU team are good. And while it seems like hocus pocus to outsiders—virtually like they are pulling a rabbit with these specific characteristics out of a hat—there's solid science and experience backing them up. I trust Rutherford's profile. They all have a little wiggle room— he estimates ages to be between late twenties to midthirties, so it might be midthirties to late thirties, but it won't be midsixties."

"Good enough for me," Webb said. "So then think about this. The name of your dog is one thing, but your grandmother's pet name? That makes me think this person has been in your house or your backyard. Or somewhere in your neighborhood. Your grandmother came to visit?"

"She did and still does. She's a widow now, but back then she and Daideó would often come together. They were Irish, born and bred, but moved to America after they got married. My father was born in New York City. Our Daideó worked in finance and Maimeó stayed in town after he died. She loves the vibrancy of the big city and all the conveniences. But, at the same time, she still loves coming out to the rescue and staying for weeks at a time to enjoy the quieter life."

"Best of both worlds," McCord said.

"Absolutely. Back when we were kids, Daideó's vacation time was sometimes limited, but he was all for Maimeó hopping on a train and coming down to stay with us. We lived in Charlottesville at the time, and she'd pop in and stay for a week or more. Sometimes longer in the summer, which let Mom and Dad occasionally get away on their own for a bit. So all our friends knew her."

"And did she call you those pet names on a regular basis?"

"All the time. And we were a busy household. Kids were always running in and out. Mom was always of the opinion the best way to keep your eye on your children was to make your home the neighborhood hub. You were overrun with kids, and your fridge was constantly being raided, but you knew where your kids were and who they interacted with. A couple of kids were nearly permanent fixtures."

Cara grinned at the memories. "Marty practically lived at our house. I swear he had a crush on you."

"*Did not.* Just because my best friend was a boy didn't mean we liked each other that way. What about Dory? She was practically your Velcro twin."

"She really was, wasn't she? I wonder what she's doing now?"

"Isn't that what you're supposed to use Facebook for?" Meg froze for a second. "Facebook! Maybe we need to look some of these kids up. Do we think someone like this would have a social media profile?"

"I have no idea, but let's see." Cara pointed at the messenger bag Webb had put down when he came in. "Clay, is your laptop in there?"

"Sure is. Let's crack it open." He got up and returned

with the bag, already pulling out his laptop. He perched it on the side of the bed, booted up, and logged on. He passed it to Cara. "You've got a Facebook account, or do you need to use mine?"

"I've got one because I need a personal account to manage the page for the school. Facebook is a necessary evil for self-promotion."

"Amen." At Cara's surprised look, McCord grinned. "Gotta promote my writing and all that."

"Makes me glad I don't have to deal with that stuff," Meg said.

"Amen," repeated Webb dryly.

Cara logged McCord out of his account and then logged into hers. "Okay, so let's think about this. We're looking at men, somewhere around our ages, with say three or four years on either side. We can search by our schools and go from there."

While Cara started paging through profiles, Meg checked her mail. "Brian's e-mail is here." She opened up the attachment. The pencil sketch filled the screen, depicting a man, very likely in his early to midthirties. He had a very square jaw, high cheekbones, and sported a Van Dyke beard. He wore a baseball cap that came down low over his forehead, partially blocking his eyes, which were darkly shaded. No hair showed from under the cap, suggesting a short haircut. The long nose ran at a slightly crooked angle, as if it had been broken and not healed correctly. His neck was thick, suggesting a muscular build. Meg took a long moment to study the sketch. There was something here, something that pulled at her, but nothing she could put her finger on. She held out the phone to Cara. "Take a look at this. There's something familiar here, but I can't place it."

Cara took the phone and spent a long moment looking down at the sketch. "Yeah, I know what you mean." She looked up to meet her sister's eyes. "We know this person,

I can feel it. He never let me see him because he was afraid I'd be able to identify him. Maybe this sketch just isn't exact enough? Karen may only have had a glimpse of him and was struggling to get away, so she didn't take in enough details?"

"It's possible, but our sketch artists are good. You'd be surprised what they can get out of a victim. No, I think the problem is we're looking at a mature man and comparing it to someone from fifteen to twenty years ago."

"Okay, let's keep that in mind while we look at people. You know what we really need? Our old yearbooks."

"That can be for tomorrow, if we don't find anything here. The problem with yearbooks is it's still the same young faces. We need to find those people now to compare them."

"I've gone through anyone associated with our elementary school. I can't see anyone there that fits. I'm now into Buford Middle School alumni." She paused, scanning the faces in the photo section. "So many memories. Penny Hollens and Marsha Brooks. Holly Simpson. Remember Mark Douglas? Everyone thought he was hot back then and wanted to date him." She tilted her head and looked at the screen. "Today he's bald and works for an accounting firm. Now I'm always going to think of him this way. Thanks for nothing, Facebook. And look, there's an old shot of Marty Garber. Look at those buckteeth. That was before the braces went on. Wonder what he's doing now. They moved away when . . ." Her voice trailed off. "Meg . . . can I see your phone?"

"Seriously? *Marty?* No way." But Meg passed over her phone.

"Wait . . . okay, here's a current picture of him." Cara held Meg's phone up beside the on-screen image. "No, you're right, it's not him. But look at this." She angled both the phone and laptop so Meg could see it.

Webb stood up and moved to stand behind Meg's chair. "You can see the similarities, but it's not quite right. You're sure we can trust the sketch?"

"Yes. Besides that, he just doesn't feel right to me. There'd be no reason for him to have this kind of hostility. He practically lived at our place some days. He'd basically hide out with us. There were sometimes problems at home with—" She cut off with a gasp, staring wide eyes at her sister.

"Derek." The two sisters said the word in unison.

"Could maybe be him, aged nearly two decades. If so, he slimmed down and muscled up a lot," Cara said. She held the phone up to the screen again. "Look at it again, not as a match, but as a relation."

"I can see it," Webb said. "Who's Derek? A brother?"

"Older brother." Meg sat down heavily in her chair. "Marty was just your everyday kid, into sports and comics. But Derek. Looking back now, I realize he was always a strange kid, a kid who always seemed to be on the outside watching, but not a part of any group. He wasn't very social, and when he was forced to be with a bunch of kids, someone always ended up getting hurt. Other kids didn't want to spend time with him, and he became even more withdrawn. It was a vicious cycle. Marty was mostly a happy-go-lucky kid, and he didn't want to get sucked into the drama or be singled out as the brother of the weird kid, so he hung out a lot with us. Honestly, even at the time, I wondered if he was scared of Derek. But as a kid, I would have just chalked it up to a big-brother relationship, not the development of a psychopath."

"Did Derek try to hang with you guys?" McCord asked.

Cara flinched. "He did. And we lied to him a few times and said Marty wasn't with us, when he was. He must have known, but he couldn't prove it."

"You don't honestly think that's the reason for this. That he's so disturbed we didn't include him that women have to die to make me pay?" Meg shook her head. "I just can't believe it."

"I agree. There has to be more to it. Have you run into him since they moved away? How old was Derek then? Thirteen?"

"Marty was twelve, so thirteen seems about right. I haven't seen him, not that I can remember, but now I really need to think about this."

"Is there anything that leads you to a Civil War connection?" McCord asked. "Did he show an interest as a kid?"

Meg shook her head and looked to Cara, who simply shrugged. "Not that I remember. It wasn't anything his father had an interest in either. But they moved to Mississippi, and I understand Confederate culture in some of the southern states is still alive and well in a big way. It may have been something he discovered as a teenager or young adult." Meg's phone chimed and she picked it up, read the message and sighed. "Oh yeah, I forgot to tell you something."

Cara narrowed her eyes at her sister's subdued stance. "What?"

"Mom and Dad will be here in five minutes. They're just parking the car."

"*You told them?*"

"How could I not tell them? They're your parents. Can you imagine how hurt they'd be if they found out about it later? You nearly died."

"You made sure I didn't." She wilted under Meg's unblinking stare. "Yeah, yeah, I know. I just didn't want to worry them. I kind of thought maybe we wouldn't tell them."

"If you're going to officially be dead in Wednesday's

paper, I think you should tell them ahead of time," Mc-Cord gently reminded her.

"You have a point. Especially if they're going to be involved in this sting you want to pull off. This might be a good time to explain it to them."

"While everyone is here to convince them of it? That might make it easier."

A few minutes later, Eda and Jake Jennings came through the door and made a beeline for the hospital bed. McCord pushed his chair back out of the way and stood, watching as Eda hugged her daughter and Jake stood with his hands on both their shoulders.

Feeling strangely separated, Meg stood on the other side of the bed, apart from her family. For the first time, she considered her parents might blame this on her and her job. That she had brought this kind of danger into Cara's life.

But Jake seemed to sense Meg's discomfort, his gaze finding his oldest daughter. He immediately circled the bed, pulling her into his arms. "Don't go there, Meggie. It's not your fault, and we would never think it was." He pulled back and tipped her chin up with his fingers. "You saved our girl."

"*We* saved her." She pulled back from her father. "Dad, I'd like you to meet two amazing men. Todd Webb, firefighter and paramedic, he saved both Cara and a second victim today, bringing them both back from certain death. And Clay McCord, the brains behind our operation today. He figured out the codes and the riddles and got us to where we needed to be in time for Hawk to find each victim and Todd to save them."

Jake moved from Webb to McCord, shaking each man's hand and expressing his sincere thanks. Then Eda hugged both of them.

A nurse came in to check on Cara, saw the added visitors, and brought in more chairs.

"Don't you want to head home and get some rest?" Eda laid a hand against Meg's cheek. "You look exhausted. You're not driving home, are you?"

"I'm driving, Mrs. Jennings," Webb said. "She can nap on the way, if she needs to."

"Actually, we'd like to talk to you and Dad." Meg sat down in one of the chairs and patted the one beside her for her mother. "We have a plan and we're going to need your help."

CHAPTER 23

Smoke screen: Smoke can be released to mask the presence or movements of military units. The blockade runner *CSS Robert E. Lee* used smoke to successfully evade the *USS Iroquois* and run the Union blockade in January 1863.

Tuesday, May 30, 11:00 AM
Fourth-floor conference room, J. Edgar Hoover Building
Washington, DC

Meg purposely timed her entrance into the conference room for the moment the meeting was supposed to start. She didn't want to be pulled into a corner by Craig or even Peters for a private reaming before she'd had time to propose her idea to the whole room. She might be fighting for her life, but she was also fighting for her career.

All the pieces were falling into place. Brian had played go-between for her, arranging the room and for all the players to be in attendance. Meg and Cara spent the morning refining their theory of the suspect. The Jenningses were on their way back to Virginia to prepare. McCord had spent a full thirty minutes closeted with his editor setting everything up from his end. And Webb, who was supposed to be on shift overlapping the beginning of the operation, had talked to his commanding officer, laid out what they were up against, and was granted the time off to join the team.

Meg entered the room with Hawk at her side, and Cara, McCord, and Webb following. A quick scan of the room told her Brian had done his job and had gotten everyone there as promised: Craig, Peters, Rutherford, the Human Scent Evidence Team, and any agents involved in the case. She met his eyes across the room and knew her thanks were conveyed by his single, subtle nod.

"Good morning. Thank you all for agreeing to meet this morning." Meg moved to the head of the table, while Cara, Webb, and McCord went to the back of the room to take chairs against the wall.

"This better be good, Jennings." Peters's words were clipped, like he was just holding on to his temper. "For someone who is twenty-four hours into a one-week suspension, you're not doing a good job of staying out of this case."

"Sir, I didn't have any choice, but I'd like to explain that to all of you." She turned to Rutherford, who sat near the head of the table, across from Peters. "Agent Rutherford, thank you for coming all the way from Quantico on such short notice. Your presence this morning is especially needed."

Rutherford silently tipped his head in acknowledgment.

Meg bent down to Hawk and quietly commanded him to go to Lacey. He trotted around the table and lay down on the floor next to the German shepherd at Brian's feet.

Meg turned to face the room, feeling the force of everyone's gaze like a tangible weight. "Yesterday morning, I was suspended by EAD Peters for my actions on Saturday morning while rescuing Karen Teller from the basement of the Teller and Sons furniture factory in Gettysburg, Pennsylvania. I was relieved of duty for a full week as a result of my failure to obey a direct order from SSA Beaumont.

However, as I was exiting EAD Peters's office, I received a number of text messages from my sister's cell phone." She pulled her cell phone from her pocket and turned on the screen. She'd previously set up the phone to display the messages as she'd seen them yesterday, starting with the picture of Cara, limp and bound, on the floor of the suspect's van. She handed the phone to Peters, who slowly scrolled through the messages, Craig reading them over his shoulder.

"I was told in no uncertain terms my sister, Cara"—she raised one hand to indicate her sister at the back of the room—"had been taken and her life was in my hands. Not only that, a second victim had been kidnapped as well. I was to tell no one in law enforcement, and was given two separate coded messages that would indicate the locations of the missing women. It was then up to me and Hawk to find and rescue the victims. To ensure both my silence and compliance, the lives of my parents were threatened." Meg paused as Peters went through the messages, waiting until he looked up and met Meg's eyes. "I had no other choice, sir. I know you offered protection for my parents, but I felt that would not be sufficient. This suspect has proven himself a competent planner. I knew he would simply wait until he had a clear shot and then he'd kill them. No game, no warning. Just murder."

Peters's laser stare pinned her for the space of several heartbeats before he gave a reluctant nod.

"I felt my only option was to proceed according to his rules, which actually gave me some leeway. I enlisted the help of two people, neither of whom is law enforcement, but both with much-needed skills. Clay McCord, the *Washington Post*'s top investigative reporter, cracked the codes and solved both riddles. Lieutenant Todd Webb, an officer with the District of Columbia's Fire and EMS Department, was paramount to our ability to save the victims once they were found."

Heads swiveled to the back of the room to where Mc-Cord and Webb sat. Even for those unfamiliar with Mc-Cord's byline picture in the *Post*, there was no mistaking the men, since Webb had come that morning dressed in his navy DCFEMS uniform to add an air of official expertise to her team.

"With the help of Mr. McCord and Lieutenant Webb, we were able to not only locate the victims who were in very disparate locations, but also to save both their lives."

"What were his methods this time?" Rutherford asked. "I assume he held to his previous method of changing the kill method each time, based on the victim."

"Your assumption is correct." Meg opted to follow Rutherford's previous lead, naming the victims by their first name to humanize them. "For Cara, it was drowning, based on the fact our great-grandfather drowned during the sinking of the *USS San Diego* during World War One. She was taken out to the remains of the American World War One Ghost Fleet in Mallows Bay, near Nanjemoy, Maryland, just upriver from the Aquia Creek Landing, a major Union Army port along the Underground Railroad in 1862. She was tied to the remains of a warship and left to drown as the tide came in. The second victim, Julie Moore, a pulmonary care nurse who cared for lung cancer patients, was actually taken earlier in the day and hidden in the Pry House Field Hospital Museum on the outskirts of the Antietam Battlefield outside Sharpsburg, Maryland. The museum is only open from Thursday to Sunday, so it was unoccupied at the time. Julie was stabbed—a single, very precise wound, exactly placed so she wouldn't bleed out. Instead, the injury induced a collapsed lung on that side—called a pneumothorax—which would lead to a very slow suffocation death, the kind of death that takes hours. Lieutenant Webb's knowledge and skills as a paramedic enabled him to save her, chiefly because Mr. McCord predicted her method of death in advance. That allowed Lieutenant Webb to have on hand the supplies needed for the required invasive procedure.

"There was a significant change in the suspect's modus operandi this time. There were no dogs involved, no public note left in my name. Instead, he had a direct conduit to me through my sister's cell phone, and it allowed him to deal directly with me for the first time."

"Mr. McCord's article in the *Post* warning women about the attacker likely precipitated that change," Rutherford stated.

"In your opinion, sir, is the suspect escalating or devolving at this time?"

"I don't know enough yet, but from what you've told us so far, he's simply compensating. You've blocked his proven method of luring his victim, so he's taking a different tack."

"This time, he didn't lure them at all. Both times, the victim was attacked from behind and overcome with inhalation anesthetics. He picked remote or low-traffic predictable areas to do so. For Julie, it was the dark parking lot at her gym at five-thirty in the morning. For Cara, it was in the deserted area where she parked her car behind her obedience school before a regular private lesson. Due to the nature of the attacks, neither victim saw the suspect. When both of them regained consciousness, they were already at the kill site and the suspect was gone."

"How did he manage to take two victims?" Brian asked. "How did he manage to put them both in life-threatening situations, where you still had time to rescue them? And why would he go to that trouble?"

"He took the victims sequentially. Julie was taken first and then moved to Sharpsburg. She was stabbed and left to die. He then got back to Arlington in time to take Cara out to Mallows Bay. As far as why go to the trouble, as best we can tell, it's all part of the game to him, and the game is sacred. It's almost like he considers it unsporting if I don't have a chance to make the save."

"It's all part of his intention to torture you," Rutherford said. "But it must be frustrating the hell out of him, because he's being trapped in his own rules."

"What do you mean?"

"You're not supposed to keep winning. Sure, he could just find women who looked like you, kill them, and hide the bodies for you to find, but where's the adrenaline rush in that? The excitement is part of the game for him. The thrill of the kidnap, of pitting his wits against yours." Rutherford turned to take in the team at the back of the room. "Or you and your team, as the case may be. This tells me the victims are incidental. Their deaths are incidental. The thrill for him is the game. He actually doesn't care if they live or die, so long as you think they might die. His thrill comes from making you suffer through the game. The victims are merely pawns."

Cara made a sound from the back of the room that was almost a growl, and Meg looked up to see her poised to spring out of her chair. McCord had one hand clamped over both of hers to keep her seated.

"Ms. Jennings, my apologies," Rutherford said smoothly. "We don't ever have this discussion with a victim in the room. Please understand our clinical analysis of the crime is what helps us catch the perpetrator."

Peters's fist thumped on the table to draw Meg's attention. "Jennings, why is she here?"

"Because I asked her to be here, sir, as an integral part of the team. Yes, Cara's a victim. She's also a survivor. But more important, as you now know, she's been a crucial part of this case practically from the beginning. And I need her to play an important role in what I hope will be the close of the case."

"And that is . . ." Peters's tone said he was reaching the limit of his patience.

"Sir, with Cara's help, we think we may have a lead on the suspect, but we don't have nearly enough evidence to actually get a warrant from a judge to pursue him. I was able to examine the sketch that came out of Karen Teller's abduction. And while it's not an exact match, I believe the suspect may be Derek Garber. He fits much of Agent Rutherford's profile. He's thirty-one and white, and has recently moved back into the area from Jackson, Mississippi. He's had some significant challenges in life, one of which was at my hands, although I didn't make the connection at the time. He completed high school with some difficulty, but was convinced his path lay in medical school. Needless to say, he was not accepted by any of the leading colleges, but managed to get into the premed program at Our Lady of the Lake College in Baton Rouge."

"He washed out, didn't he?" Rutherford asked.

"He did. He got through the first year, but was not invited back for a second. But, apparently, that was enough time to learn some specific anatomy lessons. He took that knowledge of human anatomy and then tried to apply it to animals, but the best he could manage was a diploma from Penn Foster's online courses as a vet tech. It would seem that didn't work out either, since he currently works at a county animal shelter in Rocky Mount, Virginia, which would give him access to the van used in the abductions. Shelters like that don't provide substantial veterinary care. They simply try to find homes for the animals they have and they're already overcrowded. Badly behaved or sick animals are often euthanized. That would be the technician's job."

"That explains the access to anesthetics," Craig said. "But aren't those things controlled substances? Don't they have to be tracked with each use?"

"They do, but someone who wants can play fast and loose with those drugs. Let me be clear, this is pure speculation, but we're working with someone who is essentially a serial killer, even if he's really only had one kill we know of. Is that correct, Agent Rutherford?"

"It is. And I see where you're going with this. The three big warning signs of serial killers are persistent bed-wetting, fire starting, and animal abuse. If Garber in his capacity at the shelter simply killed the animals some other way, likely with his own hands, he'd have the satisfaction of the animal's horrific death and he'd be able to pocket the drugs and no one would ever know. Are the two drugs we're looking at drugs that are specifically used in shelters like this?"

"They are. Overdoses of ketamine are used to euthanize animals, but usually this work is done by only a single tech and it needs to be a direct vein injection. They use an inhaled anesthetic like isoflurane to quiet the animal enough to do the injection. So he'd have access to both."

"He likely wouldn't use the inhaled anesthetic if his end goal was to torture an animal to death. The thrill for him would be the animal terrified and in pain."

"Bastard," Brian muttered under his breath, but still loud enough to carry.

"But at some point, that wasn't enough for him," Rutherford said. "So what caused him to focus on you? The Mannew case?"

"That's our best guess."

"So, then, why you?"

"This is where we launch into pure theory. Cara and I grew up next door to the Garber family during our elementary- and middle-school years. The younger son, Marty, was a close friend of mine. The older son, Derek . . . was not. He was not a popular child and was seen by most kids as being somewhat odd and a loner. But we never saw him as anything but harmless back then. If he was into anything darker, we missed it as children. And we lost touch after they moved away when Derek was thirteen. Until last night, when I reached out to Marty, just two old friends connecting and swapping updates on the family. That's where the information on Derek came from."

"This isn't playing for me," Peters said. "Where is his motivation?"

"I had an hour-long chat with Marty, sorry, Martin now, last night. He's worried about Derek. Nothing has gone the way he wanted, and I got the impression from Martin that he's worried Derek could just go off on someone. When he flunked out of med school, but before he became a vet tech, he then turned to a new passion—search-and-rescue. He'd set his sights on law enforcement and thought search-and-rescue could be his way in, because he didn't have the chops to actually attend the police academy. Apparently, he had a real hero complex. Wanted to be the guy to ride in wearing the white hat. He wanted to be considered important and thought he could make his name that way. And that's where I come in. Deuce and I did some volunteer work with the Virginia Search and Rescue Dog Association, the oldest volunteer SAR group in Virginia, and still one of the biggest. I went back and looked through my notes. Garber was in my class, but when it came time to test for skills to join the team, I rejected him. His skills weren't up to par and he was always staying in control, rather than letting his dog, Boomer, do the job he was trained to do. More than that, I suspected he abused Boomer, simply from the way the animal reacted to him. I blackballed him because he wasn't SAR caliber."

"You dashed his hopes," Rutherford said. "He had to settle for a job where his major role was to kill innocent, unwanted animals. He had a dream and you killed it, trapping him in his miserable existence. And then you got all the glory denied to him when you caught Mannew. So now it's time for you to pay for everything that's gone wrong in his life."

"That's what I think. Now, I hadn't seen him for more than ten years before he took those classes, and he changed from a boy into a man. I likely never saw his first name, just his last name and the name of his dog, so I never connected it with the boy I once knew. Honestly, he was so far beneath my radar when I was a kid, I'm not surprised I never made the connection."

"So you think this is our guy," Peters said, "but you have absolutely no evidence it's him."

"Correct, sir. And a suspicion won't convince any judge to invade someone's privacy because maybe, *just maybe,* it's him. But we think, based on what happened yesterday, that I'm his next target. And if that's true, then we want to take control of the situation."

"How?"

"We have a theory that yesterday was a major move on his part to put me at a disadvantage. He knows that to get me, I need to be off my guard and vulnerable. And what better way than for me to lose two women on my watch, especially if one of them is my sister? What if both Cara and Julie had died? My career with the FBI would be on the line." Meg braced both hands on the table and leaned in. "So let's let him think that's exactly what happened. That Julie died from her injury. That Cara was rescued, but died last night from a pulmonary edema brought on by secondary drowning. Lieutenant Webb assures me that while this is rare, it is possible. So now I've lost both victims, and my job is on the line because I risked their lives going vigilante. My job is at risk, and you're threatening to take away my dog. So what's my knee-jerk reaction? I quit and go home to my parents' isolated rescue in Cold Spring Hollow, Virginia, where I'm a wide-open target."

"You want to make yourself a target?" Craig's tone was thick with disbelief.

"I want to set up a sting with the help of the FBI," Meg responded. "If the theory is right that his planning is done, and he's exhausted his preselected victims, then I'm next. I can spend the next week or two looking over my shoulder at every opportunity and risk being caught unawares. Or I can be proactive and draw him out into a space where no one else will get hurt, and where we can bring in agents for the operation who will blend in."

"How?" asked Peters.

"You can't run a large rescue with just two people. My parents have volunteers who help out daily. I propose replacing some of those volunteers with undercover agents in the short term. There are only so many roads in, so when he comes for me, we'll know it. Then we simply wait."

"Let me get this straight." Peters sat back in his chair and crossed his arms over his chest. "You want to set yourself up as a target out in the country, with only a handful of agents to protect you."

"I can protect myself," Meg snapped back. She forced herself to stop, and gathered herself calmly. "I'm an ex-cop. Of any of the Human Scent Evidence Team members here, I'm the most capable of protecting myself from attack. That being said, additional agents for extra assistance would be appreciated. If we control the setting, we can take him. Then we have him on attacking a federal officer and we can get whatever search warrant we need. We can also let Karen see him and testify if that's really him or not. But we have to let him make the first move."

Peters was silent for a minute, staring at her over the closed fist he pressed against his lips. Then he leaned forward. "I like it, but we need to make sure you're safe and so is everyone else involved. So now the only problem is how to let him know where to find you."

"That's where I come in, sir." McCord pushed out of his chair to stand. "I've already cleared it with my editor. I'm going to write the story of yesterday's rescue and how it went so badly wrong in our fictional world. Add to that the fallout of Meg resigning, rather than facing consequences, and retreating to her family's rescue, which will be named in full and a location identified. That will run on the front page tomorrow. We can be ready for him tomorrow, but I bet he won't move until Thursday. If there's one thing this guy has shown us, it's he's prepared. He'll take his time, get ready, and then he'll go after her."

"And we'll be ready." Peters pushed back from the table to stand. "Jennings, put it together. Beaumont, you have clearance to get her whoever and whatever she needs. But keep it clean—I don't want any technicalities getting in the way of this arrest. Let's finish this, once and for all."

CHAPTER 24

Feigned Retreat: A feigned retreat is a planned withdrawal designed to lure an enemy force into leaving a superior defensive position in order to attack. If executed successfully, the retreating force leads the enemy into an ambush.

Thursday, June 1, 7:14 AM
Cold Spring Haven Animal Rescue
Cold Spring Hollow, Virginia

"You're sure you're ready?"

Meg looked up at Webb from where she sat on the bed, lacing up her hiking boots, Hawk at her side, watching her with interest. She stood and adjusted the unbuttoned shirt she wore over the plain white T-shirt that hid her bulletproof vest, making sure the outer shirt lay smoothly over the shoulder holster tucked under her left arm. "Yeah, I'm ready." She looked up into his eyes, seeing concern and worry there. "He's not going to win this."

"It's not that I don't have faith in you." Webb ran one hand through his short dark hair, making it stand up on end. He, too, was wearing jeans and heavy boots, with an old shirt, perfect for working in the barn and fields. "I don't have any faith in him. He's unpredictable, and, as Cara said, has no boundaries. No one is going to be that close to you if things go south. He's going to have a weapon with him."

"I'll be ready. And no one can be closer than we've already got them positioned. If he sees anyone, it's game over. He'll pull back in a heartbeat. The whole point of this op is that he thinks I'm alone and vulnerable. If I've got a half-dozen agents peeping around the nearest tree, he's going to rabbit."

"I understand what you're doing. It doesn't mean I'm comfortable with it. You're purposely inviting him to attack you from behind."

"Just like he did with Julie and Cara. In fact, I'm counting on it."

"And if he uses an inhaled anesthetic like he did on them?"

"Then I've got five seconds to step on his instep and plant my elbow in his solar plexus. He's never tried to take down someone trained in self-defense. He may be a bit surprised by the experience. Then there's the barbed wire."

"What about it?"

"It's what the fences are made of. But if he comes up behind me, I can flip him over my shoulder and right into it. Let me assure you that will slow him down. Yes, it's a hazard to me, but I can also use it as a weapon on site."

"And if he goes Indiana Jones on you and simply pulls out a gun?"

"That's what the bulletproof vest is for. Truthfully, I'd rather not have it because it will slow me down, but even I can see I need to take that precaution. Don't worry, we've got all the bases covered. Yes, I'm putting myself at risk, but he's going to try to asphyxiate me, not shoot or knife me. He's going to put a bag over my head, or a garrote around my throat. That also gives the agents time to move in. Suffocation isn't instantaneous. But I hope to never get to that point."

"Is the gun the only weapon you're carrying?"

"Oh, ye of little faith." She pulled up one pant leg to reveal the grip of a tactical knife protruding from her boot for easy retrieval. "And I've got my SAR knife here." She turned back her left cuff. The strap of a sheath encircled her forearm, the handle within easy reach. Meg pulled it quickly from the sheath. "Don't leave home without it." She laughed at Webb's raised eyebrows. "Normally, it stays folded in my SAR bag, but it's a damned good knife and will be perfectly appropriate for protection."

McCord and Cara came through the doorway at that moment and McCord abruptly stopped in his tracks at the sight of Meg holding the military knife an inch from Webb's chest. "Whoa! Put that thing away. Save that aggression for Garber, or whoever the perp is."

Meg rolled her eyes and smoothly slid the blade home again in its sheath, tugging her sleeve back down to conceal it. "I was just showing Todd, so he could see I'm ready."

"Second knife in the boot?" Cara asked. "Shoulder holster?"

"Yes and yes."

Cara glanced at McCord. "Her preferred close-combat combination. Otherwise it would be a second, smaller firearm in an ankle holster."

"You do this a lot?"

"Self-defense isn't new to me." Meg picked up a well-worn, broad-brimmed leather crusher off the bed and perched it at an angle on her head. "But even if I spot him in the bushes, I have to let him actually try to get to me. That's the point behind the 'assaulting a federal officer' charge. A gun isn't as useful in close quarters like that. A knife is much more versatile."

"Mom's got breakfast ready, so we should head down," Cara said. "Hawk, come. Breakfast! Saki and Blink are probably already eating." Ears perked, Hawk trotted out the door. "Come on, let's eat and then get out there."

"Everyone except you." McCord followed her out into the second-floor hallway. "You're dead."

"Right. I keep forgetting that." Cara glanced back at him. "Nice article, by the way. I forgot to tell you yesterday. You really captured the tragedy of my passing."

"I didn't lay the misery on too thick?"

"No, just enough. Seriously, Clay, it was a good article. It's going to draw him out, I know it."

The smile slid from McCord's face as he started down the stairs. "That's kind of what I'm afraid of."

"I'm right here," Meg said from behind them. "I can hear every word you're saying."

"I'm not hiding the fact I'm a little uncomfortable with this. I know you need to do it, but . . ."

"Yeah, I need to do it. It's time to end this." Meg glanced at Webb, caught his answering nod. "Now let's eat. No one does the big hearty breakfast like Mom, and we're going to need it. It could be a long day. The rescue opens to visitors at nine AM, but the 'volunteers' will be officially arriving at eight AM to get the animals fed and watered, and cages and stalls cleaned beforehand."

"What about the two agents who came in with me before the article was published so he couldn't track us?" Cara asked, stepping off the stairs and heading for the kitchen.

"They're going to coordinate the operation from inside the house. The agents who are stationed around the property have been there since five-thirty, while it was still dark. Dad helped get them into place and was back to the house before sunup."

They entered the kitchen, to find Eda standing at the stove in the large, sunny room. She glanced up from the eggs she was scrambling as they came in. "Good morning.

Grab a seat at the table and I'll bring the food over in a minute. Cara, can I leave you to pour the coffee?"

"Sure." Cara went to one of the cupboards and started pulling down thick clay mugs, setting them beside the coffeemaker.

Meg went to her mother and gave her a quick hug. "Thanks, Mom."

Eda gave her daughter a quick, critical once-over. "For what?"

"For agreeing to host this circus. For putting us up. For making breakfast." Her voice dropped. "For being the rock you always are when we need to lean on you a little." Bending, she gave her mother a quick kiss on the cheek.

Her mother laid a hand against her cheek. "You kick that bastard's ass for what he's done to my girls, you hear me?"

Meg smiled. "Loud and clear."

"And be safe while you're doing it. You know I won't draw an easy breath until this is over."

"I know." She gave her mother another hug and then took her shoulders and bodily turned her back to the stove. "I'm distracting you and you need to keep an eye on the stove before we're eating charcoal for breakfast."

"You take that hat off before you sit down at my table, young lady."

Smiling, Meg wandered back to the table, dropping the hat on the sideboard against the wall, and snagged a cup of coffee from Cara as she passed, already mixed to her specifications. "Bless you."

"Least I can do. I confess I'm feeling mostly useless today. I know I can't help, the whole sting would fall apart if he saw me, but . . ."

"I know. But it makes me feel better to know you're here and safe, where he can't hurt you again. He'll never hurt you again."

"No, he won't. You'll make sure of that."

"And in the meantime, you can hang with Coleson and Stross, who will be manning the command post here at the house. They'll have access to all the comms, including the wire I'll be wearing, so you'll always know what's going on. It'll practically be like you're out there with me."

"Best I can ask for, considering."

The sisters separated to take chairs across the table from each other just as Eda started carrying platters of scrambled eggs, sausage, toast, biscuits, and home fries to the table, along with a jug of cream gravy.

Jake came into the kitchen and pulled out the chair at the head of the long table, taking in the group clustered around his table. "Good morning."

"Everything ready to go outside?" Meg asked.

"Everyone who needs to be is in place and has provisions to make it through the day." He sent an affectionate smile in Eda's direction. "That was her idea. They said they didn't need anything, but she didn't think they should be out there for hours with nothing to tide them over."

"That's Mom for you."

"Sure is." He took the platter of eggs Cara passed to him, spooned out a generous portion, then passed it to Meg. "You're all ready?"

"Yes."

"You'll be safe out there."

"I promise. No grandstanding. I just want to get this guy."

"Good enough for me."

Meg considered him over the rim of her coffee mug. "You and mom are being awfully good about all this. Calm and collected all the way."

Her father turned to her, and for the first time, she saw the fury behind his eyes, which he was keeping so well concealed. "If you'd let me, I'd go after him myself and take him apart with my bare hands." He took a sip of his coffee, struggling to keep his rage tamped down. "But that wouldn't help you and would only hurt your endgame."

"It really would." Meg wrapped her hand around his clenched fist lying on the table beside his plate. "So trust me to do the job for you." She glanced down the table at Webb, who was silently studying her, while Cara, Mc-Cord, and Eda chatted. She looked back at her father. "To quote someone wiser than me on occasion, we're going to do this 'smart, not stupid.' We're not going to let him get the upper hand, and we aren't going to let him win. Thank you for trusting me in this. We will get the justice that Cara, Sandy, Michelle, Cat, Karen, and Julie deserve. He'll pay for this for the rest of his life."

"Amen to that."

Breakfast passed quickly. Cara and Eda kept the conversation light and flowing, but Meg had trouble joining in. She knew her family was trying to keep its collective chin up, but her mind was already out in the fields. Ready. Waiting.

After breakfast, she met Coleson and Stross, who were set up in the den. "Agents, thank you for coming all the way out here."

Coleson was tall and blond, and gave her a sunny smile. "Happy to. We've got the more comfortable position here in the house with your mother's good coffee." He toasted Meg with his coffee cup.

"And breakfast." Stross, stouter and darker, scraped the last of his eggs off his plate and shoveled them into his mouth. "I pity the poor bastards out there since five-thirty," he said. "They didn't get a hot breakfast."

"Then let's try to move this along for them. What have you got for me?"

"Your electronics." Coleson set down his mug and picked up a small black case. Tipping open the lid, he lifted out a small, flesh-colored, tapered cylinder. "Hold out your hand."

Meg did as directed, and Coleson dropped the object into her hand.

"That's your earpiece. Slide it right into your ear. You'll be able to hear us, loud and clear, and it won't be visible to the perp." Meg slipped the earpiece into place as Coleson removed a small, thin microphone on a fine wire, looped into a coil, and a transmitter. "This is your microphone." He eyed her critically; Meg knew he wasn't a man checking out a woman, but an agent trying to find the best way to protect a colleague. "We could put this on your shirt"— he tugged at the edge of the loose cotton button-up covering her shoulder holster—"but I think there's too much chance of you getting it caught on something and us losing the signal. As long as the plan for you to be in the far pasture to repair barbed-wire fencing hasn't changed?"

"No, that's still the plan. It puts me farthest from the house and in the most isolated area of the property. It will be the easiest place to attack me."

"Then we definitely want you to be able to talk to us. Under the T-shirt and vest?"

"Sure." Meg slipped out of the cotton shirt, unclipped and pulled off her shoulder holster, laying it carefully on a chair, and then stripped off her white T-shirt and bullet-proof vest, revealing the sports bra beneath.

Coleson expertly attached the mic under her sports bra, taping it securely against the skin between her breasts so the mic would rest just above the neckline of the vest. Then he ran the wire under the band of her bra to drop down her back. The transmitter he slipped into her back pocket. "How does that feel? Does the tape pull?"

"No, feels comfortable."

"Good." Coleson's gaze shot over her shoulder. "Can I help you?"

Meg looked over her shoulder to see Webb standing in

the open doorway, his sharp eyes taking in the scene. "I was just checking to see if Meg was ready to head out."

"Just about." Meg slipped on her vest and T-shirt, noting that Webb respectfully turned away until she was done strapping the shoulder holster back on. She picked up her other shirt. "Do we need to test this?"

Agent Stross swiveled away from the equipment spread out across her father's desk. "Yes. Find another room and we'll give it a shot."

"Sure." Meg stepped out of the den and walked down the hallway and into a large, comfortable family room with a spacious sectional and a gigantic flat-screen TV. "Testing, testing, one, two, three. Am I coming in clearly, Agent Stross?"

"You are. You can hear us fine?"

"Clear as if you were standing right beside me."

"Great. Comms are a go."

"Then I'm also a go. I'm heading out." Meg turned to Webb. "Where are you going to be?"

"I've been told McCord and I are starting in the barn." One eyebrow cocked sardonically. "We're taking Hawk there to hang out with one of your horses in her stall?"

"That would be Auria. She and Hawk are buddies. He won't notice I'm AWOL if he's with her, and I don't want him anywhere near this maniac. He could get hurt or he could actually keep the guy from going after me. The rest of the dogs will stay in the house with Cara. So once you get Hawk safely locked down, what's the plan?"

"Apparently, we're mucking out stalls and helping with feeding."

"They're trying to keep you nearby, because that was my requirement, but they're also trying to keep you out of harm's way." She laughed at the way his brows snapped together in displeasure. "I hear you. This is what they say to the man who runs into a burning building when everyone else is running out."

"Exactly my point. I could be more useful."

"Let's start here and see how things progress. Go back in there and at least get an earpiece so you know what's going on. If I need you, I'll let you know." She started to turn toward the door. "Now, I've got to get out there—"

He grabbed her by both shoulders, jerking her up on her toes as he pulled her in and kissed her. For a moment, Meg was shocked motionless, and then she relaxed into him, curling her hands into his cotton shirt.

After what seemed like mere seconds, he pulled back, lowering her down to flat feet and waiting until she had her balance before releasing her. "You be careful out there."

"I will be."

"No, I mean *careful*. Don't be cocky. Don't be overconfident. You're smart and you're strong, but sometimes smart and strong don't beat crazy, and this one is crazy in spades."

She pressed a palm to his smoothly shaved cheek. "I will. Promise." She pulled back, letting her fingertips run over his skin until her hand dropped.

"Come back and we'll pick up where that left off."

She flashed him a smile that held substantial promise. "Deal."

Meg turned and left the room. It was only then she remembered she was wearing an open mic.

CHAPTER 25

Quaker Guns: The traditional Quaker gun was a log that was trimmed, mounted, and painted black to resemble real artillery. During the Civil War, the Confederacy used Quaker guns to compensate for a lack of artillery—at Centreville, Virginia, and during the Siege of Corinth (Mississippi), Quaker guns were deployed to disguise the strategic retreats of Rebel forces.

Thursday, June 1, 11:52 AM
Cold Spring Haven Animal Rescue
Cold Spring Hollow, Virginia

Leather gloves protecting her hands, Meg carefully twisted the broken barbed wire into a loop, winding the ten-inch tail back onto itself. Picking up the fence stretcher from the ground in front of where she knelt, she slipped one end of it through the loop and then fitted the other end into a matching loop on the other section of broken wire and ratcheted the stretcher tight until it hung suspended over the long, lush grass.

She sat back on her haunches and pushed back the brim of her hat, wiping sweat off her brow with her forearm. The day was unseasonably warm, and she was overheating in the field, with no shade and the full sun beating down on her from a cloudless sky. The bulletproof vest was a heat trap, and she couldn't remove her long-sleeved shirt without revealing her shoulder holster, so she was stuck, slowly baking. She'd run out of water an hour ago.

Meg had been repairing fences out here in the east paddock for over three hours. She was purposely working slowly, trying to stretch what would be a normal half day's work into a full day, if that's what it took. Working slowly also had the added bonus of allowing her to pay more attention to her surroundings rather than the familiar, monotonous task of repairing fences. This outer pasture wasn't used often, only when the overflow of animals required the extra space. Since that hadn't happened for a while, and hands were badly needed for animals already in the rescue, these repairs were set aside. But now was the perfect time.

This was also the perfect place. She was a sitting duck out in the open, clearly on her own in the wide pasture, but the forest flanking the Jenningses' land was only thirty feet behind her and gave excellent cover for anyone attempting to sneak onto the property. The entrance to the rescue was situated at the top of the hill, with the driveway sloping down to the house and buildings below. Anyone coming in from the road would be forced downhill. But the landscape played to their advantage. From the top of the hill, the land funneled down into a hollow and then spread out into wider pastures below. Meg had arranged to have "workers" visible in the lower fields, knowing he'd see them from above and would then be forced into the hollow to keep out of sight. And that's where he'd trip over her, all by herself.

There was only a slim chance he planned to climb the eight-hundred-foot hill from the bottom to approach from below. Instead, he'd park closer and come in from one of the adjacent roads, all of which were conveniently close to I-64 and a quick getaway, once his mission was complete.

If he came in from the north, as she predicted, he'd find her conveniently close and would stay far away from the main house. *Away from Cara, and Hawk, and Mom and Dad. Away from Webb and McCord.*

Meg surreptitiously scanned the tree line again, but there was no sign of movement.

Patience. He'll come.

She unrolled a new section of wire from the roll of barbed wire in the grass and neatly cut off the desired length with her fencing pliers. A quick flick of her wrist buried the wickedly sharp, pointed pry claw of the pliers in the soft dirt, leaving the handles sticking up at a forty-five-degree angle so they were visible in the long grass. She slipped the wire through the loop on the fence stretcher, making a linking loop and winding the wire back on itself. A second loop on the far side completed the patch job. She released the fence stretcher and the new section of barbed wire swung free.

"Not bad at all."

A dust cloud in the distance caught her attention, and she spotted her father's old, beat-up pickup, only ever used on the grounds of the rescue, bumping along the dirt track that circled the perimeter of the property. Raising her hand to shade her eyes, she squinted into the distance, but all she could see was the dark shape of someone behind the wheel.

"Jennings to comm," she said softly. "I've got someone coming in, driving Dad's pickup."

"All clear, Jennings." It was Stross's voice. "We sent out some supplies to you. We don't want you passing out in the field due to dehydration or hypoglycemia. No sign of him yet, so we could be hours more."

"Thanks. Appreciate that. Jennings out."

Meg picked up her tools and the roll of barbed wire and carried them down two more sections of fence to the next break. She deposited everything in the grass as the pickup rolled to a stop behind her. She turned just as the door slammed and Webb circled around the hood of the truck, carrying a basket. "This is from your mom."

"Is there water in there? I'm parched."

Webb set the basket down, turned up one of the wicker flaps, and pulled out a chilled bottle of water, frosted with condensation.

"You're amazing." Meg grabbed the bottle, unscrewed the cap, and downed half of it in one continuous series of swallows. "It's hot as hell out here. I needed that."

"She sent food too. Nothing too heavy, but something to keep you going."

"She's amazing too."

"You okay?"

"Got lots of the fence repaired. But no sign of anything or anyone suspicious."

She froze as her earpiece crackled to life. "Perimeter Three to comm. I've got a black sedan coming up Cold Spring Road."

Meg knew from the way Webb stiffened that he must have acquired an earpiece, as she had suggested. "You got that?"

"Yeah. That's not the vehicle we expected."

A chill snaked down Meg's spine. "He doesn't need the van. He's not expecting to take me anywhere. This could be his own car."

The set of Webb's rock-hard jaw spoke of his tension more eloquently than words. "He's got to get to you first. Any other way up here besides that road?"

"Not by car. But we don't even know if that's him. There aren't many who live up the mountain here, but we aren't the only ones. Jennings to Perimeter Three. Can you get eyes on a plate? A number or state?"

"Negative. Too far off, but we'll try. Stay sharp, every-one. Perimeter Three out."

Meg calmly bent and reached into the basket and pulled out a fat sandwich on a roll. "Want to split it with me?"

He stared at her wide-eyed, as if not sure how she could eat at a time like this. "No. I want this guy to show up."

"You know you can't be here when he does." She took a big bite of the sandwich.

"Yeah, I know. Eat your sandwich. I'll scram. I just wanted to see how you were doing."

Meg took a second to chew and swallow. "Thanks for coming all the way out here. The energy boost will be just in time. I'll eat, then get back into position. He's got to find me first, so it could be another twenty or thirty min-utes. If that's even him."

She could see the conflict in his eyes, his desire to stay, to tell her one more time to be careful. But it had all been said already, and he knew she had to be out here on her own to draw the unsub out. Webb stepped back. "See you back at the house."

"You absolutely will."

She watched as he got back into the truck. He gave her one last, long look, and then drove off down the track, cir-cling the pastures on his way back to the house.

Meg quickly ate her sandwich, drained the bottle of water, and then finished up with a fat slice of her mother's legendary banana bread. She removed one more bottle of water from the basket and then repacked it and set it against a fence post away from where she was working.

"Okay, you bastard," she murmured. "Bring it on."

She went back to work, but every sense was height-ened—the barbed wire seemed sharper, the sun glared more brilliantly, and the warble of a bluebird, hidden in the trees thirty feet away, a vibrant exclamation of joy. She flinched when another voice boomed in her ear. *Had it been that loud, only minutes before?*

"Perimeter One to comm. We're pretty sure this is our guy and not someone who lives up here. He just parked the car, has exited the vehicle, and is coming through the trees onto the property. We have eyes on him, about five foot eleven, two-ten, baseball cap, and sunglasses. The license plate is unreadable from a distance. It's smeared with mud, possibly on purpose."

"Jennings to Perimeter One. Give me his current location."

"He's parked off to the side of the road, near the driveway to 2658 Cold Spring Road. And he's walking due south through the woods."

Right toward me.

Excellent.

"Jennings, stay sharp." Coleson's voice this time. "He's coming right into your area. A little east of it, but if he's got his eyes open, he'll find you."

"Roger that. Jennings out."

Here we go.

She took off her right glove, freeing her hand for either her gun or her knife. She dropped the glove in the grass, took another long swig of water, and then knelt down again and started repairing yet another section of fencing, carefully keeping her bare hand away from the barbs.

All is quiet.

Loop the wire to tie off the broken section, repeat with the other side.

Install the fence stretcher.

Too quiet.

Use the pliers to tap in new staples where the wire has been pulled from the fence post while the wire is still pulled tight. Cut a new wire section.

Close your eyes and listen for anything moving behind you.

Nothing.

Bury the fencing pliers in the grass for the next use. Tie off the new section with fresh wire, winding all ends securely. Remove the stretcher. Test the new connection.

The blow came from behind, knocking her hat off and sending her spinning into the newly repaired fence, the weight of pure rage and fury at her back driving her into the razor-sharp barbs.

CHAPTER 26

Kill Zone: A kill zone is a defensive fortification surrounded by barbed wire or natural barriers that is completely blanketed by defensive fire. Enemy troops are funneled or lured into the kill zone and either killed or captured.

Thursday, June 1, 12:26 PM
Cold Spring Haven Animal Rescue
Cold Spring Hollow, Virginia

Meg managed at the last second to get one gloved hand up in front of her face so her cheek was driven into worn leather instead of razor sharp steel. But the barbs bit deep into her other hand, wringing a cry of pain from her.

The voice exploded in her ear. "He's got her. All agents move in! Go! Go!"

The wire bowed beneath the combined weight of their bodies, bending into the field before snapping back. Using the tensile strength of the wire to her advantage, Meg blocked out the pain and pushed off from it with both hands, throwing herself backward into the grass on top of her attacker. They hit the ground hard, and Meg struggled to get away, but her attacker had one arm around her neck and the other wrapped around her right wrist. She yanked against the hold, all while trying to roll him off balance; but as she shifted her weight to the left in a roll, he took advantage of the space between their bodies to jerk her right hand up toward the middle of her back.

Meg screamed as her shoulder dislocated, nearly blacking out from the pain, but somehow managing to hold on. He released her now-limp arm and she continued her roll off him to the left, while frantically shaking off her heavy left glove, letting it fly off into the grass. She gagged as the arm still around her throat cut off what little air she had after the blinding pain of the shoulder injury.

Strangulation is still suffocation.

His final victim.

Her field of vision started to fill with black and green patches as her oxygen level dropped dangerously low.

She threw all her weight into one last attempt to roll off him, to change her position so her windpipe would fall into the crook of his elbow, releasing some of the killing pressure. The jerky movement shifted her sideways slightly, but he rolled with her, maintaining his hold.

As she struggled, she put out her left hand to catch herself in the grass. But instead of grass, her hand fell onto something solid, knocking it sideways, and her fingers closed over the grips of the fencing pliers. Without a thought, she grabbed them tight and, pulling back to swing with all her remaining strength, she buried the wickedly sharp pry claw into the flesh of his upper thigh.

This time, it was his turn to scream in agony and the arm around her neck abruptly released. She rolled away, scrambling to her feet, gasping with the effort of pulling air through her bruised throat and into her lungs. By the time she looked up, the man was also on his feet, the pliers swinging free in his left hand, the pry claw dark and wet with blood.

"Bitch," he spat.

She only had the briefest moment to take him in, but a slide show of images shot through her mind in that second.

The silent boy standing behind Marty, staring at her with narrowed eyes.

Coming around the corner of the house to find him crouched over a spider, systematically pulling legs from the wriggling body.

Standing on the other side of the open doorway from him, Marty flat against the wall, out of sight, only feet away. "He's not here, Derek. Are you sure he didn't go down to the park?"

Watching the man follow his German shepherd through the long grass, the dog's head down searching for the scent trail. The harsh jerk of the leash as he tried to get the dog's attention. The cold look in the handler's eyes at the end of the unsuccessful trial.

"Why, Derek?"

The man's eyebrows curved upward in surprise. "So you do recognize me? I wasn't sure you would. You didn't seem to, the last time I saw you."

"I didn't then. But I know exactly who you are now." As she talked, Meg tried to get her right arm to move. Both the large knife and her gun were on her left side for right-handed access. She could get her fingers to wiggle, but large arm movements were not possible without blinding pain. She couldn't use her right arm with any force, assuming she could even get a knife into her right hand. She definitely wouldn't be able to aim her gun.

She knew then that he'd done it on purpose. This was a man who could induce an hours-long pneumothorax. Dislocating a shoulder was a snap for anyone with medical training. But the crippling results could be catastrophic.

When he tried again to strangle her with his bare hands, she wouldn't be able to fight him off.

The key was going to be the knife in her boot, pressed against the outside of her right ankle within easy reach of her now-useless right hand. But it was also within reach of her left hand if she had about two full seconds to crouch down, reach over, and grab it. She was going to have to make that time. The agents out there were coming, but she'd planned on having the ability to fight hand-to-hand with Garber to buy herself time. He'd gotten the better of her there, but she was not out of the running.

"Smart, not stupid." Webb's voice suddenly rang in her head.

"I know exactly who you are," she repeated. "And I even know why."

He held the fencing pliers up, examining them with a detached air. "Really?" His cold blue gaze snapped from the bloody pliers to her face. "Why?"

"Because you want the glory. You want to be the guy who rides in, wearing a white hat to save the day. You want to be important. Instead, you clean up the dead and the unwanted. You're unimportant and forgettable to anyone who crosses your path."

The rage with which he flung the pliers away told her more about his state of mind than actual words. *Not thinking clearly. He just threw away a proven weapon.* She scanned his body, seeing a lump under his sweatshirt that could be a gun in a holster. *But he's not using it. Is he keeping his hands free to wrap around my throat at any moment?*

"You know nothing about me," he spat.

"But I do, Derek, I do. I had a great conversation with Marty last night about you. Always did love Marty. So smart, so successful. Oh, and the funny thing? Cara was with me at the time. She was really thrilled to hear how great Marty is doing. That must be hard for you, knowing how you always paled in comparison to him."

His eyes narrowed to slits, but the hatred still radiated clearly. "Impossible. She died. I know she did." Triumph glowed in his eyes. "I killed her."

"You'd like to think that. Unfortunately for you, the FBI has a reporter for the *Washington Post* in its pocket. They print what we tell them to, because that's the kind of power we have. Oh, by the way, Julie Moore also survived. You failed, Derek, in so many ways. Wait! Let me count them." She raised her left hand and started numbering off names on thumb and fingers. "Michelle, Cat, Karen, Julie, Cara." She met his eyes and extended one additional finger. "Might as well add 'Meg' to that list, since you've failed here too." She tipped her chin high and ran the fingers of her left hand over the smooth, unblemished skin of her throat. "Marty would be mortified. How does it feel to be the family failure agai—"

With a roar, Garber leapt for her, but she was ready. As he lunged, she rolled low, pulling her injured arm close to her body. The roll took Garber down, tripping him just as he was reaching for her upper body, which was suddenly not there. Swallowing a groan of pain, she rolled over the grass, her left hand scrabbling at her pants leg and finally getting beneath, her fingers closing over the hilt of the knife. She'd just pulled it free, when he came at her again.

He threw himself on top of her, his hands closing over her throat with crushing pressure. This time, though, she was ready for him. A swift knee between his legs had him gasping and she rolled him. As he settled beneath her, she brought the knife up, the edge of it pressed to the soft skin under his jaw. He froze, his eyes going wide with a combination of surprise, rage, and fear.

"I suggest you let go," she rasped. "Or I'll end you right here."

His hands loosened to fall to the grass on either side of his shoulders.

"And don't even try going for your gun. Or maybe you should? It'll be just the excuse I need."

From the corner of her eye, she saw two men sprinting for her from out of the trees: Webb and McCord.

This was her last ten seconds alone with the man who made her life hell for far too long. The knife pressed harder into Garber's flesh and he gasped, his face going bloodless.

This is the man who tried to kill my sister. Who threatened my parents. One "slip" of the hand and I could end it all right now.

"Meg, put down the knife."

She raised half-wild eyes to Webb. He was crouched beside her, one hand partially extended toward her.

"Hold still. I'm going to reach over to take your gun." Webb slipped his hand under her shirt, pulling out her service weapon. He trained the weapon on Garber's head. "Don't move, or I won't hesitate to shoot, you piece of shit." He didn't take his eyes off the man under Meg's knife, but he gentled his voice and directed his words back to the woman holding the weapon. "We've got him. Let the system deal with him now. He'll never be granted bail. He'll never see the light of day again."

The hand holding the knife trembled for a second as competing definitions of "justice" warred in Meg's head. Finally logic and training won out over raw emotion. Keeping her eyes locked on the gun in Webb's hand, she pulled the knife away.

"Let me take that." McCord reached in from the other side and slipped the knife from her fingers. "Give me your hand. Let me help you up." He held out his hand, palm up, for her.

She slapped her left hand into his and let him tug her to her feet and off Garber. "Check him. I think he's carrying on the right side."

Webb reached under the shirt with his free hand and pulled out a small handgun. He passed it over to McCord. "He never bothered to use this?"

"No, he wanted to literally kill me with his bare hands. Asphyxiation was always his thing." She lifted her left hand to lightly prod her throat and winced.

"Have you got cuffs?" Webb asked Meg.

Meg wordlessly turned and flipped up her shirt so McCord could pull out the cuffs from the small leather pouch at the small of her back. Webb and McCord turned Garber over, cuffed him, and left Garber lying facedown in the grass. Neither seemed to care much if they were a little rough with him.

With a shout, two agents broke from the trees, running flat out, straight for them.

"How did you get here first?" Meg asked Webb and McCord.

"We don't have orders to follow." Webb didn't look even remotely repentant. "After I got back to the house with the truck, McCord and I decided we'd head back here on foot so we could be closer. Your dad slipped us a pair of binoculars and sent us off with directions on how to stay hidden. We both had earpieces so we knew where he was coming in and could make sure we didn't inadvertently intercept him early. Your FBI boys were only looking for something in motion outside the property, not inside, so, in the end, we could be closer than they were because they were telling us where not to be. We watched him break from the trees and go for you and were on the move before the FBI order was given."

The two agents ran up, panting, and took control of the site and the suspect. In the distance, a large dust cloud announced the arrival of at least one vehicle.

Meg stepped back to move farther out of their way, and a small moan broke inadvertently from her lips, drawing Webb's clinical gaze.

"Come here." He led her about twenty feet away, into the small amount of shade along the forest line at midday. Slipping fingers under her chin, he gently tipped her head up before running his fingertips over her throat. "That's going to be colorful tomorrow." He ran careful hands over her shoulder. "This is the more immediate problem. I'm sure you already know it's dislocated."

"The blinding pain and uselessness kind of gave it away. He knew exactly what he was doing. He was putting me out of commission from the first moment."

"Bastard didn't want to use the gun he had, unless he had no choice, because he was fixated on watching the life leave your eyes while he strangled you to death with his own hands. But he knew he'd never be able to fight you and win if you were able to use your combat skills. So he used the medical training he had to cripple you. Let me fix that shoulder for you."

"You can put it back?"

Webb simply gave her a nonplussed look.

"Of course you can. Sorry. Yes, please."

"Let's get you out of this shirt first." Webb helped her slide the shirt off her shoulders and arms, moving her right arm as little as possible. But she still couldn't help the hiss of pain from escaping between her clenched teeth. It was then that Webb saw her punctured and bloody right hand and whistled.

"That's from when I hit the barbed wire. I still had the left glove on, so I could cushion my face with it. But I'd taken my right glove off so I was free to go for a weapon."

"We know McCord's up to date on his tetanus, how about you?"

"Always. SAR handlers never know where we'll be and what conditions are like, so we stay up to date."

Webb gently picked up her hand, taking care not to jostle the arm, and examined it. "Not as bad as it could have been. Abrasions and a few small punctures. They'll need a proper cleaning at the ER."

"No ER. We'd be stuck there for hours. You're already doing my shoulder—you can do it all. Just tear a strip off the shirt to bind it for now." She watched as he tore a long strip from the bottom of the shirt and methodically wrapped her right hand. "Okay, let's do this. I have a feeling this isn't going to be fun."

"Definitely not. Fair warning, it's going to hurt like hell, because I don't have any anesthetic. I need you to lie down." He helped her sit; then he slipped one hand behind her neck and lowered her down into the grass.

Footsteps announced another arrival and McCord entered Meg's field of view.

McCord bent over her, bracing both hands on his knees. "You okay?"

Webb answered for her. "I'm going to reduce her shoulder. Put it back into place. She's in a lot of pain and this will instantly help. If we wait until she gets to the hospital—"

"I said *no hospital*," Meg grated through a locked jaw. "If you do it, then I don't need a hospital."

"If we theoretically waited until she got to a hospital, there'd be significant swelling and it would be harder to do. But they'd have anesthetics."

"Less talk, more action."

"You got it. I need you to relax the muscles in your shoulder." He smiled at her cynical bark of laughter. "That's the spirit. I know it's going to be hard to do, but do your best or else I'm fighting your muscles and that will make it harder on both of us." He wrapped one hand around her bandaged hand, raising it into the air so her arm was bent at a ninety-degree angle, and cupped his other hand under her elbow. "I'm going to apply traction to your arm while rotating it down toward the grass. This is the easiest way to do it without sedation, but it's still going to hurt. During the rotation, you'll feel the ball of the humerus slip back into place and the pain should drop right off. Ready?"

She nodded.

He gripped her hand tightly. "Okay, relax that shoulder as much as you can." He pulled her elbow down toward his hip as he started to rotate the arm outward.

Meg gasped as the pain spiked in nauseating waves; she bit her lip to hold back a cry, but held very still.

"Doing great. Try to stay loose, just a little farther and—" There was an audible *click* as the bone slipped back into place.

Meg's body went slack as the pain suddenly seemed to evaporate.

"There we are." Webb rotated the arm back and laid her hand flat on her stomach. A quick tactile exam of her shoulder had him nodding his approval. "That worked nicely. You're back where you should be. Can you sit up?" When she nodded, he helped her rise off the grass. "Okay?"

"Pain's not gone, but it's much better, thanks."

Webb quickly fashioned a makeshift sling out of her discarded shirt. Then he and McCord helped her stand and catch her balance.

"Thanks." Meg raised her left hand to shield her eyes from the sun as an SUV and her father's pickup pulled up. Before it had even stopped, Cara was out the passenger door and running toward her. Meg threw up a hand before Cara could throw her arms around her.

"I'm okay, but hugs are out for a bit."

"Bet me." Cara came around to her left side, slid her arm around her waist, and gave her an awkward one-handed hug. "See?"

Meg laughed. "Never could keep you down."

"You either, apparently. It was terrifying listening remotely to what was going on. I loved when you baited him with the fact I was alive."

"Speaking of which, and maybe I'm being spiteful—but I kind of feel it's my right currently—want to go say 'hi'?"

Cara's grin was part joy, part calculation. "To show him in the flesh? *Yes.*"

"This way then." Meg led the way back across the grass, stopping briefly to greet her father, kissing his cheek and saying she'd be right back. Then she left Webb and McCord with him as she and Cara walked over to the now half-dozen agents who were walking the handcuffed Garber over toward the SUV. "Agents? Just a moment, please."

As a group, they halted and turned to her.

"My sister wanted to say hello to an old friend." Meg and Cara circled the group to stand in front of Garber. "Hey, Derek. Remember Cara? Oh, of course you do, you just saw her two days ago."

Before anyone could react fast enough to stop her, Cara slapped Garber full across the face with all her strength. Then she leaned in close to him. "Remember that the next time you think you ever had the upper hand. Six women survived your hideous urges. You lose in every way. You failed. More than that, you're nothing. Just a footnote we'll forget by next week."

She turned on her heel, threaded her arm through Meg's uninjured one, and together they walked away from the man who'd made their lives hell, heads high and eyes fixed firmly on the future.

CHAPTER 27

Appomattox Court House: Contrary to common belief, Lee's surrender at Appomattox Court House on April 9, 1865, did not mark the end of the Civil War. In fact, the last battle to be fought was won by the Confederate forces on May 13 at Palmito Ranch near the Texas-Mexico border; and the last Confederate forces to surrender were the men of the Cherokee Rifle brigade, under Brigadier General Stand Watie, on June 23 in what is now the state of Oklahoma.

Friday, June 2, 8:20 PM
Jennings residence
Arlington, Virginia

Brian stood up from where he sat with Ryan on the love seat, Lacey at his feet. "I'd like to make a toast." The room quieted and all eyes turned to him. "It's been a tough few weeks, but Meg has really shown us how to get the job done. To keep a level head, work the case, and save the victims, all while under immense stress. We could all learn from the master." He raised his wineglass. "To a job well done. To Meg!" Bending, he clinked glasses with Ryan.

The room echoed with "To Meg!"

The idea of the small celebration had come from Cara,

but had ballooned into a bigger get-together as word spread. Now instead of just family, it included Webb and McCord, as well as the whole Human Scent Evidence Team, Craig and Peters, and everyone's partners and dogs. Blink, originally terrified by all the people, had attached himself to Webb, but was now happily flopped on the floor next to Rocco, lying beside Lauren and her current boyfriend of the month. The living room and the kitchen were full of dogs, but no one minded.

Meg stood from where she sat on the couch between her mother and Cara, her right arm now in a proper sling, her bruised throat a bloom of dark tones of fuchsia and purple-black above the scooped neckline of her top. "Too kind, Brian, too kind." She grinned when he simply inclined his head and then drained his wineglass before settling back on the couch and whispering something to Ryan that made him laugh. "Brian left out a few details. Mysteriously, one of the details he left out was his own contribution to the case. Amazing." Brian took a dramatic mock bow amid the snickers of his coworkers. "But it's not just Brian. It's Lauren, and Scott, and Craig. It's Hawk, Lacey, Rocco, and Theo." Rocco, hearing his name, let out an enthusiastic bark.

"Shhhh, knucklehead," Lauren said affectionately, ruffling his fur. "No one asked for your opinion."

"It's also EAD Peters . . ." She scanned the room. "Has he disappeared again?"

"In the kitchen, refilling my glass." Peters's voice carried through the kitchen doorway. "You people drive me to drink, and I can't do it on the job."

The room exploded with laughter as Peters strolled out back into the living room with a very full glass of red wine. He raised the glass in salute to Meg as he wound back through the room toward his wife. Meg shook her head in disbelief. Peters the hard-ass was proving to be a very sociable person, once you got him out of the office and out of his suit.

"It's also EAD Peters," Meg repeated, "who green-lighted the final takedown and gave us more leeway than other supervisors. That leeway allowed us to be success-ful." She turned to where McCord sat on the arm of the sofa beside Cara, and toward Webb, who stood behind him, nursing a beer. "And the case would be nowhere, *absolutely nowhere,* without Clay McCord and Todd Webb. I owe you two more than I'll ever be able to repay. You gave me back my sister."

McCord, no doubt hearing the emotion in her voice, leapt into the fray to lighten the tension. "No worries. Next time I need a scoop on a case, you'll be there for me." He sent her a cheesy smile full of white teeth. "Right?"

"Wrong." Peters's voice boomed from the back of the room.

"Shoot. Well, at least I can write about this case. Especially my favorite part of it."

"And what was that?" Webb asked. "When you solved the riddle and saved the day?"

"Nah. I was thinking more along the lines of when Cara hauled off and slapped the bastard and then told him off. That was absolutely glorious."

Cara repeated Brian's mock bow amid clapping and cheering.

"Of course, early on," Meg continued, once the room finally got quieter, "my sister, Cara, was crucial to solving many of the riddles. Many thanks for lending me your big, beautiful brain. And, last but not least, thanks to our parents, who opened up their home and beloved rescue to a dangerous op and all the FBI agents who came with it. We couldn't have done it without you."

Her father simply squeezed her mother's shoulder and gave a solemn nod.

"So all I can say is this." She raised the glass in her gauze-wrapped right hand. "You all made a difference in this case and I am grateful to each and every one of you for it. To teamwork!"

"To teamwork!" And everyone drank.

Time to get out of the spotlight. "We don't normally close a case with a party like this, but this one is special. So refill your glasses, please"—at the back of the room, Peters raised his now half-empty glass—"and help yourself to food. Enjoy!" She sat back down on the couch and let the chatter rise up around her as her mother gave her a half hug from her left and her father's hand comfortingly rubbed her back.

A few minutes later, as talk and laughter abounded, Meg quietly slipped from the sofa and moved toward the door. Hawk, who always had one eye on her, got up to follow, and when she slid open the screen door to the deck, he slipped out with her.

She stepped out onto the quiet deck with her glass of wine. She crossed over to the railing on the far side and set her glass down. Hawk followed her and flopped down beside her, drawing in a lungful of cool late spring air and letting it out with a contented sigh. Meg looked up at the cloudless sky, where the stars sparkled and the sliver of moon tipped the backyard in ghostly white.

The sound of the sliding door opening and closing had her looking over her shoulder. "Hey."

"Hey," said Webb, still standing with one hand on the handle. "Want company or would you prefer some peace and quiet?"

"I'd like your company. But, yes, I needed a break from the chaos in there. Big parties sometimes make me a little crazy. Too much noise, too many people—I just needed a moment."

Webb crossed the deck and put his beer down beside her

wine, then set his hands down on the railing on either side of her hips. Not quite embracing her, giving her the freedom to keep her distance, but opening the door for her.

She walked through it, leaning back against him, and his arms moved to encircle her stomach.

"Just before the party started, we heard Michelle came out of her coma. Doctors are very encouraged and think she'll make a full recovery."

"That's fantastic news. Another life saved by you and the teams. So what's next?" he asked.

"Next at work? Well, I get two full weeks off, to let this shoulder heal. Then, assuming I have the doctor's approval and promise to continue with my physical therapy, I can come back to light duties. Full duties in four weeks. Peters considers this a win-win situation because it takes care of my concussion too."

"How's your head feeling?"

"Not bad, considering it got thrown around a bit yesterday."

"Good." He was silent for a moment, staring off into the shadows draping the yard. "You know, I think McCord has a thing for your sister."

She turned in surprise to look at him over her shoulder. "I thought I was the only one who saw that. I realized the day she went missing that he was more deeply worried than I expected. And then there was his level of desperation when you two were trying to keep her alive underwater, and the way he was hanging over her when we pulled her out. Put it all together and I think there might be something there."

"For him. What about for her?"

"She's always seemed to like him. There's always been a lot of healthy sarcasm between them, but that could just be the way they relate."

"Kind of like in third grade when you like a girl so you tease her, just to get her to look at you?"

Meg laughed. "Something like that. I guess time will tell."

"And what about us?"

"What about us?"

"We still haven't managed an actual date yet. Every time we make plans, something comes up."

"It won't in the next two weeks. Stake your claim now and I promise to show up. It would be nice to do something fun, not something stressful or that has a life depending on it."

"That would be novel for us, wouldn't it?"

"It really would be. But, for now, I'm just happy to enjoy a little quiet with you."

He pulled her in close and she tipped her head back against his chest and looked up at the stars.

The buzz of conversation filtered through the sliding glass door and Meg took comfort in Brian's booming laugh, the sound of Cara at the blender making more mixed drinks, the relaxed breathing of the dog at her feet, and the strength of the man at her back.

There was no danger, no missing persons, and no puzzles. For tonight, there was only peace.

Acknowledgments

Writing a novel is never a solitary job, and this one was no exception. I was helped along the journey by a number of historical and technical experts, and owe them many thanks for their assistance: Johnny Johnsson, a local expert on the Choate Mine at Soldiers Delight Environment Area who generously shared his personal pictures of the mine, as well as several professional papers on its history; Lynell Tobler, vice president of the Soldiers Delight Conservation Inc. for her research assistance; Captain Lisa Giblin of the South Placer Fire Department for sharing her knowledge of firefighter/paramedic training, as well as for medical consultations; South Placer Fire Department's Battalion Chief Jason Brooks, Engineer Paramedic Darrin Mayo, and Intern Firefighter Lyubov Gavrilyuk for an interesting roundtable discussion about the best ways to kill someone by positional asphyxiation; and Round Rock police officer Noah Moncivais and his pit bull partner, Harley, for sharing their training and experience as a drug, scent detection, and tracking team.

My writing has been supported by a fantastic group of people from the publishing industry and beyond: Peter Senftleben, who not only started the series with me, but encouraged this particular novel; Esi Sogah, who enthusiastically jumped into the fray and was instrumental in shaping the final story; my agent, Nicole Resciniti, who is always working diligently behind the scenes in every way possible; and my critique team—Lisa Giblin, Jenny Lidstrom, Rick Newton, and Sharon Taylor—for once again offering their time and talents to take a rough first draft and turn it into a polished, cohesive manuscript.